just for now

ALSO BY ABBI GLINES

The Vincent Boys

The Vincent Brothers

OTHER SEA BREEZE NOVELS

Breathe

Because of Low

While It Lasts

just for now

ABBI GLINES

Simon Pulse

New York London Toronto Sydney New Delhi

SIMON PULSE

An imprint of Simon & Schuster Children's Publishing Division
1230 Avenue of the Americas, New York, NY 10020
First Simon Pulse edition April 2013
Copyright © 2013 by Abbi Glines
Cover photograph copyright © 2013 by Michael Frost
All rights reserved, including the right of reproduction
in whole or in part in any form.
SIMON PULSE and colophon are registered trademarks
of Simon & Schuster, Inc.
For information about special discounts for bulk purchases, please
contact Simon & Schuster Special Sales at 1-866-506-1949 or
business@simonandschuster.com. The Simon & Schuster Speakers
Bureau can bring authors to your live event. For more information
or to book an event contact the Simon & Schuster Speakers Bureau
at 1-866-248-3049 or visit our website at www.simonspeakers.com.
Cover designed by Jessica Handelman
Interior designed by Mike Rosamilia
The text of this book was set in Adobe Caslon Pro.
Manufactured in the United States of America
2 4 6 8 10 9 7 5 3
This book has been cataloged with the Library of Congress.
ISBN 978-1-4424-8861-8 (hc)
ISBN 978-1-4424-8860-1 (pbk)
ISBN 978-1-4424-8862-5 (eBook)

To my friend, Autumn Hull,
who listened to me (for countless hours)
while I thought through Preston and Amanda's story.
Her enthusiasm for this book cheered me
on when I needed it the most.

ACKNOWLEDGMENTS

I have to start by thanking Keith, my husband, who tolerated the dirty house, lack of clean clothes, and my mood swings, while I wrote this book (and all my other books).

My three precious kiddos, who ate a lot of corn dogs, pizza, and Frosted Flakes because I was locked away writing. I promise, I cooked them many good hot meals once I finished.

Tammara Webber and Elizabeth Reyes for reading and critiquing *Just For Now*. Thanks for your help, ladies!

To the coolest agent to ever grace the literary world, Jane Dystel. I adore her. It is that simple. And a shout out to Lauren Abramo, my foreign rights agent who is doing an amazing job at getting my books worldwide. She rocks.

Bethany Buck and the rest of the Simon Pulse staff have all

been amazing throughout the creation of this book. I couldn't have pulled this off without their brilliance.

And ALWAYS to my FP girls. Love y'all, and I'm thankful every day that I have each of you.

Prologue

"Well, if it ain't li'l Manda, all dressed up and coming out to play."

The water I'd been sipping chose this moment to strangle me. Covering my mouth to muffle my hacking cough, I turned away from the warm breath against my ear. I had shown up here tonight for one reason: to see Preston Drake. Wasn't it just my luck that when he finally decided to notice I was alive, I started coughing up a freaking lung?

Preston's amused chuckle as he patted my back didn't help my humiliation any. "Sorry, Manda, I didn't know my presence would get you all choked up."

Once I was able to speak again, I turned around to face the guy who had been making a grand appearance in my late-night fantasies for a couple of years now. All the primping I'd suffered through so that I looked irresistible tonight was pointless.

Preston was grinning at me like he always did. I amused him. He didn't see me as anything more than the innocent little sister of his best friend, Marcus Hardy. It was cliché. How many bad romance novels had I read about the girl falling hopelessly in love with her brother's best friend? Countless.

"You startled me." I wanted to explain my sudden burst of coughing.

Preston tipped a bottle of beer to his lips and took a drink while keeping his eyes cut toward me. "Are you sure it wasn't my sexy-as-hell voice whispering in your ear that caused your momentary lack of oxygen?"

Yes, that was probably it. But the guy knew he was beautiful. I wasn't going to add to his ego. Crossing my arms over my stomach, I struck a defensive pose. I never knew how to talk to Preston or what to say to him. I was so afraid he'd look me in the eye and know that I closed my eyes at night and imagined doing very bad things to his body.

"Damn, Manda," he said in a low, husky voice as his eyes lowered to my breasts. I'd worn a low-cut white blouse tonight, and a really good push-up bra, in hopes of at least getting Preston to see that my body was all grown up. Besides, I knew he had a thing for boobs. It was obvious by the girls he dated. . . . Well, he didn't really date. He just screwed them. My boobs were not big, but, a good push-up bra and the right position and they weren't too bad.

"That's a real nice shirt you got on."

He was really looking at me. Or at them—but they were a part of me, so it was the same thing. "Thank you," I replied in a normal voice that betrayed the fact I was breathing a little faster now.

Preston took another step toward me, closing the small area that had separated us. His eyes were still directed at the cleavage I had pushing up in full view. "Maybe wearing a shirt like that ain't real smart, Manda." His deep voice caused me to shiver. "Aw hell, girl, don't do that. No shivering."

One large hand touched my waist. His thumb brushed against my stomach and gently pushed the hem of my shirt up. "I've been drinkin' since four, sweetheart. You need to push me away and send me packing, 'cause I don't think I can stop this on my own."

Small whimper. Oh, yes. Should I start begging now?

Preston lifted his eyes to meet mine. His long, pale blond hair that girls everywhere wanted to get their hands in fell forward over one of his eyes. I couldn't help it. I reached up and tucked the loose strands behind his ear. He closed his eyes and made a small, pleased sound in his throat.

"Manda, you're real sweet. Real fucking sweet, and I'm not the kind of guy you're supposed to let get this close." His voice was almost a whisper now as his eyes bore into mine. I could see the slight glassy look that confirmed he'd had too much to drink.

"I'm a big girl. I can decide who I let get close," I replied, shifting my hips so that he had a better view directly down my shirt if he wanted it.

"Mmmm, see, this is where I think you might be wrong, 'cause untouched little bodies like yours, all fresh and sweet, shouldn't tempt guys who are only looking for another hot fuck."

Something about hearing Preston Drake say "fuck" out of those full, pink lips of his was a major turn-on. He was too pretty. He always had been. His lashes too long, his face too sculpted, and you add that in with his lips and hair, you get one lethal package.

"Maybe I'm not as untouched as you think," I said, hoping he didn't detect the lie. I wanted to be one of those bad girls he didn't mind taking in a back room up against a wall.

Preston lowered his mouth to barely graze the skin on my shoulder that was revealed by the shirt I'd chosen. "You telling me that this sweetness has been played with?"

No. "Yes," I replied.

"Come take a ride with me," he asked close to my ear as his teeth pulled gently on my earlobe.

"Okay."

Preston moved back and nodded toward the door. "Let's go."

That probably wasn't such a good idea. If Rock, Dewayne, or any other of my brother's friends saw us leaving together, they'd stop anything from happening. And I wanted something to happen. Alone time under the covers thinking about Preston

Drake was getting old. I wanted the actual man. I wonder why Preston hadn't thought about our exit. Did he want the guys to stop us? I glanced over at their usual table, and Rock wasn't paying us any attention. Dewayne winked at me, then went back to talking to some girl.

I looked back at the bartender. "I have to pay my tab first."

Preston nudged me toward the door. "I got your tab. You go get in my Jeep."

Okay. Yes. I wanted to go get in his Jeep. This would also have us leaving separately. Nodding, I hurried for the door, thinking I may have just won the lottery.

Glancing around the parking lot, I searched for Preston's Jeep. When I didn't see it out front, I headed for the back of the building to see if he'd parked back there. Most people didn't because there were no lights around.

Stepping into the darkness, I wondered if this was smart. A girl really shouldn't be out here by herself at night. Maybe I should just go back to the part of the parking lot were it was well lit.

"Don't you back out on me now. I'm already going half mad thinking about this." Preston's hands came around my waist and pulled me tightly up against his chest. Both of his hands slid up and covered my boobs, squeezing them, then tugging on my top until it was low enough that he could feel the exposed skin of my cleavage.

"Sweet God Almighty, real ones feel so damn good," he murmured.

I couldn't take a deep breath. Preston's hands were touching me. I wanted him to touch more. Reaching up, I undid the buttons on my shirt and let it fall open. I found the front clasp of my bra and quickly unfastened it before I could back out. We were in the middle of a very dark parking lot, and I was being a complete slut.

"Damn, baby. Get your ass in my Jeep," Preston growled as he pushed me forward a few more steps, then turned me left by directing my hips. His Jeep appeared in front of us. I was pretty sure we couldn't do this in a Jeep.

"Can we, uh, do this in here?" I asked as he turned me around to face him. Even in the dark, his light hair stood out. His eyelids were lowered, and those long lashes of his almost brushed his cheeks.

"Do what, baby? What is it you wanna do? 'Cause showing me these pretty titties has me going a little crazy." He pressed me back up against his Jeep as he lowered his head and pulled one of my nipples into his mouth and sucked hard before flicking it with his tongue.

No one had ever kissed my boobs. The immediate explosion that went off in my panties as I cried his name hadn't been on purpose. My head was pressed back on the Jeep window, and my knees had completely given out. Preston's hands holding firmly to my waist had kept me from ending up a heap on the gravel.

"Motherfucker," Preston growled, and I started to apologize when his hands cupped my butt and he picked me up. I grabbed his shoulders and wrapped my legs around his waist, afraid he would drop me.

"Where are we going?" I asked as he stalked deeper into the parking lot. Had I made him mad?

"I'm getting your sexy ass back here so I can strip off your clothes and bury my dick into that tight little pussy. You can't go do shit like that, Manda, and expect a guy to control himself. It don't fucking work that way, baby girl."

He was going to "fuck" me. Finally. Not exactly what I wanted him to refer to it as when we finally did it, but Preston wasn't one for roses and candlelight. He was all about the pleasure. I knew that already.

Preston reached out and opened a door behind me. We stepped into a dark and slightly chilly room.

"Where are we?" I asked as he sat me down on a box.

"Outside storage unit. It's okay. I've used it before."

He'd used it before? Oh.

I could hardly see him, but I knew from the shadow of his movements that he was taking off his clothes. First his shirt. I wanted to see his chest. I'd heard from girls giggling around town that he had one of the tightest, most ripped stomachs they'd ever seen. Rumor was, even Mrs. Gunner, the wife of one of the city council members, had slept with Preston. I didn't believe that, though. He was just too pretty to have sex with someone her age. I heard a crinkle and started to ask what he was doing when it dawned on me—he'd opened a condom wrapper.

His hands started running up the insides of my legs, and I didn't care so much about Mrs. Gunner or the other rumors I'd heard about his sex life.

"Open up." His husky demand had the desired effect. I let my legs fall open. His hand slipped right up to the edge of my panties. With one finger he ran down the center of my warmth. "These panties are fucking soaked." The approval in his voice eased any embarrassment I might have felt from a comment like that.

Both his hands reached up and slipped my panties down until they were at my ankles. Preston knelt down and slipped each of my high heels through the holes. Then he stood up and leaned over me. "I'm keeping these."

My panties?

"Lay back," Preston said as his body came over mine.

I reached back to make sure that the box was large enough for me to lie all the way back. "You got plenty of room, Manda. Lay back," Preston repeated.

I didn't want him to change his mind or possibly sober up, so

I did as I was told. The cardboard was sturdy and full of something firm and heavy, because we didn't even put a dent in it.

Preston's mouth lowered to mine and I prepared myself for our first kiss, when he stopped. His lips hovered over mine only for a second before he moved away and began kissing my neck. What had just happened? Did my breath smell bad? I'd just had a peppermint inside the bar.

The little licks and nibbles he was making along my collarbone made it hard for me to think too clearly about it.

Then his hips lowered and both of his hands shoved my skirt up around my waist. I didn't have too much time to prepare myself before he was pressing against my entrance.

"Tight, fuck, fuck, it's so tight," Preston whispered, and his body trembled over me, making the sharp pain between my legs a little more bearable. "I can't hold back, Manda. Fuck it . . . I can't."

Pain sliced through me, and I screamed and bucked underneath him. He was cursing while saying my name as he slid in and out of me. The pain slowly started to ease, and I felt the first tremor of pleasure.

"AHHH, holy shit," Preston cried out, and his body jerked over me. I wasn't sure what exactly had just happened, but from the small moans coming from him, he enjoyed it.

When he didn't move anymore and the hard length inside of me began to go away, I realized it was over. Preston pushed himself away from me and slowly pulled out of me as he muttered more curse words. He moved, and from what I could see, he was putting on his shirt. Already?

I sat up and pushed my skirt down. The fact that I was on display suddenly mattered. When I heard the zipper on his jeans, I quickly fastened my bra and started buttoning my shirt.

"Manda." His voice sounded sad. "I'm sorry."

I opened my mouth to ask him what for, because what we'd just done I'd completely asked for, when he opened the door and walked off into the darkness.

Chapter One

Three months later . . .

PRESTON

The bottom step was rotten. I needed to put fixing that on my priority list. One of the kids was going to run down it and end up with a twisted ankle—or worse, a broken leg—if I ignored it. Stepping over it, I walked the rest of the way up the steps to my mother's trailer.

It had been a week since I'd stopped by and checked on things. Mom's latest boyfriend had been drunk, and I'd ended up taking a swing at him when he'd called my seven-year-old sister, Daisy, a chickenshit for spilling her glass of orange juice. I'd busted his lip. Mom had screamed at me and told me to get out. I figured a week was enough time for her to get over it.

The screen door swung open, and a big gap-toothed smile greeted me.

"Preston's here!" Brent, my eight-year-old brother, called out before wrapping his arms around my legs.

"Hey, bud, what's up?" I asked, unable to return the hug. My arms were full of groceries for the week.

"He brought food," Jimmy, my eleven-year-old brother, announced, and stepped outside and reached for one of the bags I was carrying.

"I got these. There's more in the Jeep. Go get 'em, but watch that bottom step. It's about to go. I gotta fix it."

Jimmy nodded and hurried off toward the Jeep.

"Did you get me dose Fwooty Pebbles I wyke?" Daisy asked as I stepped into the living room. Daisy was developmentally delayed in her speech. I blamed my mother's lack of caring.

"Yep, Daisy May, I got you two boxes," I assured her, and walked across the worn, faded blue carpet to set the bags down on the kitchen counter. The place reeked of cigarette smoke and nasty.

"Momma?" I called out. I knew she was here. The old beat-up Chevelle she drove was in the yard. I wasn't going to let her avoid me. The rent was due. I needed any other bills that may have come in the mail.

"She's sweepin'," Daisy said in a whisper.

I couldn't keep the scowl off my face. She was always sleeping. If she wasn't sleeping, she was off drinking.

"The dickhead left her yesterday. She's been holed up pouting ever since," Jimmy said as he put the other groceries down beside mine.

Good riddance. The man was a mooch. If it wasn't for the kids, I'd never show up at this place. But my mom had full custody because in Alabama as long as you have a roof and you aren't abusing your kids, then you get to keep them. It's some fucked-up shit.

"You bought free gaddons of milk?" Daisy asked in awe as I pulled out all three gallons of milk from a paper bag.

"'Course I did. How are you gonna eat two boxes of Fruity Pebbles if you don't have any milk?" I asked, bending down to look her in the eyes.

"Pweston, I don't think I can dwink all free," she said in another whisper. Dang, she was cute.

I ruffled her brown curls and stood up. "Well, I guess you'll have to share with the boys, then."

Daisy nodded seriously like she agreed that was a good idea.

"You bought pizza rolls! YES! Score," Jimmy cheered as he pulled out the large box of his favorite food and ran to the freezer with it.

Seeing them get excited over food made everything else okay. I'd gone weeks with nothing but white bread and water when I was their age. Momma hadn't cared if I ate or not. If it hadn't been for my best friend, Marcus Hardy, sharing his lunch with me every day at school, I'd have probably died from malnutrition. I wasn't about to let that happen to the kids.

"I thought I told you to get out. You caused enough trouble 'round here. You run off, Randy. He's gone. Can't blame him after you broke his nose for nothin'." Momma was awake.

I put the last of the cans of ravioli in the cabinet before I turned around to acknowledge her. She was wearing a stained robe that was once white. Now it was more of a tan color. Her hair was a matted, tangled mess, and the mascara she'd been wearing a few days ago was smeared under her eyes. This was the only parent I'd ever known. It was a miracle I'd survived to adulthood.

"Hello, Momma," I replied, and grabbed a box of cheese crackers to put away.

"You bribing them with food. You little shit. They only love you 'cause you feed them that fancy stuff. I can feed my own kids. Don't need you spoilin' 'em," she grumbled as she shuffled her bare feet over to the closest kitchen chair and sat down.

"I'm gonna pay rent before I leave, but I know you have some other bills. Where are they?"

She reached for the pack of cigarettes sitting in the ashtray in the middle of her small brown Formica table. "The bills are on top of the fridge. I hid 'em from Randy. They made him pissy."

Great. The electricity bill and water bill pissed the man off. My mother sure knew how to pick them.

"Oh, Pweston, can I have one of dese now?" Daisy asked, holding up an orange.

"Of course you can. Come here and I'll peel it," I replied, holding out my hand for her to give it to me.

"Stop babying her. You come in here and baby her, then leave, and I'm left to deal with her spoiled ass. She needs to grow up and do shit herself." Momma's bitter words weren't anything new. However, watching Daisy flinch and her eyes fill up with tears I knew she wouldn't shed for fear of getting slapped caused my blood to boil.

I bent down and kissed the top of her head before taking the orange from her and peeling it. Confronting Momma would only make her worse. When I left, it would be up to Jimmy to make sure Daisy was safe. Leaving them here wasn't easy, but I didn't have the kind of money it would take to go to court over it. And the lifestyle I'd chosen in order to make sure they were okay and taken care of wasn't one that the courts would look favorably on. There wasn't a snowball's chance in hell I'd ever get them. The best I could do was come here once a week and feed them and make sure their bills were paid. I couldn't be around Momma more than that.

"When's Daisy's next doctor's appointment?" I asked, wanting to change the subject and find out when I needed to come pick her up and take her.

"I think it's last week. Why don't you call the doc yourself and find out, if you're so damn worried about it. She ain't sick. She's just lazy."

I finished peeling the orange and grabbed a paper towel, then handed it to Daisy.

"Tank you, Pweston."

I knelt down to her level. "You're welcome. Eat that up. It's good for you. I bet Jimmy will go out on the porch with you if you want."

Daisy frowned and leaned forward. "Jimmy won't go outside 'cause Becky Ann lives next doowah. He tinks she's pwetty."

Grinning, I glanced back at Jimmy, whose cheeks were bright red.

"Dammit, Daisy, why you have to go and tell him that?"

"Watch the language with your sister," I warned, and stood up. "Ain't no reason to be embarrassed 'cause you think some girl is good-looking."

"Don't listen to him. He's in a different one's panties ever' night. Just like his daddy was." Momma loved to make me look bad in front of the kids.

Jimmy grinned. "I know. I'm gonna be just like Preston when I grow up."

I slapped him on the back of the head. "Keep it in your pants, boy."

Jimmy laughed and headed for the door. "Come on, Daisy May. I'll go outside with you for a while."

I didn't look back at Momma as I finished putting away the food, then retrieved the bills from the top of the fridge. Brent sat silently on the bar stool, watching me. I would have to spend a little time with him before I left. He was the middle one, the one who didn't push for my attention. I'd sent the other two outside knowing he liked to have me to himself.

"So what's new?" I asked, leaning on the bar across from him.

He smiled and shrugged. "Nothing much. I wanna play football this year, but Momma says it costs too much and I'd be bad at it 'cause I'm scrawny."

God, she was a bitch.

"Is that so? Well, I disagree. I think you'd make an awesome corner or wide receiver. Why don't you get me the info on this and I'll check into it?"

Brent's eyes lit up. "For real? 'Cause Greg and Joe are playing, and they live in the trailers back there." He pointed toward the back of the trailer park. "Their daddy said I could ride with them and stuff. I just needed someone to fill out the paper and pay for it."

"Go on ahead and pay for it. Let him get hurt, and see whose fault it'll be," Momma said through the cigarette hanging out of her mouth.

"I'm sure they have coaches and adults overseeing this so that it is rare someone gets really hurt at this age," I said, shooting a warning glare back at her.

"You're making me raise the sorriest bunch of brats in town.

When they all need bailed outta jail in a few years, that shit is all on you." She stood up and walked back to her room. Once the door slammed behind her, I looked back at Brent.

"Ignore that. You hear me? You're smart, and you're gonna make something of yourself. I believe in you."

Brent nodded. "I know. Thank you for football."

I reached out and patted his head. "You're welcome. Now why don't you come on outside and walk me to my Jeep?"

AMANDA

Marcus, my older brother, was mad at me. He was convinced I was staying home instead of going to Auburn like I'd planned because of Mom. I wasn't. Not really. Well, maybe a little bit. At first it had been for completely selfish reasons. I'd wanted to get Preston Drake to notice me. Well, three months ago I'd gotten my wish for about forty minutes. Since then he hadn't looked my way once. After several pitiful attempts to get his attention, I stopped trying.

Unfortunately, it was a little too late to decide I wanted to go to Auburn instead of the local junior college. I was almost relieved I couldn't go away, though. My mom was dealing with the betrayal and desertion of my dad. He now lived an hour away with his new young girlfriend and their child.

Leaving home meant leaving Mom all alone in this big house. If I hadn't made the decision to stay and try to get Preston's attention, I'd be leaving today for Auburn. Mom would be crying and I would be sick to my stomach with worry. She just wasn't strong enough to be left alone just yet. Maybe next year.

"You can't live here forever, Amanda," Marcus said as he paced in front of me. I had come outside to the pool with the new copy of *People* magazine hoping to get some sun, but Marcus had shown up. "At some point we're going to have to let Mom learn to cope. I know it's hard. Look at me, I'm still stopping by four to five times a week just to make sure she's okay. But I don't want you giving up your dreams because you feel responsible for our mother."

I'd managed to keep my not going away to Auburn a secret from him until today. Normally, he was so wrapped up in his world with his fiancée, Willow, and his online courses to keep up with what I was doing.

"I know this, but maybe I just wasn't ready to leave home. Maybe this is all about me. You ever think of that?"

Marcus frowned and rubbed his chin hard, which meant he was frustrated. "Okay. Fine. Say you don't want to go away just yet. Have you considered maybe going in January? Getting your feet wet with college while at home, then venturing out?"

Sighing, I laid my magazine in my lap. I might as well give up on reading it until he'd gotten this off his chest. "No, I haven't, because that is stupid. I can go an entire year here, then transfer next year. It works for me. I know people here, and I want to be here for the wedding. I want to help Willow plan it. I don't want to be four hours away missing all this."

I'd hit him below the belt. Anything to do with his wedding and he went all soft. Marcus stopped his endless pacing and sat down on the end of the lounge chair beside me. "So this is really about you wanting to stay at home? You're just not ready to leave yet? Because if that is really the case, then I'm good with that. I don't want you going off if you're not ready. Sure as hell don't want you going to Auburn. But if this is what you want—*you* want—then I'm happy. I just don't want what Dad did to take away any more of our lives than it already has."

He was such a good guy. Why couldn't I be infatuated with a good guy like my overprotective, loving brother? There were guys out there like him. I'd met a few. Why did I have to be hung up on a male slut?"

"It *is* all about me. I swear."

Marcus nodded, then slapped my foot before standing back up. "Good. I feel better now. Since you're not moving away today, you're invited to the engagement party the guys are throwing for me and Low."

Guys? "What guys?"

"You know, the guys. Rock, Preston, Dewayne—well, the truth is, mostly Trisha is throwing it and the guys are all planning the alcohol."

"Does she need help?" I asked, thinking how ridiculous it

was that I was asking in hopes that I would be thrown together with Preston in some part of the planning.

"Yeah, I'm sure she does. Why don't you give her a call?"

I would do that. Today. "Okay, cool. When is it?"

"This Friday night."

Chapter Two

PRESTON

"Where do I put these large paper balls, and what the hell are these, anyway?"

Trisha, the only other female who'd managed to get one of my friends to tie the knot, glanced back at me from her perch on top of the ladder and laughed. "Put the box of lanterns on the table over there beside the flowers," Trisha instructed me before turning back to tying ribbon from the ceiling.

When I'd agreed to help with this party for Marcus and Low, I'd thought that meant I was chipping in for the beer. Not carrying shit and hanging it up all day long. Trisha had demanded we all be here at eight this morning. She'd barely given us a break for lunch. The next time one of my dumbass friends got engaged, I wasn't making the mistake of offering to help again.

"Five more boxes in the truck, Preston. What're you standing around for?" Rock asked as he walked in behind me and dropped a box on the table.

"I'm trying to find a way to get the hell out of here."

Rock chuckled. "Good luck with that. My woman ain't letting anyone free until we've got this thing looking just the way she wants it."

"A warning that Trisha was a party-decorating Nazi would have been nice."

Rock slapped my back. "Nope. Then it'd just be me and Trisha. I wanted y'all to suffer through it with me."

Fine. Five more boxes, and then I was finding a way to sneak out. I followed Rock back outside to the truck. A familiar little Mercedes coupe pulled into the drive. What the hell was Amanda doing here? She was supposed to be safely tucked away at college by now. I wouldn't have come to the Hardys' beach condo if I'd thought there was a chance she could be here. Damn it. The girl was driving me crazy. She'd started flirting with me heavily about three months ago. And she hadn't let up. I wasn't someone she needed to be flirting with. My life was too fucked up for the likes of an innocent like Amanda.

Her car door swung open, and out came a very long tanned leg. I stopped. I was weak where she was concerned. After a very vivid dream about what she'd feel like and taste like, I'd been closing my eyes and pretending like every other woman I ended

up fucking was Amanda. I was sorry scum for doing it, but . . .
ah, hell . . .

Amanda stood up, and the tiny little red shorts she was
wearing made those long legs that ended in a pair of red heels
look endless. Fuck, I was going to get a boner. I'd been thinking about those legs wrapped around me for three months too
long. If she'd treat me like the creep I was, then it would be
easier to ignore, but she didn't. She smiled and batted her long
eyelashes and flipped her blond hair over her shoulder. Even the
few nights she'd managed to get drunk at Live Bay, the local
club, the innocence pouring off her was a major red flag.

"Get a box!" Rock yelled at me as he pulled out another one
of the boxes from the truck. I didn't make eye contact with her.
I couldn't. She'd smile, and I'd be an ass trying to get her to
go away. Ignoring her worked better. I didn't like to see that
sweet little flirty gleam in her eyes suddenly turn to hurt when
I opened my mouth and spewed lies. I'd seen it too many times
this summer. I was staying the hell away from that. My heart
couldn't take it.

Grabbing a box, I headed back to her daddy's condo. It was
set directly on the beach, and a perfect spot for tonight's party.
The patio opened up to the condo's pool—we had reserved it for
a private party.

"Hello, Preston." Amanda was beside me.

She was relentless. "Manda, aren't you supposed to be off at college by now?" Please, God, let her be leaving and getting far away from my dirty mind.

"I'm staying here this year. I decided I wasn't ready to leave home just yet."

Well, fuck me. She was staying here? *No!* I needed her to leave before I did something stupid. Like hauling her ass into the nearest bedroom and stripping off them red shorts, then tasting every last inch of her.

"Gonna have to grow up sometime, Manda. Can't stay at home with Mommy forever." I was a prick.

I didn't have to glance over to know Amanda had stopped walking beside me. I'd done it again. All I ever managed to do was say things to hurt her feelings. I needed to leave it like this, just go inside and pretend like we hadn't even spoken. But I couldn't.

I stopped and turned to look back at her. She was standing there with her hands clasped tightly in front of her, making her tits push together and—holy fucking shit! She wasn't wearing a bra under that flimsy little shirt she had on. You could see her nipples poking through the fabric. What was she doing? She didn't need to dress like that.

"Manda, go put on a bra. I know your boobs aren't that big, but *that* shirt requires a bra."

Her big green eyes welled up with unshed tears. It was a punch to the gut. I hated that every word I said to her was cruel, but I needed her to stay away from me. She had no idea exactly who I was. No one did, really. I was many different things to many different people. Sometimes I didn't even know who the hell I was anymore.

She ducked her head, and long blond hair fell over her shoulders. She crossed her arms over her chest and walked briskly past me and into the condo. I set the box down at the door, then turned and headed out to my Jeep. I couldn't stay here. I needed to go beat the shit out of something before I lost it.

AMANDA

I was done. No more. I couldn't continue to try to make Preston like me. He acted as if I was still his best friend's kid sister and he hadn't screwed my brains out behind a club. This was just hurting me more and more. It was past time I moved on. Let this one go. He'd just let me know how lacking my body was. I would just put the memory of how I lost my virginity away. Forget about it and never look back. Besides, it wasn't like I could ever share the experience with anyone. It was humiliating enough just to know I'd sent him running. He hadn't even kissed me. The idea of kissing me had repulsed him that much.

I didn't need to face anyone just yet. I ran up the steps instead of going into the living room, where everyone was getting ready. Sadie White, my best friend, would be here tonight.

I wouldn't be alone in this crowd of people. Closing the door to my bedroom in my dad's place, I pulled my phone out of my purse and called Sadie.

I hadn't told her everything. She had no idea I'd given Preston my virginity in a storage unit like some cheap slut. I was too ashamed to tell her that part of the awful truth. But she did know he had flirted heavily with me and we'd gone out to his Jeep and made out a bit before he walked off and left me.

"Hello." Sadie's voice was happy and cheerful. Jax, her rock-star boyfriend, was in town. She was always on cloud nine when he came to visit. He was here this time to pack her up and move her off to California. I was trying not to think about that.

"I know you and lover boy are packing you up and all, but I wanted to make sure you're coming tonight." I hadn't been able to mask the hurt in my voice. She was going to pick up on it.

"Yes. What's wrong, Amanda?" I could hear the concern in her voice.

Swallowing through the lump in my throat, I gripped the phone tightly and tried real hard to control my emotions. "I just didn't want to be alone. With . . . everyone."

Sadie sighed. "Is this about Preston? I swear I want to kick his butt."

"No. It . . . okay, well, maybe it is. But it's my fault. I should have stayed away from him. I knew he was like this." Maybe I hadn't known he would actually screw me and walk away, never to be nice to me again. But I had known he was a player. This was his brush-off.

"I'll be there. You won't be alone. In fact, you'll have a date."

I stopped blinking back tears and waited for an explanation of her last statement. What did she mean by "a date"? Was she sharing Jax? No . . . that made no sense.

"Huh?"

Sadie cleared her throat, then covered the phone with her hand, and I heard her muffled voice. I waited patiently for her to stop her private conversation and clue me in.

"Okay. Here's the thing. Jason, Jax's brother, is here too. You met him about six months ago, remember? He was at the birthday party I threw for Jax at the beach house."

"Of course I remember Jason. He's hard to forget." He looked a lot like Jax. He just had a quieter demeanor. I'd had to talk to him that night because he didn't say a whole lot.

"Well, he's been asking about you. I knew you were hung up on Preston, which I can't really figure out. He's cute and all, but he's a man whore. Jason mentioned you again today."

Jason Stone, younger brother to the world's biggest teenage heartthrob, liked me? "Uh, well, um, okay. I think. I mean, really? Jason? He dates models and stuff. I saw him on *Teen Heat* last week with Kipley McKnowel. I can't compete with that. I've seen her makeup commercial."

Sadie laughed. "She's airbrushed in that commercial.

She's really not that fabulous in real life. I met her. Trust me. Besides, he was with her that one time. He said she was missing intelligence. He wasn't interested."

"Jason Stone . . . really?" I was just having too hard a time comprehending this. I'd just recently gotten used to Jax Stone randomly showing up at my house on Sadie's arm. Now to actually go on a date with his brother?

"Yes, really. I take it that you're interested." Sadie's amused tone made me smile. Maybe this was what I needed to get over Preston. He didn't want me. I needed to face that.

"Okay. Yeah, I mean, if he's sure."

"You are clueless, Amanda Hardy. Just because you can't get the attention of a guy hell-bent on sleeping his way through the United States doesn't mean you aren't gorgeous and smart and extremely appealing to any guy with two eyes and a brain. Trust me. 'Kay?"

The heaviness in my chest eased some. The ache was still there, but the hope that I could move on and stop getting hurt by Preston was a relief. I still couldn't believe it was going to be with Jason Stone. Tonight didn't seem so bad anymore.

"I trust you. Now, what do I wear?"

Chapter Three

PRESTON

I'd ignored the few calls from Rock I got after I'd sped out of the condo like a man running for his life. He would have to get over it. I couldn't explain. I would just pitch in more money than I'd originally intended to make up for bailing on helping them set up. Staying that close to Amanda and not going after her and falling on my knees and begging her to forgive me for the stupid shit I said would have been impossible. I hated to see her hurt. I hated doing it. I was a shithead. But I couldn't let her near me. She was too sweet and innocent.

Closing my Jeep door, I took a deep breath before heading toward the condo. The music was already pouring out the windows, and the parking lot was filling up. I'd come a little early so I could slip Rock some money so he'd get over the fact that I'd left him high and dry earlier.

Before I reached the door, it swung open and Rock stepped out. His frown looked more concerned than pissed. Shit.

"You okay?" were the first words out of his mouth.

I reached into my back pocket and pulled out a couple of hundreds. "Here. Take this. It's my part for the party. I had some shit come up earlier and I had to run."

Rock reached out and took it, but he didn't put it in his pocket. He held it between his fingers. "You fucked up with some shit and can't get out of it?"

What? Wait . . . did he mean drugs? "Uh, no."

Rock's eyebrows lowered, and he pointed the money I'd given him at me. "Then where the hell do you get the cash you never seem to run out of? 'Cause I know where you come from, boy, and it ain't an inheritance."

This was not the first time I'd dodged this question. But it was the first time I'd had to deal with it sober. "It ain't drugs, Rock. Now put the shit in your pocket and let me inside."

Rock shifted on his feet, but he didn't move. "You know if you need help getting out of anything, I got your back. Right?"

He'd had my back since we were kids. He was also the only friend I'd ever had over to my trailer growing up. I'd just had him over the one time, though. Momma had been high as a kite and throwing the few dishes we had across the kitchen because

I'd forgotten to pick up her empty bottles of whiskey and throw them away the night before. I could still see the look of horror in Rock's eyes that day. It had been the first and last time I let someone come over.

I nodded, stepped around him, and headed inside the door. He slapped my back as I passed, and I knew we were okay.

The place looked amazing. Those paper balls were hanging from the ceiling, and it looked pretty damn good. Flowers in vases wrapped with white lights were everywhere. It wasn't too incredibly packed yet, but I knew everyone would be here soon enough. I scanned the room quickly for any sign of Amanda. She wasn't here yet. I had time to get a drink and find a female to latch on to before she showed up.

There were several stations with bartenders outside on the patio and around the pool. I made my way out there. Fresh air and a shot of Cuervo would be nice.

"You bailed on me. I should push you in that pool," Trisha said threateningly as she walked toward me.

"I know. I'm sorry. I gave Rock some money to make up for my running off. Something came up. I had to go."

Trisha rolled her eyes. "Cheap sluts aren't an emergency. They're a dime a dozen."

Let her think I'd run off to get laid. It was better than the truth. That I'd run off because Amanda Hardy was so fucking under my skin I couldn't think straight. She'd been the only thing in my head while I'd relieved some tension in the shower before I left for the party.

"Don't push me in. I might get naked and get this party started," I replied with a wink.

"I wouldn't be surprised," she replied, and walked off.

I stopped at the first drinking station when I saw Dewayne, another of my best friends since elementary school. Me, Rock, Marcus, and Dewayne had been close since the day we'd all been suspended in the second grade for fighting on the playground. It had formed a bond that I'd never take for granted. I'd needed a family. They'd become that for me.

"If it ain't the pussy king," Dewayne said. "I show up to help out, and your ass is already run off. 'Course, I wasn't surprised. I'd have been more surprised if you'd actually stayed and worked all day."

"Shut up. You lazy ass, I know you didn't stay all day," I replied with a grin, and looked over at the young guy in a tuxedo standing behind the bar. "I need a shot of tequila."

"Already hitting it hard, huh? Damn."

I started to respond when Dewayne's eyes widened and he let out a low whistle. I followed his gaze and almost swallowed my damn tongue.

Amanda was here. Wearing a short, clingy white dress. Her long tanned legs looked even longer with the bronze high-heeled sandals she was wearing. Her silky blond hair was curled and pulled up on her head, while several curls had fallen loose and grazed her bare neck and shoulders. Ah, hell.

"Is she with Jason Stone? Fuck, I hope not. Marcus is gonna be pissed." Dewayne's words slapped me in the face. I tore my eyes off her and looked to see whose arm she was holding on to. Jax Stone's brother was smiling down at her, saying something. He was making her laugh. She was gazing up at him like he was fascinating. Fuck. A red haze settled over my vision, and I started to move. A hand clamped down on my arm and jerked me back.

"What the hell are you doing?" Dewayne's hard tone surprised me. What was I doing?

"I, he, she . . . I don't know."

I didn't look back at Dewayne. I couldn't explain that asinine answer. Instead I turned to the bartender. "Make that a double, and keep 'em coming."

AMANDA

Jason was everything Preston wasn't. He was polite. He liked talking to me. He made me feel attractive. He didn't say hurtful, mean things. He wasn't scanning the crowd looking for a female to haul off and screw. He was with me. Completely. It was nice. I liked feeling wanted.

So why did I keep looking back at Preston? He was drinking

heavily already, and Marcus and Low hadn't even arrived yet.

"You want something to drink?" Jason asked from beside me. I tore my gaze off Preston and turned it back to my date.

"Not really. Unless you do," I replied. I really didn't want to go anywhere near the bar in front of us. Far away from Preston was best.

"Did Trisha do all this? She did a fantastic job. This place looks magical. Very romantic," Sadie said in awe as she and Jax came up beside us. He'd been stopped at the door, and the request for autographs had begun. I needed to find Trisha and have her put a stop to that. A lot of the people here were accustomed to Jax coming around, but this would be new for some guests and I knew it got to Sadie.

"Yeah, she worked on it all day. She directed and we followed," I replied.

Sadie grabbed my arm and tugged me close to her. "Preston is looking this way. He doesn't appear to be happy. We need to move," she whispered.

I agreed. "Come on, let's go down to the beach and see what Trisha decided to do under the tent she has out there. I know they are playing music and that's where the dance floor is."

"Oh, wait. Marcus and Low are here," Sadie said, pointing back toward the door we'd come out of. They were inside talking to guests. We needed to go speak to them before we escaped to the beach.

"Let's go say hello first," I replied, looking up at Jason to see if he was okay with this.

"Yeah, let's get the big brother thing over with. That way I can be less nervous." The amused tone in his voice didn't take away the serious expression in his eyes. He was nervous. Marcus was pretty good about letting me date as long as he approved. He didn't breathe down guys' necks or embarrass me.

"He will be nice. Come on."

"I don't know that I'd believe her. Your last name is Stone," Jax drawled.

"Oh, stop it. You know he has moved on from that. Look at him. He's infatuated with Willow," Sadie replied.

Once upon a time Marcus had been crazy about Sadie. That was how I knew her. But Jax Stone had been the only guy ever to win Sadie's heart. Marcus never even stood a chance. When Willow had come into his life, I'd been so happy for him. She was just as gorgeous on the inside as she was on the outside. They'd had a major hurdle to get over thanks to our father and Willow's sister, but they'd loved each other enough. More than enough. I wanted that one day too.

"I'll just be happy when he's married. Maybe with a kid or two," Jax replied. The crooked smile on his face assured everyone he was kidding. Well, maybe a little bit of that was true. Jax was incredibly possessive of Sadie. He didn't like any guy getting too close. Marcus had gotten too close once.

Sadie laughed and kissed his cheek. Thanks to the stiletto heels she was wearing, she didn't have to stand on her tippy toes. "I'm moving away with you tomorrow. What more do you want?"

Jax raised an eyebrow at her question. "You really want me to answer that with an audience?"

Sadie blushed and ducked her head, causing Jax to chuckle.

"Let's go see Marcus. These two are only going to get more disgustingly sweet the longer we stand here," Jason said, leading me past Sadie and his brother.

Marcus and Low were standing under the white lights that Trisha and I had strung together earlier and wrapped around several of the paper lanterns in the center of the main room. The smile on Marcus's face made me tear up. I loved seeing him this happy. I loved that he'd found Low. If anyone deserved a happily ever after, it was my bighearted older brother.

"You're sure he isn't going to take a swing at me?" Jason asked with his mouth very close to my ear.

I nodded. "Yes, I'm sure. Come on."

As if he could hear the whispering, Marcus lifted his eyes to meet mine. The smile on his face froze as he shifted his gaze from me to Jason, but only for a moment. The sincerely happy expression returned as he made eye contact with Jason. Apparently, he approved.

"Wasn't expecting you to show up with a date," Marcus said as we stopped in front of him and Low.

"It was a last-minute thing. Jason saved me from coming here alone," I explained.

"Or your sister agreed to go out with me, and I took the opportunity and ran with it," Jason replied.

Marcus smirked and nodded. "I just might like you."

Low held her hand out to Jason. "I'm Willow, and it is very nice to meet you. If you are lucky enough to get Amanda on a date, then you must be a great guy."

Jason shook Low's hand, then glanced over at me with a smile. "I've been working on getting up the nerve to ask for a while now. Tonight was my lucky break."

Really? He'd been interested in me for a while? Wow. I hadn't expected that. He was Jason Stone. He was splashed all over the news, and gossip magazines loved him.

"Well, we are glad you're here," Willow assured him.

"What's he doing?" Marcus asked, taking a step forward, his attention directed outside.

"Shit," Rock growled, running by us and toward the doors leading out to the pool. Marcus took off after him. What in the world was going on?

Then I saw Dewayne standing between Preston, who was leaned up against the bar with an amused grin on his face, and some guy who was yelling at Preston and pointing at him over Dewayne's shoulder.

I started to follow Marcus. Something was wrong. Was

Preston starting a fight? Why was he doing this? And why the heck did I care so much?

"Wait, don't go out there, Amanda," Low called out as I started after my brother. I wanted to run outside and ignore her, but I was leaving Jason behind too. Sadie's big eyes met mine, as she and Jax had stopped just behind Jason and me to give their congratulations to Marcus and Low. I needed to give all of them a reason why I needed to be outside. I needed to see if Preston was okay.

"I'll be back. They may need me." It was the best I could come up with before running after Marcus.

Chapter Four

PRESTON

This was not the kind of shit I needed right now. I'd been focused on drinking Amanda Hardy out of my system tonight. That's all I wanted to focus on. That and her legs. Damn, her legs.

Then something like this happens. Not what I was in the mood for.

"Tell him you didn't touch his mom, Preston," Dewayne demanded from in front of me. He was acting like my fucking bodyguard. I could take this guy. I didn't need someone to protect me.

"Tell. Him," Dewayne repeated.

I couldn't do that. Me and the guy threatening to beat my ass both knew I couldn't deny it. He'd caught me with his mom last week. I could remember his face. Couldn't remember his mom's face but did remember the fury in his eyes. I'd seen it one too many times.

"What's going on?" Rock asked as he and Marcus ran out and also stood between me and the guy. I didn't have the heart to tell the guy his dear mom had paid me very well for that Sunday afternoon roll around her sheets. I wasn't into older women. I used them. That was it. They had cash, and I fulfilled their fantasies. The dude wouldn't be able to handle the truth, though.

"Trying to stop a fight," Dewayne explained as both Rock and Marcus stood beside him, blocking me even more from the angry son of one of my clients. This was just another reason I needed to start demanding that I not handle business in clients' houses. This shit happens.

"What did he do?" Marcus asked, glancing back at me.

I shrugged and took another shot of tequila.

"Guy says Preston slept with his mom, and he's out for blood," Dewayne explained.

"Shit," Rock mumbled, and shot a warning glare back my way.

"Go ahead, Preston. Explain that ain't the case," Dewayne demanded again.

I was getting tired of that. I hadn't spoken up yet. Had they not figured out that there was truth to this? Did they want me to lie to the guy and piss him off more? This guy and I had made eye contact that day as I'd pulled my jeans back on and headed out his mother's bedroom door while she made excuses to her son. I hadn't stayed around to deal with the drama. I just got the hell out.

"You got the wrong guy," a voice interrupted. "He's mine. He wouldn't be sleeping with someone's mom when he has me to come home to. So back off. I don't want to hear any more of this."

What the fucking hell?

Amanda walked around the wall of guys standing guard in front of me and crooked her finger my way. "Come on, baby. Let's go. This guy's confused you with someone else, and you've had too much to drink."

Had I passed out? Maybe I'd had more shots than I intended.

"Manda, what the hell—?"

"Back off, Marcus. I got this," she snapped, cutting off her brother's angry question.

"Come on, Preston. *Now.*"

I didn't question her. I set down my shot glass and stood up, then walked over to her. What was she doing? She slipped her hand around my waist and steered me away from the angry son and my friends.

"Follow me," she said, and led me through the crowd and toward the stairs leading up to the bedrooms. Probably not the best idea. I didn't need to have Amanda Hardy anywhere near a bed. Especially as drunk as I was at the moment. But then again, maybe this was all a drunken dream. Which meant I could strip her hot little body of this clingy, sexy-ass dress and kiss all the places my dreams haunted me with at night.

Amanda opened a door and pushed me inside a pink-and-white bedroom with ruffles on the bed and a white teddy bear resting against the pillows. Hell, yeah. This was hot. Amanda naked on that bed. Fuck, I was hard.

"Sit down." She shoved me toward the bed and then backed away from me. Not the best dream I'd ever had.

She put her hands on her hips and glared at me from across the room. Sexy. As. Hell.

"What are you doing? This is Marcus's engagement party. You can't go picking fights. What is wrong with you? Is everything a joke to you? Life's just one big party for you, isn't it? Well, wake up! You have friends down there who love you. They stand up for you even when they know you probably did screw that poor guy's mom." She stopped and shook her head in disgust. "God, please tell me she wasn't married." Then she put up her hand to stop anything I might say in reply. "No. Don't tell me anything. I don't want to know. Just stay in here. Sleep it off. Don't ruin this night for Marcus and Low. They deserve to be happy. Marcus loves you, Preston. Don't do something stupid to hurt him."

She dropped her hands to her side and let out a sigh. She was disappointed in me. This was a good thing. Maybe she was even disgusted with me. That would be even better. I needed her to stop flirting. I needed her to stop making me want things I couldn't have. Because, dammit, I wanted her. So very bad.

"I've got a date that I've run out on to save the testosterone party down there from throwing down one big ugly fight. All because you can't keep your pants up around a female." She dropped her eyes as she said the last part, and her cheeks flamed red. Did the idea of me having sex embarrass her?

She turned and walked back to the door. Her perfect round ass swayed under the thin material of the dress, mocking me with what I couldn't ever have. What I'd never be good enough for.

"He better be good to you," I said just loud enough for her to hear me if she was really listening. She stopped. She'd heard me.

Slowly she turned back around and stared at me with a confused expression. "What does that mean?" she asked, studying my face like it had all the answers she needed.

"It means that I don't give a shit who his brother is. If he hurts you, I'll hurt him."

Amanda let out a short, hard laugh and shook her head. "Really? *Really*, Preston? You care if Jason hurts me? Because I find it very hard to believe that you care about my feelings at all." Then she spun around and walked away, slamming the door behind her.

AMANDA

I would not cry. And I would stop this stupid shaking. There was a very hot, attractive, somewhat famous guy downstairs waiting on me. He didn't make me feel cheap and unwanted. Taking a deep breath, I straightened my shoulders and smoothed the wrinkles out of my dress, then walked back down the stairs. Scanning the crowd, I found Jason immediately. He was with Sadie and Jax. They were all probably talking about me. I'm sure Sadie was explaining my performance with Preston.

Speaking to guests as I made my way through the crowd, I kept a permanent smile plastered on my face. No one would know that what I'd just done had been for anyone else but Marcus. I'd never let them see I had any feelings for Preston. My pride would keep me safe.

"I'm so sorry. I was worried that if I didn't step in and help, we'd have a fight on our hands, and I don't want anything to ruin tonight for Marcus and Willow," I explained once I got to Jason, before anyone could say anything.

Jason was frowning, but it was a concerned frown. "That's fine. You did a good job ending things."

"Please tell me you locked him in a room so he can't come out," Sadie said. She was annoyed. I could hear it in her voice.

"Yeah, he is locked up. Hopefully passed out by now," I assured her.

"I'm sorry. I have to ask this—did the guy really sleep with someone's mom?" Jason asked.

Jax reached over and punched Jason in the arm. "Dude. Don't."

"I was just curious."

"It's her brother's best friend. Let it go."

"No. It's okay. He may be one of Marcus's best friends, but I'm aware he has issues. And yes, Jason, he probably did. You would be hard-pressed to find a female here Preston hasn't slept with."

Sadie's eyebrows shot up, and I realized what I'd said. I was venting. I needed to watch my mouth. My mom always said, "Loose lips sink ships." She was right. I needed to be more careful what I spewed from my mouth.

"Weren't we going to go down to the beach and check out the tent and band?" I asked, needing to get everyone's mind off what I'd just said.

"Yeah, we were," Jax replied, reaching for Sadie's arm and leading her toward the door.

"Sounds like a good idea to me," Jason agreed, and offered me his arm. I slipped my hand into the crook of his arm, and we all headed outside.

Marcus was standing with Willow in his arms, talking to Dewayne, Rock, and Trisha pretty intensely when we walked back out the doors. Cage York, Willow's best friend, and his girlfriend, Eva, had arrived too. They must've been getting filled in on the situation. Cage and Preston play baseball together, so they're pretty tight.

"Come here, Amanda," Marcus called out to me. I was hoping he'd forget what I'd just done, but apparently he wasn't going to. I wasn't sure what he was going to say, but I didn't feel right letting Jason hear them talk about Preston. He wasn't here to defend himself, and I'd already bashed him enough.

"Let me go reassure my brother that Preston is fine, and then I'll meet y'all down there."

Jason nodded. "Of course."

If Marcus frowned any harder, the crease in his forehead was going to crack. Not a good sign. "Don't scold me. I got him out of here, didn't I?"

"You don't need to stick your nose into any of Preston's crap. He has issues you need to stay miles away from. I get that you were trying to help save the party, but I don't like you stepping in to help Preston out. We got it. You stay away from his messes."

I might have had an absent father for the most part, but I had Marcus to make up for it. Where my daddy ignored me, Marcus hovered over me. I love him, I really do, but I don't like being told what I can and can't do. It was time he backed off a little. I was eighteen years old.

"She made a smart move. Lay off and give her a little credit." Cage stepped over and defended me. Like that would help. Marcus tolerated Cage because of Willow. He didn't exactly care what his opinion was.

"Listen. I saw a way to help, and I did. Not a big deal. I didn't go have a heart-to-heart with Preston. So back off. I'm a big girl now." I shot Marcus a tight smile, and then left him standing there before he or any of the other guys could speak up. I had a date waiting on me. I wasn't going to waste another minute talking about Preston Drake.

A hand shot out and grabbed my arm, and I glanced back to see it was Dewayne who'd stopped me, not my brother. What was his deal? Was I now going to get a lecture from him, too?

"Preston talks when he's drunk. He talks a lot. About a lot of shit. You know what I mean? Keep your distance. I love him, but he ain't good for you." Dewayne's low voice almost sounded like a rumble, but I heard every word. He'd spoken low enough that Marcus and the others couldn't hear him. I felt my face heat up, and I jerked my arm out of his hold.

What did Dewayne know about me and Preston? Could he possibly know about that night? I'd thought it was my secret. Apparently not. My stomach turned, and I prayed I wasn't about to get sick. It was bad enough knowing Preston had taken my virginity in a storage building on a bunch of boxes and then walked away, leaving me there alone. But knowing that someone else knew of my shame was even worse.

I had to force myself to keep from running as I walked swiftly through the crowd. I didn't smile and pretend like everything was great. The dark beach up ahead on the outskirts of the tent and lighting was my goal. Hiding away for a few minutes while I got a grip on things was necessary.

I could hear Sadie call my name from somewhere up ahead, but I pretended like I didn't hear her. I ran for the sand and the shadows.

I just needed a moment.

Tears burned my eyes, and I tilted my head back and blinked into the ocean breeze in an attempt to dry my tears before they ruined my face. The small sliver of hope I'd had that Preston had felt something for me was now completely extinguished. He had told someone. A moment that I wanted to remember yet wanted to wash my memory of at the same time wasn't as private as I'd thought. Preston had talked about it, while drunk. God, I hated him. How could I have been so crazy about him when he has no redeeming qualities? I was the biggest idiot on the face of the earth.

"Amanda?" Jason's concerned voice startled me. I hadn't expected him to follow me out here. Although we'd met before, this was really our first time together without a crowd around us. I wanted to be alone. Not pretending for my date.

Taking a deep breath, I blinked away my tears and turned to face Jason. "Hey, sorry. The crowd and everything got to me. Fresh air and a quiet moment seemed like a good idea."

"I just thought I'd check on you. I can go if you want to be alone."

Yes. I wanted to be alone. But I couldn't be rude. Jason had been really understanding so far tonight. I hadn't been the best date. It was time to suck it up and get over myself.

"No, I'm glad you came out here. You can enjoy the quiet with me." I smiled up at him. It was odd how similar he looked to Jax. He didn't have the rocker swagger that Jax did, though. He was more polite and studious, almost.

"I like hiding from crowds. It's been my thing since crowds became an issue with my brother's fame." The grin on his face was really cute.

"I can imagine. You don't appear to be as outgoing as Jax."

Jason chuckled. "No. Not even a little. Jax was always the one who liked an audience."

"So are you leaving with Jax and Sadie when they move her to LA?" It was still hard for me to accept the fact that Sadie was leaving. I was going to miss her so much.

"Yeah. Classes start next week for me, too."

Jason would be going to college in California too. That was one of the reasons I didn't feel guilty for using him to get over Preston. Not that it was working.

"Well, I think I'm ready to go back to the crowd now. You want to dance?" I asked, deciding it was time I stopped hiding at my brother's engagement party.

"Sounds good."

Chapter Five

PRESTON

You can't leave a guy to "sleep it off" when he's barely had anything to drink. A few shots of tequila does not a drunk Preston make. I lay back on the bed and stared at the white ceiling fan slowly spinning. Letting everyone around me think that I was just living from one party to the next had always been easy. It covered up the truth. I liked pretending to be carefree. It had always been better than the truth.

Letting Amanda Hardy think I was as shallow as I'd convinced her I was hurt like a son of a bitch. I didn't want to see the disappointment and disgust in her eyes. The only thing that kept me from blurting out the truth while she went on and on about my sucky behavior was the fact that the truth was worse.

Reaching over, I picked up the white teddy bear lying beside my head and held it up to my nose. It was Amanda's. It smelled like her. This was her sorry-ass father's condo, but this had to be Amanda's room. Staying in here wasn't going to be possible. I'd just think about all I couldn't have. I placed the bear back in its spot and stood up.

Marcus was my best friend. Sure, there was a group of us, but Marcus was the one I loved the most. He'd always seemed to know more than I wanted him to, but he never said anything. Instead of asking me questions like Rock had when we were kids, Marcus had brought me an extra lunch every day. He never mentioned it. He just did it. When I'd been bruised from one of my mom's boyfriends' drunken fits, Dewayne and Rock had asked why. Marcus had changed the subject and then slipped into the school office to get me an aspirin that he'd casually placed in my hands without explanation.

The guys were my family, but Marcus was my brother. Blood didn't matter. He'd cared when no one else had known there was something to care about. I had to let this fascination I had with his sister go. I also needed to get downstairs and celebrate with him. He'd found someone worthy of him. Being locked away and sulking over Jason Stone showing up with Amanda was unfair. Marcus didn't deserve this.

I walked down the stairs and into the living room. As I entered the room, Willow smiled at me and motioned me over. She was surrounded by guests, but her attention was on me. I could see the

53

concern in her eyes. If anyone understood my life even a little, it would be Willow. She'd had a suck-ass family tree too.

"You're back," she replied, with a smile to let me know she was glad I'd returned.

"Yeah, I figured things had time to cool off. I didn't want to miss tonight. I'm sorry about earlier." I stopped at that. I couldn't explain any more to her.

Willow shrugged one shoulder. "No worries. I think the guys were just worried about that guy causing a stir. He was a friend of a guest. He's been escorted out."

I reached behind her to the bartender and grabbed a beer. It was safer than the tequila shots.

Willow raised an eyebrow. "Ever heard the saying 'Liquor before beer, never sicker'?"

I tipped the bottle to my lips, took a swig, and grinned. "Sweetheart, it's liquor before beer, never fear."

Willow laughed. "Guess you'd know this better than anyone."

"He's been drinking before he was old enough to shave," Marcus drawled as he came up behind Willow and wrapped his arms around her waist.

Willow tilted her head back, and I watched as Marcus bent his head to capture her mouth with his. They were so fucking sweet it made me sick. It also made me jealous as hell. I would never get that. I could never love like that. Ever.

"Glad you came back down to the party. I knew you weren't

drunk when Amanda took you up there," Marcus said, once he'd released his fiancée's lips.

"Yeah, I figured I'd given the guy time to leave or calm down."

Marcus nodded. "I walked him to the door. Trisha said she was sorry. She told Krit he could bring a few friends. That was one of them."

Krit was Trisha's brother and the lead singer in a band. He didn't normally have the best crowd surrounding him, and he traveled with a posse.

"Well, Krit's friends have gotten classier. That guy was the son of a neurosurgeon in Mobile."

Women always talked. They told me about their husbands and how they were neglected. I didn't need to hear an excuse as to why they hired me, but they always felt like they had to give me one. It had been my first time with that woman. Normally, I kept my client list small. I had the usuals, but she'd been a friend of a client, so I'd agreed.

"So you did sleep with his mom?" Marcus asked. The disbelief wasn't there. He knew. He always knew.

I sighed and took another drink of my beer. Of course I did. I wasn't going to answer this, though. Not tonight.

"Listen, either you dance with your girl, or I'm going to," I said, shooting Willow a grin. She knew I was kidding, but I loved getting Marcus all riled up.

"Back off, lover boy, or I'll be the one kicking your ass," he replied in an amused tone.

"Dancing sounds like fun. I want to go see Amanda and her new friend, too. I saw them walk down there," Willow replied.

My somewhat good mood vanished. I wouldn't be going down to the dance floor. I couldn't handle that. I'd want to dance with her just to see if she felt as good as I knew she would.

"She's with a Stone. Pisses me off. She don't need to get mixed up in that world. He might not be a rock star, but he is awfully close to it," Marcus snarled.

Willow laughed and slapped his arm. "He seems like a nice guy. Don't judge him because of his family."

I wanted to argue that, yes, you should judge him because of his family, but I kept my mouth shut. I couldn't show any concern. Marcus would catch on, and he'd be shoving Amanda at Jason Stone. There was no way he'd ever agree to let his little sister near me, and I couldn't blame him.

"I'm being good," Marcus replied. "Besides, he leaves to fly off to LA soon, I'm sure. This is just a friendly thing. Amanda doesn't seem real interested. Which is good, because he ain't flying my baby sister out to LA with him. I'll let her go five hours away, but that is as far as I'm allowing her to go."

Willow sighed. "She'll need room to breathe soon enough, Marcus. You can love her and care about her while you stand back and let her make her own decisions. She isn't the little girl you took care of all your life. She's a big girl now. Don't forget that."

Marcus bent down and kissed Willow's head. "I don't want to talk about family tonight. I just want to hold you in my arms. Let's go."

I gave them a small good-bye wave with my beer in hand and watched them walk toward the doors leading outside.

I could leave now and they'd never know. That way, I wouldn't have to drink until I no longer cared about Amanda and Jason Fucking Stone.

"Hey, sexy. Why haven't you called?" The cooing sound came from behind me, and I glanced back over my shoulder to see a familiar-looking brunette.

"Because I'm the asshole who never calls," I replied with a wink.

She giggled and closed the space between us. Large fake rack. Big brown eyes. I'd screwed her before. She was a Jackdown groupie—I'd hooked up with her at the club one night while Jackdown was playing.

"I'm the forgiving type," she whispered in my ear and then moved in front of me, slipping her hands in the back pockets of my jeans. "Real forgiving."

"Is that so?" I asked, taking a drink and watching her. She'd been one of those who knew exactly what she was doing. But then, typically band groupies were talented in the sex department. They had to be to keep the interest of guys who had new girls throwing themselves at them every night.

"You come here tonight with Krit?" I asked, looking around for Trisha's younger brother.

"No. I'm friends with Trisha, and I went to school with Willow," she explained, and slipped her other hand over the crotch of my jeans. "I came here looking for you."

Sure she did. She came looking for action, and I was the first one she'd found who she was interested in. I wasn't an idiot. "What do you have in mind? You might just convince me if you can make it sound real good." She was going to have to be a talented dirty talker to get me interested. My mind was still focused on Amanda Hardy. I needed the distraction.

She stood on her tiptoes and pressed her mouth to my ear. "Come back to a room with me, and I can remind you just how talented my mouth is."

Ah. Yeah. She was the one. I remembered her. She had one big-ass mouth. I'd never even fucked her. She'd just sucked me off. I could close my eyes and pretend.

I reached down and grabbed her hand. "I think that sounds like a real good idea."

She smiled up at me as I led her through the crowd. I couldn't take her upstairs. It felt wrong. We were going to the bathroom. This wouldn't take long. Not with the image I had locked away from the dirty dreams I'd been having of Amanda.

AMANDA

My feet hurt from these heels I'd been determined to wear. Jason was a great dancer, and he had made me forget other things and laugh. Willow and Marcus were cuddled up with each other at the corner of the dance floor, talking. I loved seeing them like that. I wouldn't go interrupt them to tell them bye. I'd more than likely see Marcus tomorrow anyway.

"This was so much fun," Sadie said as she and Jax walked up to us. They had danced most of the night too. Someone came up and asked for Jax's autograph, and I heard Jason sigh. It had eased up earlier, but I guess now that we looked like we were leaving, people were anxious to get close to him before he was gone.

"Yeah, it was. I haven't had this much fun dancing in a long time," Jason agreed. I could feel his eyes on me, and I glanced up at him and returned his smile. I'd been really good about not worrying if Preston was asleep in my room or if he was back at the party. But now we were about to walk back through the condo, and I was concerned about what I might find.

"We've got a day of packing tomorrow, or I'd say we should stay and close the place down," Sadie said in a wistful tone. I knew she was excited about moving close to Jax.

"I'm ready to get out of these heels anyway," I assured her. I was more than ready to go home.

"Let's go," Jax said as he handed the picture he had just signed back to the guest.

Jason and I led the way down the candlelit path leading back to the condo from the beach. His hand held mine and it was nice.

When we reached the doors to the condo, I took a deep breath, hoping I wouldn't see Preston. Praying he was asleep.

The party was still going strong inside the condo too. I spoke to several people as we passed by, and waved at those too far away. Just before we reached the front door, I saw in the corner of the room the shaggy blond hair that was impossible to miss. His back was to everyone else, and from the hands on his shoulders I could tell he had someone in front of him backed into that corner. My stomach twisted, and I tightened my hold on Jason's hand, then picked up speed. Getting out of here was suddenly very important. I didn't want that image in my head.

Just as I was about to turn my head away, Preston glanced back over his shoulder and our eyes met. The glassy look in his eyes was one that I was all too familiar with. His attention shifted from me to Jason, and then he winked at me. What was he doing?

I glared at him in return and opened the door, then stepped outside. He was such a jerk. A stupid, sexy, hard-to-get-over jerk.

The ringing of the telephone woke me up. Rubbing my eyes, I rolled over and reached for the cordless phone beside my bed.

Mom had to be gone somewhere. She rarely let the phone ring more than three times.

"Hello."

"Hey, you still sleeping?" Marcus asked on the other end of the phone.

"Yeah."

"Wake up, sleepyhead. It's after ten."

"Mmm-hmm, whatya want?" My eyes were still heavy. I'd been up all night talking to Sadie. She'd left early this morning for LA. It would be months before I saw her again.

"I need a favor. I hate to ask you, but I don't know who else to call."

Sitting up, I covered my yawn. "Okay, I'm listening."

"I know you aren't crazy about Preston after what he did at the party, but he's my best friend, and I need your help."

My eyes snapped open wide, and I slung my legs over the side of the bed. I was instantly alert.

"Yeah," I replied, wanting him to get on with it.

"He is passed out on my sofa. He showed up at our apartment late last night and said he was a bastard and a few other things, then walked over and curled up on the sofa and went to sleep. Anyway, Low is gone to get Larissa, and I'm at work. Can you go over there and get him up and gone? I don't want Low to have to deal with him. She'll have Larissa, and, well, you are probably going to have to throw water on him and help him get home. She can't do all that and take care of Larissa, too. I tried waking him up before I left, but he wouldn't budge and I was running late."

Explaining to my brother the reasons why I didn't want to do this would be bad. That was a secret that he'd never know. I would do this for him one last time. That was it, though. After today, I was keeping my distance. I was. I meant it.

"Okay, fine. I'll get him up and gone."

"Thanks so much. I owe you one."

He had no idea.

"Yeah, you do. Bye."

"Bye."

I hung up the phone and frowned at it. Going to see Preston was a bad idea. However, I couldn't leave Willow there to handle him while she had Larissa to take care of.

Larissa was the daughter of Willow's sister and my father. My dad's affair with Willow's sister had almost destroyed Marcus and Willow when they'd found out. It was bad enough that our dad was cheating on our mom, but to find out that he also had another child—it had been really tough to deal with. Willow's sister was hard to like. For everyone. Including Willow. She'd mistreated Willow for years. But Larissa was innocent in all this.

Willow was like a mother to Larissa. She was little and would want my attention too. I hadn't seen her in a couple of weeks. I missed her sweet face. I could get rid of Preston, then hang out with Willow and Larissa awhile.

I dialed Willow's number to let her know I was going to be at their apartment when she got back with Larissa. Once I was done, I got out of bed and decided I'd forgo a shower and just pull my hair up. I didn't want to impress anyone, anyway.

Chapter Six

PRESTON

"Get up" followed by a hard slap to my arm broke into my warm, happy dreams. The same sexy voice that had been begging me, "Don't stop," was now yelling at me. Shaking my head to clear it, I slowly forced my eyes open.

Amanda was glaring down at me with a glass in her hands. She stuck her hand into the glass, then flicked cold water at my face. What the hell?

"What are you doing?" I croaked out, moving my arm to cover my face from any more attacks.

"Trying to wake you up," she replied.

She was annoyed and she was gorgeous. Her hair was pulled back in a ponytail, and she was wearing shorts and a T-shirt. No makeup. Nothing. She was perfect. I wanted to stare up at her very perfect body and face, but I was afraid of her tipping the entire glass of water over my head.

"Come on, Preston. Get up," she begged. I liked that sound. Moving my arm away, I smiled up at her.

"You could always come down here," I replied, unable to stop myself.

Her eyes flew open and then instantly narrowed. "The only reason I haven't poured this entire glass of ice water on your head is because Marcus loves this old couch. But I'm about to not care."

I sat up quickly. As sexy as she looked standing there all pissy, I didn't want ice water thrown at me. "I'm up, sweetheart. Why don't you put that glass down?"

"Good. Now get on your shirt and leave. I saw your Jeep downstairs. You don't need a ride. Bye," she replied, then spun around. Her cute little ass was barely covered by those cutoff jean shorts. I was weak, and I'd just been woken up by the star of my very naughty dream. I jumped up and wrapped my arms around her waist, pulling her back against my chest. Mmmm, she felt real good.

"What . . . what are you doing?" she asked in a flustered tone.

"I'm sorry."

I hadn't realized I was going to apologize. I didn't need to apologize, dammit—I needed her to hate me. But she smelled so good and her bottom was pressing back against my morning hard-on, and I couldn't let her go without making sure she didn't hate me for being an ass the other day.

"Why?" she asked in a cautious tone.

"I was an asshole the other day. I shouldn't have talked to you that way. I don't want you to be so angry at me. I was having a bad day, and I took it out on you. I'm so sorry." I was the one begging now.

She let out a heavy sigh, and her chest rose and fell under her snug-fitting T-shirt.

"Those titties are actually real nice. They're real, and I'm betting they're soft and feel like fucking heaven." Shit, why'd I say that?

Amanda stiffened in my arms. I should let go of her and move away. It was the right thing to do. I'd apologized, and we needed to leave it at that. I was in her brother's apartment. I had an appointment with a client in three hours. Amanda was too sweet for me to touch.

"Okay," she said in a whisper.

I could slide my hands up her stomach and cup her tits right now. She was going all relaxed in my arms. Leaning in to me. Ah, so good. *NO!*

I dropped my hands and stepped back. Amanda's posture went stiff. She didn't look back at me. I stood there trying to think of something to say, but nothing came to me.

"Get on your shirt and leave. Willow and Larissa are on

their way back. Marcus wanted you gone before they got here," she said in a flat voice before walking away. I watched her until she walked into the guest bedroom and closed the door behind her.

I sank back down on the couch and dropped my head into my hands. Why did I keep doing this? I had to remember she was off-limits. Why did she have to come to me so easily? Didn't she know better than to get close to boys like me? She didn't need to let me touch her—she needed to fight me off. But, damn, knowing she would welcome my touch was driving me fucking insane.

I looked around the room for my shirt and found it folded on the end of the sofa. Willow must have done that. I slipped it on, then felt in my pockets for my phone and my keys. Only my phone was there. My keys were probably in the Jeep. I should just go. Not say anything. Just go. She was right to hide from me.

I moved my feet to walk to the door and ended up heading for the room that Amanda had gone into. I just couldn't leave it like this.

"Manda," I called out, and knocked once before opening the door.

She was sitting on the bed with her legs folded up underneath her, staring out the window. She didn't turn and look back at me.

"I'm sorry," I said, stepping into the room.

She shrugged and kept her gaze fixed on the window looking out over the water.

"Are you not going to talk to me now?" I asked, taking a few more steps closer to the bed.

"Our conversations don't typically end well," she replied.

And that was all my fault.

"I know."

She didn't respond right away. I watched her as she sat there. The late-morning sun was shining through the window, making her already perfect face look even more angelic. How did I always mange to hurt her? She didn't deserve to be hurt. Her dad had ripped her world apart this past year. She needed friends. People who would love her and not continually hurt her. Why couldn't I do that?

"This time you have nothing to be sorry for," she said. "I got too close; you moved away. I got the hint. Not really a big deal. I'm fine. Now just go."

Dammit. She really didn't understand guys at all.

"Manda, I backed away because I was letting something happen that shouldn't. You're too good for me. You realize that, don't you? I'm fucked up. My life is one screwed-up mess. As much as I'd like to touch you—because, baby, you're all kinds of irresistible—I can't. I will never be good enough for you."

Finally she turned her head and met my pleading gaze. I

needed her to understand this. I'd let her play this game too long, and I'd enjoyed the hell out of it. Having her flirt with me had been something I looked forward to and dreaded at the same time.

"Fine. You don't want to be good enough for me, then you will never be. I deserve someone who wants to be what I need. It isn't like you will be my only crush. You were just my first. You taught me a lot about guys." She stood up and walked over to me. "You're right. I deserve more. So much more than a guy who won't even kiss me while he's sliding in and out of me. I'm good enough to be a quick fuck, but I'm not good enough to kiss? Got it. Lesson learned."

What the *hell* was she talking about? We hadn't had sex. I would *not* forget having sex with Amanda Hardy.

"Bye, Preston. We're done here. Conversation over."

"Amanda, what are you talk—"

The front door opened, interrupting me, and a little voice started calling out, "Mana! Mana! Are you?" Larissa and Willow had returned.

Amanda walked past me and into the living room.

My head was spinning. What the fucking hell was she talking about?

"Hey you, pretty girl. I missed you," Amanda cooed.

"Martus at work," Larissa told Amanda.

"Yes, he is."

Larissa lifted her green eyes, and she found me standing back, watching them.

"Pweston here," she replied happily, and clapped her hands.

I couldn't think through the spinning in my head to carry on a conversation with the kid. I had to get out of here. I wasn't going to get answers with Willow standing here between us.

"Hey there, gorgeous. You have fun with Manda and Low today, okay?" I told her, then smiled at her as she waved at me.

"'Kay," she replied.

"Thanks, Willow, for the sofa. Sorry I showed up here. It wasn't a good night," I explained.

I couldn't tell her that I'd been to check on my brothers and sister and found out my mom had been gone for two days and they'd been left alone at night. I'd had to go hunt her down and threaten her with jail if she didn't get back home. She hated me more and more each day. But at least she was home now. I'd also made sure Jimmy had a cell phone that he could keep hidden in his room so he could call me the next time something like this happened.

I'd ended up drinking too much at the bar because I'd been mad at myself for not going and checking on the kids sooner. I was turning out just like my mom. I had to stop drinking so damn much.

"No worries. It's always open if you need it," Willow replied.

"Thanks," I said again, then headed for the door. I didn't look back at Amanda. She was done with me. Finally I'd managed to push away the one female who may have actually given a shit. But what had she meant about "lesson learned"? I needed the answer to that.

AMANDA

"The tension was so thick I could cut it with a butter knife. What the heck was that all about?" Willow asked, after the door closed behind Preston. I didn't want to tell her any of this. She would never understand, anyway. Then there was the chance she could slip up and tell Marcus, which would be horrible. As hurt and as angry as I was with Preston, I didn't want Marcus to hate him. Marcus was one of the few people who Preston had to turn to. I didn't like the idea of him being alone.

"He was pissed I woke him up with cold water. We argued. Y'all came back in the middle of him being grumpy."

Willow didn't look like she believed me, but she nodded anyway. "Okay. I won't pry. But let me just say that Preston is dangerous. He is adorable and sweet and fun loving, but something about him is dark. He has had a bad past. I know because he grew up down the road from me. I think he may have had things worse than I did. Just be careful about that, okay? You're still young, and you have been sheltered from so much. It isn't my business, but just be careful."

There was no need for this warning. But I nodded. "Okay."

"Now, what are we girls gonna do today?" Willow asked, smiling down at Larissa.

"Swim!" Larissa cried out happily.

"Swim it is," Willow agreed.

I would have to borrow one of Willow's swimsuits. I started to ask, when my cell phone started ringing in my purse. I walked over to the table where I'd dropped my purse when I walked in, and pulled my phone out. Glancing down at the screen, I sighed when I saw Preston's name. What was he doing?

"Hello," I said in the most annoyed tone I could manage.

"I can't find my keys. They aren't in the apartment or in my Jeep. Can I have a ride?"

Dang it. When was I going to get some space from him? He was everywhere. I couldn't get over this thing I had for him if I was always having to be near him.

"Okay," I replied, and hung up.

I looked back at Willow, who was standing there watching me. "He can't find his keys. I'm going to drive him home. I'm sure he has a spare set there."

Willow chewed nervously on her bottom lip. I knew she didn't like this, but then, neither did I.

"Well, be careful. I'll let Marcus know you had to give him a ride."

I understood that innocent warning. It wasn't meant for me,

but for Preston. I bent down and gave Larissa a kiss on the head. "I'll be back later. Save some water for me."

"Swim," she repeated.

Smiling down at her, I headed for the door and downstairs. Maybe after I got him home I could put some distance between us.

Preston was leaning up against the passenger-side door of my car. He had on his Oakley sunglasses, and his arms were crossed over his chest, making the muscles flex. Why, oh why, did he have to be so freaking beautiful?

Even though I couldn't see his eyes through the dark lenses, I knew he was watching me. I could feel it. And unfortunately, I liked it. Or at least my body did.

"Sorry about this. Someone must have taken them so I wouldn't drive. Don't know who, though."

I unlocked the doors with my remote. I didn't have to talk to him if I didn't want to. I was giving him a ride only.

Sliding into the driver's seat, I buckled up and ignored him while he got in beside me. The black leather was warm already from the sunshine. Reaching over, I turned on the seat vents to cool them down. My dad may not be good for a lot of things, but he sure came in handy when I needed a car. His owning several Mercedes dealerships assured me that I'd have the best when it came to vehicles.

"What did you mean upstairs about not kissing you while I, uh, did other things?"

What kind of game was he playing? Did he really want to relive this with me?

"Exactly what you think it means, Preston. You were there. You should know."

He was staring at me. I didn't glance over at him. I focused on driving.

"I wouldn't be asking if I wasn't as confused as fucking hell right now."

How was he confused? I had been very specific. He hadn't kissed me once while we had sex. That was pretty dang clear.

"I really don't want to rehash this. It happened. We were acting like it didn't up until just now, so let's go back to that. M'kay?

I tightened my hold on the steering wheel and turned into the traffic. Neither of us said anything for a few moments. Maybe he'd decided to grant my request.

"Manda, are you telling me that we . . . had sex?"

The disbelief in his voice was my first clue. Well, maybe it was the first clue that I'd picked up on. I had missed the other clues. The ones where he didn't explain or frowned like I was crazy. But slowly it was dawning on me. He didn't remember!

If the humiliation could get any worse, it just did. He had forgotten we'd had sex. I'd given the jerk my virginity like an idiot, and he'd been with so many girls he couldn't remember me. Wow. I thought I was over this rejection, but this new knowledge caused a lump in my throat. How could he?

"Manda, answer me, please. Before I force you to pull this car over and look at me." Preston's voice sounded panicked. Why? Didn't he forget girls he'd screwed all the time? I was now one of many.

"I just want to take you home and leave. Let's not talk about this."

"Fuck," Preston growled beside me, and threw his head back against the headrest. "It wasn't a dream. It's a memory. *Shit.*"

A dream? What was he talking about? Now I was confused.

"Manda, please tell me I didn't . . ." He stopped and swallowed loudly, then took a deep breath. "Please tell me I didn't . . . I didn't have sex with you in a storage room. On boxes."

I couldn't exactly tell him that. So I didn't respond. I kept on driving.

"Fuck me!" Preston roared, and balled up his hands into fists on his legs.

"I already did that. Didn't end well," I replied.

"Don't say that. Please don't say that." The emotion in his voice surprised me. Was it that big a deal that we'd had sex? It hadn't been very memorable for him, obviously. So why was he having a breakdown about it now? I was the one who should be upset. Not him.

"I'm just being honest," I replied as I pulled into the parking lot of his apartment building.

"I thought it was a dream," he said in a low voice. His head was still back on the headrest and his eyes were closed tightly. I felt a little sorry for him.

"I'm not going to tell Marcus. If I was going to tell him, I would have done so by now." I was reassuring him. I couldn't help myself. I hated seeing him so upset.

Preston opened his eyes and looked at me. "I'm not upset because I think you're going to tell your brother." He let out a ragged sigh. "But I guess you'd think that of me. Why wouldn't you?"

"You have sex with different girls every night. I was one of them one night. Maybe just the first one that night. Who knows?" The bitterness in my voice couldn't be helped.

Preston's expression looked tortured. "Manda. I was drunk. Very, very drunk. I woke up the next morning and thought it was all a dream. I've actually relived it many times in my dreams since then. I never realized I'd . . . *God*, I can't believe I took you to a storage unit behind a bar." He ran his hand through his hair in frustration.

Okay. I couldn't take this anymore. He was beating himself up over this, and it was partly my fault. I'd been the idiot, to go outside with him and allow what had happened to happen. I could have put a stop to it.

"I could have stopped it. I didn't want to," I said. I wasn't going to tell him that I'd been fantasizing about having sex with him for years. That was the one piece of this secret I could keep to myself.

"Why? Why would you let me do that? You deserve so much more than that." He paused and stared at me intently. "Tell me that wasn't your first time."

Did I lie here? Or did I tell him the truth? Lying would make us both feel better. Or at least, it would make him feel better. I would think about it all the time.

"I chose to do it. I wasn't drinking. I was completely sober that night, and I chose to let it be you."

Preston slung the car door open and got out. I sat there and watched him as he paced in front of the car. He ran his hands through his hair several times, and I caught myself wishing I could do that. I loved the way his hair felt. That night might be something I regret later in life when I meet the guy I marry, but right now I couldn't make myself regret it. I had a really good memory of Preston. Even if he hadn't kissed me and he'd walked away and left me when it was over.

I sat in the car and watched Preston deal with this information more dramatically than I'd expected him to. When he finally stopped pacing and looked at me, I opened the car door and got out.

"I was your first. That night. I took your virginity in a shitty storage unit on a bunch of boxes." It wasn't a question. He was just stating the facts.

I nodded.

"Did you *know* I was completely trashed?"

No. I hadn't known that. I'd known he had been drinking, but apparently I hadn't known he had been drinking that much. I shook my head.

"I'm never drinking again. That's it. I swear. I'm done." He put both hands on the hood of my car and hung his head. "I can never tell you how sorry I am. You should hate me for the rest of your life. That is no way for you to have lost your innocence. Damn, Manda. Someone needs to shoot me."

I couldn't be mad at him. Not when he was like this. I closed my door and walked over to stand beside him. Tentatively, I touched his shoulder. "I wanted it to be you. I realize now that in order for it to be you, the way it happened was the only way it would ever happen. I think I'm okay with it now."

Preston lifted his head and looked at me. "Why me? Why would you pick me?"

The raw emotion in his voice was the only reason I decided to be honest. "Because I trusted you. I wanted you. I'd wanted you for a very long time."

Preston shook his head and stood up. "You don't want me, Manda. You do not want me. Do you understand? I am not for you."

That hurt. I forced myself to nod. I got it. He didn't want anything to happen between us. I needed to move on.

"I know," I managed to say firmly.

"I'm not gonna be able to forgive myself."

Hearing him say that hurt even more. He was much more upset about this than I would have thought. I'd known he didn't want to cross any lines with me, but I'd just realized how sincere that desire was. He truly never intended to allow anything to happen with us. It was a painful realization.

"There's nothing to forgive. I got what I wanted. It's over," I told him, then turned and walked back to my car. I was moving on from this now. This was my closure.

He didn't say anything to stop me. He just stood there and watched me drive away.

Chapter Seven

PRESTON

It was off-season for me. Other than workouts, I was free after classes. Last year I'd started partying early every day. This year things would be different.

I pulled up in front of the youth football fields. According to the paperwork I'd filled out for Brent to play, his practices would be here every Tuesday and Thursday from five thirty to seven.

I made my way over to the side of the fence where parents were sitting on lawn chairs and watching. When I finally got to play baseball, parents had always shown up for our practices too. My mom, of course, never came. I knew she'd never come to Brent's practices or his games. I didn't want him to feel as unwanted as I had. I could change that for him.

I could be here. Cheering him on. He wouldn't know that kind of rejection and loneliness.

When I got to the gate, I watched the boys warming up and doing stretches and tried to figure out which little guy was Brent. Little boys in football pads and helmets all look the same.

"You don't look old enough to have a son out there. You must be someone's big brother," an older female voice said from behind me.

I glanced back over my shoulder to see someone's mom smiling up at me from her chair. She was close to forty, but she was dressed like she was in her early twenties. I could tell from her inexpensive, snug-fitting clothing that she couldn't afford me. Besides, I wasn't working right now. I was here for Brent.

"Yes, ma'am. My brother is playing this year," I replied. Women her age hated it when I called them "ma'am." It made me smile. She'd back off now.

I turned back to the field just as the coach called out, "Go get water."

The boys pulled off their helmets and came running over to the fence where the large containers of water were lined up.

Brent's eyes locked with mine, and he paused before a big smile broke out on his face. He passed the line for water and came straight for me.

"Preston! You're here." The excitement in his voice made my heart ache a little.

"Of course I'm here. You're practicing. I didn't want to miss this."

Brent's chest puffed up. "I get to play running back. Coach said I got speed."

"Hell yeah, you got speed. You're related to me."

The toothy grin on his face just got bigger. "I gotta get water and get back out there. You gonna be here until I'm done?"

If I'd had any other plans, I'd have canceled them. The hopeful look on his face was impossible to ignore.

"Yep. You and me are gonna go get a big fat cheeseburger when this is over, and then I'll take you back home."

Brent whooped, then waved before running over to the water line. He kept glancing over at me to make sure I hadn't moved. I wasn't going anywhere.

"You're related to Brent Carey?" The surprised tone in the woman's voice behind me didn't go unnoticed.

My protective instincts kicked in, and I turned around to look at her. "Yes, I am. He's my little brother," I replied, daring her to say anything about him. I didn't care if she was a woman. I wasn't going to let her catty, gossiping mouth say or do anything to hurt Brent.

"Oh, well. It's just that no one ever comes around for him. Not at school or anything. I didn't realize he had an older brother."

She didn't deserve an explanation. But dammit, I didn't

want her talking about my family. I knew what it was like to have the mothers of the other kids talk about you and your family. It hurt. Kids shouldn't have to deal with that.

"He does" was my only reply. I turned my attention back to the field. Brent was watching me as he got into position. I was going to ignore the snide comments from idiots who had nothing better to do than talk about other people.

For the next hour and a half I watched Brent practice. He was good. Better than good, and his coach was right. The kid was fast. He needed some gloves if he was going to be handling the ball that much. We'd go get those tonight.

After we purchased the receiving gloves and Brent was one happy kid, we made our way to the Pickle Shack. This was the one place in town to get a good burger. That, and I knew Brent liked the arcade games inside.

I followed Brent inside and told the hostess we needed a table for two.

"A booth okay?" she asked, batting her eyelashes at me.

The girl was maybe sixteen. Damn, they learned young. I nodded, and she spun around and strutted toward a booth in the corner. I fell in step behind Brent, but my feet stopped when my eyes locked with Amanda's. She was sitting at a large curved booth with three other girls and two guys. I hadn't seen her since she'd left me in the parking lot of my apartment building three days ago. I'd thought about her endlessly but I had kept my distance. Seeing her here was a jolt. The time away from her had almost helped me deal with what I'd done, but looking into her pretty green eyes now, I knew I'd never get over it. She was so damn sweet, and I was the world's largest ass.

"You coming, Preston?" Brent asked, shaking me out of my trance. I tore my gaze off Amanda and made my way to our booth. I wanted tonight to be about Brent. I didn't need images of Amanda's hurt expression haunting me. I also didn't need to see her sitting so close to some dipshit who wasn't good enough for her.

I didn't know him, but I knew he wasn't good enough. No one was.

"Who're they?" Brent asked, looking at me curiously, then back at the booth where Amanda was now studying her drink and twisting her straw nervously.

"Uh, no one," I replied, opening my menu.

"That pretty blond girl keeps looking at you," Brent said, a little too loudly.

I couldn't help myself. I glanced over at her again. Brent was right. She was looking at me. A small smile tugged at the corner of her very full lips. I hadn't kissed those lips. She didn't understand why, but I did. Even drunk, I'd known some things were too good for me. Those perfect lips were off-limits to someone like me. I didn't deserve to get a taste. I wished to God I'd been

that smart about the rest of her body. Instead I'd taken her completely. I had dreams to prove it.

"She's a friend's sister," I explained, and shifted my attention
back to my menu.

"Which friend?" Brent asked curiously. I wanted to tell him
to drop it, but I didn't want to upset him. He was sensitive about
things like that. Our mother being an uninvolved parent made
him careful who he trusted. Normally, he was quiet. With me he
talked. I liked that.

"Marcus Hardy. You haven't met him."

Brent nodded. "I've heard you talk about Marcus before.
Momma says he has lots of money. Does that mean she has lots
of money too? 'Cause she's really pretty, and I think she likes
you."

I couldn't help but laugh. Kids were way too observant.
"Yeah. She has money, but you're wrong about liking me. She
actually doesn't care for me that much."

Brent let out a sigh. "It stinks being poor. The pretty girls
never like you."

Dammit. I hated hearing him say something like that.

"When you get older, it won't be about money. Right now
girls listen to what their mommas tell them. That won't always
be the case."

Brent frowned, then looked back over to the table where
Amanda was sitting. "She's gonna leave with that guy. He's

whispering in her ear, but she's still watching you."

It was real hard to ignore her when Brent was giving me a detailed description of what she was doing now. I looked over at her, and she was standing up with the group she'd been sitting with. The guy's head was bent and he was saying something awfully close to her ear, but Brent was right. Her attention was focused on me. And I liked it. No use in denying it. I loved the hell out of it. I wanted her attention. I wanted her to want me, because I sure as hell wanted her.

She shook her head to whatever the guy said, and then told him bye. I was relieved. The idea of her going anywhere with some guy alone made me ill. I knew what he was wanting. I didn't blame him, but I sure as hell didn't like it.

Amanda started toward us. Shit.

"She's coming over here," Brent announced in awe.

I was a little surprised too. I hadn't expected her to actually acknowledge me. She wasn't wearing shorts tonight. All those legs were covered up by a pair of very snug jeans. Didn't help. It only fueled my imagination.

"Hello, Preston," she said, smiling at me. The nervous look in her eyes was the only thing that gave away the fact that this hadn't been an easy decision. She looked over at Brent. "Hello. I'm Amanda."

Brent beamed up at her. "Hi. I'm Brent. Preston is my big brother."

A softness touched Amanda's smile. The tightness from her nerves was now gone. Well, damn. Having her see anything redeeming about me was not a good thing. I needed her to want to stay away from me, because God knew I wasn't strong enough to tell her no.

"It's nice to meet you, Brent. I can see the resemblance."

"Really?" Brent asked, surprised.

Amanda laughed, and it made my heart rate pick up. "Yes, really."

"You wanna sit with us?" Brent asked, scooting over to give her some room to sit down.

Amanda shifted her eyes to me, and I could see the uncertainty there. "I . . . um . . ."

"We'd both like you to join us if you want to," I assured her.

She smiled and slid into the booth beside Brent.

"Have you already eaten?" Brent asked, shoving the menu into her hands. He was anxious to get her to stay. It was pretty damn funny. The kid had good taste.

"I might eat a dessert. I've already had a burger and fries," she replied, smiling over at him.

"Okay. Cool," Brent said, taking the menu back to look at it.

I couldn't stop looking at her. She was so close. I'd had three days to let it sink in that the hot, intense dream I kept having about Amanda was very real. I'd touched her. I'd been inside her. All I could think about now was how I wanted to do it again sober. I wanted to kiss her and make sure she knew just how much I wanted her. I wanted to hear those sexy sounds that had been haunting my dreams clearly so I could remember them when I was alone.

"How are you?" she asked, breaking into my thoughts about how much I wanted her naked and under me again.

"Good. I guess. I've been thinking about things."

I stopped and shifted my eyes to Brent, who was reading the menu, before looking back at her.

"Me too. I'm sorry about how things came out."

Why was she sorry? I was the only one who should be sorry. "Manda, you have nothing to be sorry about. That was all on me."

A small grin tugged at the corner of her lips. Could they be any sexier? "Maybe. But I wasn't thinking clearly either."

"I want a cheeseburger," Brent announced, handing the menu to me. I needed the reminder that we had an audience. I'd almost said something Brent didn't need to hear.

"Good choice. It's what I always get," Amanda told him.

"Preston brought me here once before and I had a cheeseburger. It was good. But I had to share my fries with Daisy 'cause she forgot to ask for some and wanted some once I got mine. It was annoying."

Amanda glanced back at me. "Who's Daisy?"

"My little sister. Preston treats her like a baby. She ain't, though."

The smile on Amanda's face softened. She liked that.

"Preston has a thing for females. I'm sure his little sister is no different," Amanda told Brent.

Brent nodded. "Yeah, I know. Momma says he's got a different girl every night—"

"That's enough, Brent." I stopped him before he could get too out of hand. Brent grinned and ducked his head. He knew what he'd said.

Amanda stifled a laugh, and her eyes twinkled with amusement as she looked at me through her long lashes.

AMANDA

Brent was adorable. He was Preston's Mini-Me. I listened to him tell me about football practice and how his first game was coming up. Preston had signed Brent up and paid for him to play football this year, and Brent was extremely grateful. Something that small was a big deal to him. It made me wonder just how bad off Preston's family was. I knew he'd grown up on the rough side of town, but I didn't know exactly how bad it was.

"So can you come to my game next Saturday?" Brent asked, breaking into my thoughts. I hadn't been expecting an invite. Peeking over at Preston, who was watching me closely, I wasn't sure how to answer. I didn't want to let Brent down, but I also didn't want Preston to think I was using his brother to get to him. I didn't want to get to him again. I'd done that. It hadn't ended well.

"Um, well, I'd love to come to your game. If that's okay . . . with everyone. . . ." I trailed off, waiting for Preston to tell Brent why this wouldn't be okay.

"Cool, yeah, it's fine. Preston will be there too. You can sit with him."

"Okay, bud, that's enough. Don't pressure Manda into anything. I'm sure she has plans."

There was the excuse I was waiting on Preston to throw in the path. I watched as Brent's face fell, and I didn't care anymore what Preston wanted. If he was worried about me coming there for him, then he could get over it. I wasn't turning down Brent's innocent invitation just to appease Preston.

"I'll be there. Can I bring a friend? He likes football too." I had no idea who I was bringing, but it felt like the right thing to say at the moment. Letting Preston know I didn't plan on coming to see him or sit by him was my main goal. I'd find a "friend" later.

"Yeah! Cool. Bring whoever you want." Brent's eyes lit up. I could ignore the adult Preston, but the little boy who looked so much like him, with innocent hope in his eyes—I couldn't turn that down.

A short snippet of "Wanted" by Hunter Hayes played on my phone, alerting me to a text message. I needed the small distraction. I pulled my phone out of my purse and looked down to see Jason Stone's name on the screen.

Jason: Can I call you?

The reminder I needed that getting near Preston Drake was a bad idea. Jason was a good idea. He was safe. I glanced up at Preston. "I'm going to leave you two to your dinner. I've got a call to make, and I need to get home. I have an early class in the morning."

Preston's forced smile didn't go unnoticed. Why was he annoyed? I turned my attention to Brent. "I'll be at your game. Have Preston text me the details," I told him.

His big grin was worth the uncomfortable situation he had put me in.

"I will. See ya then," Brent replied.

I nodded and slid out of the seat. I waved bye to both of them and headed for the door. Once I was outside, I texted Jason.

Me: Yes.

My phone rang just as I was buckling my seat belt.
"Hello."
"I'm not disturbing you, am I?" Jason asked.

"Not at all." *More like giving me a good reason to get the hell away from Preston.*

"Okay, good. How were your first two days of classes?"

I pulled out onto the almost deserted road. During the summer you couldn't get out on this road this time of night. It would take hours to get a couple miles. But all the vacationers had gone home for the new school year. Although the weather was still warm, the crowds were gone.

"They've been good so far. Tomorrow may change things, though. I'm taking calculus, and I am getting supernervous about it. What about you? Are your classes going well?"

Jason chuckled into the phone. "I've had two classes so far, and I hate them both. Maybe tomorrow will be better. But calculus first year? Really? I'm impressed."

Math was my thing. "Yeah. I'm a math person."

"Me too."

"Really? What's your major?"

There was a pause. "Um, I'm having a few arguments with my parents about that. I'll get back to you on it." Weird. His parents were arguing with him about his major? "The reason I called wasn't to bore you with talk about our courses. I was wondering if maybe you'd be free anytime in the next month?" He ended his question with an amused chuckle.

"Um, yeah . . . I think I have some openings in my schedule," I replied, smiling.

"Then my next question is, how soon would your schedule be opening up? I was thinking of flying down . . . soon."

This was the right thing to do. Jason liked me. He wasn't pushing me away and giving me warnings. "How about next weekend?"

"Perfect."

Chapter Eight

PRESTON

Calculus. Why the hell did I agree to calculus? Passing this class would be a miracle. Keeping my grades up was part of the deal with my scholarship. If I failed a class, then I lost it. I couldn't lose this. If I played this season the way I played last season, I should have my next two years at a state college covered. I had to pass this one class first. I'd been putting it off. It was time I faced it.

Walking into the room, I did a quick scan for a desk close to the front. Instead my eyes found Amanda. She was laughing at something another girl was telling her, while some guy was leaning on her desk looking directly down her shirt while laughing along with whatever the other girl was saying. The douche.

Amanda was close enough to the front. A few girls called

out my name as I walked toward her, but I ignored them. I kept my focus on Amanda. Her eyes lifted to meet mine as I made my way to her. The smile on her lips faltered. She was trying to keep her distance because she was smart. I was the asshole not allowing it. I should be letting her run, but every little inch she pulled back I confused her. I was a shithead. This realization wasn't going to keep me from sitting beside her, though. The other guy needed to back the fuck off. His eyes were looking places they hadn't been invited. Manda needed a damn bodyguard.

"Hey, Preston," the brunette who had been making Amanda laugh greeted me first. The cooing tone of her voice was familiar. She was interested. She knew what I was like, and she was still willing. I got that a lot. I managed a small smile and nodded, but I didn't take my eyes off Amanda's.

"Hey, Manda," I said as I took the seat on the other side of her.

"Preston. Uh, hey." Her nervous reply was expected. She didn't want me near her. I couldn't blame her or take offense.

"You taking calculus first semester of college? I'm impressed. I've been putting it off."

Amanda shrugged a shoulder. " I like math."

Calculus was not math. It was a fucking science experiment gone wrong. I started to reply when the guy standing beside her cleared his throat. I glanced up at him with an annoyed snarl. Why was he still standing there?

"You took my seat," he said.

Now that made me smile. "Then I guess you should have been sitting in it."

I turned my attention back to Amanda, whose bright pink cheeks told me this was embarrassing her. I didn't want to do that, either.

"I may need help. I'm glad you're good with numbers," I told her, leaning back and getting comfortable. The guy started to say something else, and I cut my eyes back his way in a silent warning. I wasn't moving, but I'd sure as hell move his ass.

He let out a loud sigh and moved away. Smart boy.

"What are you doing, Preston?" Amanda whispered as she leaned over toward me.

"What exactly do you mean, Manda?"

"You know what I mean. Why are you sitting here? I thought we'd agreed to keep our distance. After . . . everything."

I didn't want to keep my distance. I might not get to have her again, but I liked being near her. She made me happy. She made the darkness not seem too smothering. "I want to be friends," I explained, watching her chew her bottom lip nervously.

"How can we do that?" she asked in a low voice.

I had no idea. All I wanted to do was cuddle her up and keep her. That wasn't an option, though. "We just do."

The worried look in her eyes made me feel guilty. I was asking her for something that she wasn't ready for. But I needed it.

"Okay. If that's what you want," she finally replied.

The professor walked in and started talking, so our conversation was over. For now.

She didn't look at me during the entire class, and I had a problem looking at anything but her. Was the memory of what we'd done going to drive me insane? Normally, once I slept with a girl and I was over any attraction, I moved on. But something about Amanda was holding me. Was it because I was drunk and the memories are so blurry?

Once class was over, Amanda stood up quickly, grabbed her books, and shoved them into her backpack. She was in a hurry to get away from me.

Not what I wanted.

"You have another class?" I asked, standing up and stretching.

Amanda looked over at me and her eyes zeroed in on my lower stomach. I lowered my arms slowly and my shirt covered back up the patch of skin she'd been checking out. The appreciative gleam in her eyes had me wanting to strip the damn shirt off. If that was what it took to hold her attention, I'd do it.

"Um, I—uh—no. Not right now," she stammered as she pulled her backpack up higher on her shoulder.

"Want to go get some coffee? I didn't have time for any this morning."

Amanda glanced back at the door, and the girl who'd been

talking to her before class stood waiting on her. "I was going to the library, but I wouldn't mind some caffeine first," she replied, looking back at me.

Yes. She had caved easy enough. "Can we go alone? I wanted to talk to you about some things."

Her eyes widened a bit, and I could see the understanding. Did she want to pretend it hadn't happened? I wasn't going to be able to do that.

"Okay. Let me go tell Kelsey I'll meet up with her later."

AMANDA

Why was I doing this? I deserved the Stupid Award. But then again, how was a girl supposed to tell those pretty blue eyes of Preston's no? It was impossible. When he set out to get your attention, he was insanely hard to ignore. He hadn't made peace with what had happened between us. I knew that was what all this was about. He needed to feel okay with everything. He and Marcus were close. He probably felt guilty. The sooner I eased his guilt, the sooner I could get my distance. This friends thing was not what he wanted. He wasn't friends with girls. He had friends. Lots of friends. None of them were female.

Once we got outside the math building, I grabbed Preston's arm and pulled him away from the crowd and underneath an oak tree. There was no need for us to go get coffee and pretend.

It would only give him a chance to get more under my skin than he already was.

"Listen, I know what's bothering you. I get it. This is about Marcus. So whatever you need me to do to ease your conscience so you can go on with your happy-go-lucky self, just tell me. Let's not pretend that we're going to be friends. Because honestly, I can't be your friend. It would never work."

Preston stood silently staring at me while my little "clearing of the air" became a full-blown rant. I hadn't meant to get carried away, but I had. Just looking at him and feeling my body get all excited by his nearness made me mad. What did the guy have to do to me to make me hate him?

"This isn't about Marcus. I wish to hell it was. But it isn't." Preston reached out and put a hand on my waist and pulled me closer to him. Oh my. Not what I was expecting. "I can't stop thinking about you, Manda. I try. I try all the damn time, but I can't."

Wow. My knees were a little weak.

"I want to be near you. I can't seem to keep away."

Double wow. I couldn't form words at the moment. A strand of his pale blond hair was falling in his eye, and I wanted to tuck it behind his ear. To touch it. But I didn't. He pulled me closer.

"Can we be friends? Will you forgive me for that night?"

The word "friends" was back again. I hated that word. I had

never been friends with anyone who made my heart race and my body tingle. How could I even manage that kind of relationship?

"We can try," I choked out.

His hand slid behind my back and settled on the curve above my bottom. Friends didn't stand like this. He wasn't doing a very good job with this friends thing.

"I'll be good. I promise. I'll be the best damn friend you've ever had." His voice had lowered into a husky whisper. I shivered from the sexy sound. "Mmmm, I'm gonna have to work on that," Preston added. "Feeling you shiver. I like it. I'm gonna want to feel it more."

I swallowed hard and tried to control the emotion in my voice. "Friends don't get this close, Preston," I said, and I started to take a step back when he pulled me tightly against him.

"No, Manda, they don't. But I can't stop wanting you close. Can we be close friends?" He asked, lowering his head until his warm breath tickled my ear. Closing my eyes tightly, I grabbed his arms to keep myself steady. What was he doing? "I like you close. Real close."

"Have you lost your fucking mind?" Cage York's voice broke the spell I'd fallen under, and I found the power to shove away from Preston.

"Stay out of this, Cage," Preston snarled, turning his heavy-lidded eyes from me to Cage.

"And let you get the shit beat out of you? 'Cause if you touch her, not one of those buddies of yours is gonna have your back when Marcus kills you."

"I said to back the hell off."

Cage smirked and shook his head. "I ain't gonna do that. You can go find another fuck buddy. Amanda is off-limits. You hurt her, then you hurt Low. I can't let that happen. So you see, this gets personal."

Cage had always been protective of Willow. They'd grown up together and were best friends. Marcus had issues with it sometimes, but over time he had started accepting it more and more. Especially since Cage had fallen in love with Eva.

"We're friends. Leave this alone." Preston turned to face Cage. This wasn't looking good.

"Cage, he's right. We are just friends. Let it go. We aren't and will never be anything more than friends. I promise."

Cage shifted his eyes from Preston to me. The concern and disbelief in his eyes as he met my pleading gaze was hard to miss. He didn't believe either of us. But this really wasn't his business.

"Fine," Cage drawled. "But I'd make sure it stays that way."

Preston's hands fisted at his sides.

"It will," I assured him.

Cage gave me one last nod, then turned and headed for the math building we'd just exited.

"And that is one of the many reasons our being friends

might be a problem. Everyone knows you aren't friends with girls." It wasn't like we could tell them that he'd already bagged me and was over it.

"Cage York is the last person on earth either of us needs to take advice from. Sure, I've never been friends with a girl before, but there has never been anyone I wanted to be friends with. You're different. I want to keep you close."

I wasn't going to do the right thing here. I was going to do the stupid thing.

"Okay. Friends it is, then."

Preston's face broke into a big grin that made my stupid decision seem brilliant in the moment.

"Can we go get that coffee now?" he asked.

"Sure. Lead the way," I replied.

Several girls looked our way as we walked across the street to the campus coffee shop. Preston did a real good job of ignoring them. I'd known him long enough to know he normally didn't ignore it at all. He typically measured them up with one quick glance and decided he was interested or not.

"What do you drink?" Preston asked as he walked us over to a table inside in the back corner.

"One of those icy coffee things. Anything mocha." I hadn't tried the coffee options out here yet, so I didn't have a specific order.

"Got it. The girliest drink they have," he replied with a wink, and turned to head to the counter to order. There weren't a lot of people inside. Several were outside under the umbrellas, but inside it was almost empty.

My phone played, alerting me to a text message. Pulling my phone out, I glanced down to see Kelsey reminding me that we had study group for economics tonight. When a class came with a built-in tutor to help you get through it, then you knew you were in trouble. I intended to make every study group the tutor offered.

"It's called an Ice Rageous, for future orders," Preston said as he set a drink in front of me that was topped with whipped cream and caramel.

"Thank you," I replied as I watched him sink down into the seat across from me.

"You can also order 'girlie drink' and the guy behind the counter knows what you mean." The teasing tone of his voice made me laugh. I'd never really had an actual conversation with Preston that didn't involve pre-sex or drama. This was nice.

"I'll keep that in mind."

Preston took a drink of his coffee and leaned forward on his elbows, watching me. "Why do I make you nervous, Manda?"

Why did he make me nervous? How was I supposed to answer that? Maybe because I'd had a crush on him for years, I'd given him my virginity, and he was gorgeous.

"You don't. Well, I mean, you do, but we've never really talked before. Not like this."

Preston set his cup down, but his eyes never left my face. "Then why did you go outside with me at the club? I can't let that go. I keep going back to the fact that you went out there with me. Why?"

If we were going to be friends, I needed to be honest with him. At least mostly honest with him. I was working on getting over him, so that wouldn't be an entire lie.

"I had a crush on you. I'd had one for years. I wanted to be the one you took home that night. That didn't happen, exactly. We made it to your Jeep, and then you hauled me off to the storage shed. I got over my crush after that night."

Not exactly true, but close enough. He didn't need the gory details. Or to know that I still used him as inspiration at night when I needed to feel him again. I wasn't sharing that piece of info either.

"You had a crush on me?" he repeated, and muttered a curse. "Manda, I'm so sorry. I wish I'd been sober."

I laughed for the first time since we'd started this uncomfortable conversation again. "Had you been sober, I would still be living in my fantasy world that one day you'd look at me and want me too. That night finally rid me of that delusion."

"You figured out you were too good for me that night." The tight, pained look in Preston's eyes confused me.

"No, I figured out that I am never going to be 'that girl'—the kind you're attracted to. I'm okay with that now."

Preston reached out and took my chin in his hands, and lifted my face until my eyes met his. "There are a lot of things that I'm not. But trust me when I tell you I'm more attracted to you than is safe for either of us."

"Amanda, hey!" someone interrupted us. "I haven't seen you in a while. And Preston Drake, let go of Marcus's little sister before I slap you for her." Jess, Rock's cousin and the town slut, pulled out the chair on the other side of Preston.

"Hey, Jess," I replied.

"Leave, Jess," Preston said in an annoyed tone as his hand left my face.

"*Tsk-tsk*, touchy, touchy. Cool down, lover boy. You're barking up the wrong tree with this one. She ain't your type."

"I *know* that. We're friends," he snapped, leaning back in his chair and taking a drink of his coffee.

"You stopped coming to Live Bay and drinking with me, Amanda. Wondered what happened to you. We had a few fun nights," Jess said, grinning at me with a wicked twinkle in her eye.

Back this summer, after Preston had left me in that storage room, I'd done everything I could to get his attention, including drinking and partying with Jess. But one night when a guy had gotten a little too out of hand and Dewayne had showed up and beat his face in—that had been my last night out with Jess. It had been the wake-up call I'd needed. I wasn't that kind of girl. I never would be. And no amount of partying was going to get Preston to look at me again. He'd had his fill.

"Yeah, I've been busy," I replied.

"Weren't you going off to college? Auburn or some crazy shit like that?"

The main reason I wasn't going was sitting across from me listening to every word I said. "Yeah, I was. But I didn't want to miss the wedding planning for Marcus and Willow. And my mom still needs me. She isn't ready for me to leave her just yet. Especially with Marcus getting married."

"Sure about that?" Jess asked with a knowing look on her face.

I'd probably told her something I shouldn't have one of the nights I drank too much. Dang it. I hadn't thought about that. Maybe my little secret wasn't as secret as I'd thought. I was no better than Preston. Dewayne knew something. Now Jess. Crap.

"I'm positive," I replied with a forced smile.

"If you're done with the twenty questions, Jess, we were talking about calculus. You can leave now," Preston said, setting his cup down on the table. His long tanned fingers wrapped around the cup made me think of the other things I'd felt those hands do.

"Calculus my ass," Jess replied, standing up. "You don't normally go sniffing back around where you've already been."

Preston's annoyed frown transformed into a furious glare, and he slowly stood up. "Whatever the hell you think you know, you don't. I don't care who your cousin is. Friend or not. You won't repeat any of it to anyone."

Jess raised her eyebrows and met his glare with one of her own. "I'd never repeat a word. But not because your sorry ass threatened me—because I like Amanda. That's the only reason. 'Cause, Preston Drake, I'd love to see you hung up by your balls." Jess swung her gaze to me and smiled. "I'll see ya around, Amanda."

I nodded, but I was afraid to say anything else. I'd obviously told Jess about Preston and me. This was humiliating. Who else had I told while I'd had my few weeks of drunkenness?"

Jess spun around and strutted out the door. It took all my courage to look at Preston again. He was studying his coffee cup. Guess he was wondering who all I'd told too.

"I can't believe you won the loyalty of that one. She's a mean bitch," Preston finally said, lifting his gaze to meet my anxious one.

I shrugged. I wasn't sure how I'd managed that either. But we'd bonded over vodka. Weird but true. "Jess is misunderstood. That's all."

Preston chuckled. "No, Manda. Jess is a conniving, manipulative slut. She doesn't make friends with females. Ever."

"She's not that bad," I replied, needing to defend her.

Preston raised one eyebrow and twisted his cup around in his hands as he held my gaze. "We'll agree to disagree. How's that?"

I nodded.

He let out a weary sigh. "I didn't know those drunk episodes of yours this summer were with Jess. I thought those two times I found you and took you home were flukes. It was your attempt at rebelling."

"They were my attempt at rebelling. I figured out pretty quick it wasn't for me."

"Why'd you do it?" he asked.

I knew he wasn't ready for this answer. Giving him something else to feel guilty about wasn't what I wanted. Instead I shrugged, reached for my drink, and took a sip through the straw.

"Please tell me it wasn't because of what I did. . . ."

I didn't want to lie to him, but this was one of those instances when lying was the best policy. "No, Preston. It had nothing to do with you."

The relief on his face made me glad I'd lied.

"Do you have any more classes today?" he asked.

I didn't. I was going with Willow to pick out bridesmaid dresses, and we were taking Larissa with us to find her a flower girl dress. "No, this is my easiest day of the week."

Preston tucked a strand of hair behind his ear. "I've got to head to the gym to work out with the team, but later you want to do something? Maybe help me figure out what the hell we did in class today? I'll buy you a meal."

He was really determined to do this friends thing and get free tutoring out of it too. As much as I'd like to spend time with him, I knew it was bad. "I can't. I'm going with Willow and Larissa to pick out bridesmaid dresses and Larissa's flower girl dress."

Preston titled his head to the side, and the blond hair that brushed his shoulders drew my attention. He looked like one of those airbrushed models in a magazine. No guy should be that perfect-looking. It wasn't fair.

"What about after? Stores close at six. You should be free then."

He was right. I'd probably be home even earlier than that, but I had to have some self-preservation. "Yes, they do, but I have an economics study group tonight," I said, slipping my purse back up on my shoulder. I needed to head to Willow and Marcus's to pick her and Larissa up. And I needed to get out of here before Preston convinced me to forgo my good sense.

"Okay," he replied. He leaned back in his chair and stared up at me with those sexy you-know-you-want-me eyes of his.

With a firm nod, I said, "See you around," before walking swiftly to the door.

Chapter Nine

PRESTON

As much as I'd wanted Amanda to take me up on tonight, I was glad she'd shot me down. Thirty minutes after she'd left me in the coffee shop, I'd gotten a call from a client. This one was single, in her mid-forties, and had had enough plastic surgery to look like she'd just turned thirty. She owned a few upscale salons and was in town on business. I never had advance notice with her, but she paid well, so when she called, I went. Funds were low because I'd just paid my mom's rent. Plus I'd had to cover the initial payment for Jimmy's braces.

Walking into Live Bay, where I knew at least one of my friends would be, I decided that after doing what I'd just had to do, a drink was called for. This didn't used to bother me. I could go entertain a paying MILF with no problem. But when

Amanda surfaced this summer in my dreams, I'd had to start playing a role. Sex for money was suddenly dirty. It was wrong. I had a fucking conscience I hadn't asked for, all thanks to a pair of pretty green eyes and full, all-natural lips.

I stopped by the bar and picked up the shot of tequila waiting on me. They knew me well around here. We'd been coming to this place since before it was legal for us to drink. Small coastal towns didn't have a lot of entertainment. Live Bay was it.

Dewayne was at our table watching me as I walked over to them. Cage had Eva in his lap, whispering in her ear, completely blind to anyone other than her. Ever since she'd shown up at Live Bay and sung him that song a few weeks back, they'd been all over each other. You rarely saw one without the other. Cage watched her every move like she was the most fascinating thing in the world.

"I was wondering if you were gonna show up tonight," Dewayne said as he lifted his beer and saluted me.

"I'm here. Where else is there to be?" I didn't let the frustration come out through my words. Or at least, I didn't think I did. However, the way Eva turned her head and stared at me curiously made me question that.

"Glad you're here," Cage said with that knowing gleam in his eyes. He wanted to see me with anyone except Amanda. Although Cage hadn't been one of our crew while growing up, since we were now teammates and his best friend was about to be a married-in member of the group, Cage kind of just fit. He was a part now. He also knew that my screwing around with Marcus's little sister was off-limits. Pissed me off that he could just freely be with who he wanted. No one and nothing standing in the way.

"You look down," Eva said, still studying me.

"I'm tired," I replied, looking over at Dewayne. "Where's Rock?"

"Not sure. I figured Trisha would want to be here tonight since Jackdown is playing." Trisha rarely missed her brother's performances. She'd practically raised Krit, so they had more of a mother-son relationship than a sibling one. She was like the proud parent.

"Keep wiggling like that, and we're gonna have to leave," Cage growled as he took a nip at Eva's ear. She giggled and stood up.

"Then come dance with me." She held out her hand, and he went willingly. They were a little too much for me right now. I didn't need to see that shit.

"Can Cage be any more pussy whipped?" I grumbled, taking the shot of tequila the waitress had set down in front of me.

"Someone's pissy tonight. Don't tell me you got the hots for Eva now," Dewayne drawled.

I didn't even look over at him. He was trying to goad me. It was his thing.

"What did I tell you about Manda?" I could remember some

drunken ramblings one night after I'd been with Amanda, but I wasn't sure what it was I'd said.

"More than I wanted to know," he replied.

I looked over at him. "I need to know what that is, Dewayne. I did something, and I can't remember it clearly."

Dewayne shook his head. "I think it's best you only have those sketchy memories. No use in reminding you."

I slammed my glass onto the table. "Tell me what I said, dammit."

Dewayne leaned on the table with his elbows and glared at me. "No. You were drunk as shit. I don't want to remember it. She's like my little sister, you stupid fucker. She should be the same to you. How you could do something with her like some cheap slut I am still trying to wrap my head around. I know you got issues. But that ain't an excuse. She looks at you in a way that can only mean you can hurt her. You *have* hurt her, and she still looks at you with that wistful, dreamy look of hers. It makes me so mad I could beat the shit out of you. *Okay?*"

"It's different with her, D." I couldn't tell him more than that because I couldn't accept it. There was no way I'd ever be able to have anything more than a friendship with her, but I needed him to know she wasn't like the others.

"Maybe. But she's sweet. She's good. She's also innocent. Back off before Marcus figures out there is a reason he should put a bullet in your head."

I couldn't back off completely. I needed her friendship. I wanted to be near her. "We're friends now. That's something he'll have to accept. Nothing more."

"Friends? Bullshit."

I didn't expect him to believe me. Why should he?

AMANDA

By the time I left the study group, it was after nine. Today had been busy and somewhat successful. We'd found a flower girl dress. However, the bridesmaid dresses hadn't been so easy to find. We had another day planned next week to go to Mobile to see if we could find something there.

I noticed a familiar Jeep parked in the driveway. What was Preston doing? Mom was at home. I'd talked to her already once tonight. Had he been sitting there long?

I pulled up beside him and got out. I had to get him out of here before Mom saw him. She would have a fit if she saw me hanging around with Preston Drake. He was okay as one of Marcus's friends, but that was all. She had never let it be a secret that she wasn't a fan of his.

Preston was grinning when I got close enough to make out his face. The top to his Jeep was off, and he was leaning back with his head turned in my direction.

"You're finally home," he said. There was no slur to his

voice, so he wasn't drunk. That was a good thing.

"Yeah, um, what are you doing here?"

"Go for a ride with me" was his response.

I glanced back at the house. Mom's bedroom light was off, and that normally meant she'd taken her sleeping pill already. But he didn't know that. "Mom is expecting me."

"Please," he replied.

"My mom—"

"Is asleep," he interrupted.

Sighing, I shifted my feet and stayed a good foot away from him and his Jeep. "Why? It's late and I'm exhausted."

"Because I want to spend time with you. I missed you tonight."

He missed me? Really? "I don't think this is a good idea."

"It is probably one of the worst ideas I've ever had. Please come with me," he pleaded.

I was a female. How was I supposed to ignore that? "Fine. But just a short ride, and then I need to go to bed."

I walked around the Jeep and climbed in. I'd never made it into his Jeep the last time he'd asked me to take a ride with him. When I looked over at him, he was staring at the door I'd just closed and his eyes moved to me.

"Did you . . ." He swallowed loudly. "Did you have an orgasm up against my Jeep that night?"

He was remembering more and more of our night together.

I doubted we'd be done talking about it anytime soon. The more he remembered, the more he was going to want to ask me about it. Then I'd have to relive it.

I turned my head to look outside before answering. "Yes."

"Your shirt was off," he replied slowly.

"Yes, Preston, it was. Can we please not talk about this?"

Preston shifted the Jeep into reverse, and we backed out of the driveway.

"I'm sorry. It's just . . . pieces keep coming back to me, and I just remembered you clearly coming for me while I had you pressed up against the Jeep."

I would not be embarrassed. I would not.

"No one had ever done those things to me before. It was a given that I was going to get off easy," I replied.

"I was just kissing your tits. No one had ever done that before?" The surprise in his voice made me wish I'd stayed at home. Getting in this Jeep had been yet another bad move.

"Subject change, please."

Preston didn't say anything else. He drove to the public beach that was deserted this time of night and pulled down onto the gravel parking lot just before the sand starts. The moonlight on the waves was always something I loved to watch. It was romantic, and as many times as I'd wished I could sit and watch it with Preston, I didn't want to right now. Romance and Preston had to be kept completely separate.

Preston opened his door and came around the front of the Jeep, then opened my door. He held out his hand. "Come watch the waves with me, Manda."

"It's late," I replied.

"Just for a few minutes. Please?"

Giving in, I placed my hand in his and let him help me out of the Jeep.

I left my sandaled heels on the floor and got out barefoot. Preston closed the door to the Jeep, then stared at it before looking at me. The heavy, hooded expression in his eyes told me what he was thinking. Knowing it was turning him on only made my pulse rate pick up. I couldn't help the fact that I wanted Preston to want me. To at least be attracted to me.

"Come on," he said, reaching for my hand and threading his fingers through mine. We walked out to the sandy shore until Preston found a spot close enough for us to see the waves clearly but far enough back that we wouldn't get wet.

He tugged me down with him until we were both sitting.

"Why are we here, Preston?" I asked.

"I don't know. I wanted to come out here to think. It's where I think best. And I wanted you to be with me."

My traitorous heart skipped a beat. He could say the sweetest things. I just needed to remember he could also say some of the meanest things. His mouth was dangerous. In many, many ways.

"Why me?"

He turned his head to the side and grinned over at me. "You don't want the answer to that question."

Yes, I did. I wanted it very much. "Let me be the judge of that."

Preston's grin turned into a sexy smirk, and he slid his hand across the sand until it was resting on my bare knee. "Because I can't get you out of my head. Normally, after I'm with a girl, I move on. I'm done. But you . . ." He paused and glanced back at the water, breaking eye contact with me. "You're different. I still want you. I think about you all the time."

Uh-oh. I was a goner. Those kinds of things coming from a player like Preston Drake would make any female melt. He wasn't playing fair. "It's just because you were drunk and don't remember it." I was reminding myself as much as I was him.

"No, Manda. The more I remember, the more I want you."

His hand slid up my thigh as he slowly slid it between my legs. I should be pushing him away. I couldn't bring myself to, though.

"Every night, Manda. Every damn night I dream about you. About how sweet you tasted. How incredible you felt. It's driving me crazy."

I stopped breathing as his hand slid further up my inner thigh. I was beyond the ability to form words. The last time, Preston hadn't said sweet, romantic things to me. He'd just sent me outside and we'd gone at it. This time he was pulling out all the stops, and I wasn't going to be able to ignore this.

"Where all did I taste you, Manda?"

Oh, no. I wasn't answering that question. I couldn't go there. Not with his hand almost at the edge of my shorts.

"If it was anything like my dreams, it was fucking unbelievable. I've been trying real hard to stay away. Marcus would never be okay with this. And if you knew me—the real me—you'd run. I'm not what you think. I'm so much worse."

That, I couldn't take. Hearing him degrading himself like that. So he slept around. A lot of guys did. He was sowing his wild oats. It was okay to do that. Most girls knew what they were up against with him.

"Stop it. I do know you. I've been watching you for years. You're no worse than Cage, and look at him. He has Eva. She's madly in love with him, and she knows all about his playboy days."

Preston eased his fingers up the inside the leg of my shorts. "Stop me, Manda," he whispered.

Stop him? How was I gonna do that? He had me panting with anticipation. How could I stop him?

I dropped my gaze to watch his hand disappear up my shorts just as the tips of his fingers grazed the silk of my panties. It had been awhile, so the immediate reaction of closing my eyes and letting out a moan from the pleasure was to be expected.

Preston was on top of me with both my hands pressed back above my head with one of his hands while the other one continued to tease me relentlessly.

"I'm gonna kiss you this time, sweetheart. I can't help it," he whispered as his mouth lowered and covered mine.

From the look on his face, I expected his kiss to be demanding. Instead his soft lips were gentle. Almost like he was savoring me. His tongue slipped into my mouth and tangled with mine. Each caress had me bucking my body to get closer to him. I couldn't touch him. He had my hands still pinned back with one of his. So I kissed him back as wildly and freely as I could. Everything I felt for him came pouring out of me. The groan that vibrated his chest as he eased one finger inside the edge of my panties made my body tremble. I'd only ever done things like this with Preston. I'd only imagined him when I'd fantasized about doing these things. It was always his face I saw.

"Manda, please, baby, tell me to stop," he begged in a deep, husky voice while he trailed kisses from my mouth to my neck, where he began licking and nipping the tender skin.

"I don't want to." I gasped out as his finger entered me easily against the wetness already there.

"So sweet. So wet. I shouldn't be able to touch you. I'm not good enough." His tortured voice only turned me on more. I opened my legs more, and he sank down between them as his fingers eased in and out of me.

"You're so fucking warm," he murmured as he kissed me down my chest, and he finally let go of my hands so that he could use his free hand to slide up inside my shirt. He chose that moment to start rubbing his thumb over my clit. I cried out and clung to both his arms. I was so close.

"No," he bit out, and then he was gone.

My breathing was labored, and my body parts started screaming in protest. I wanted him back. Touching me.

"No! I can't do this. I shouldn't have started it." Preston was standing up when I opened my eyes. His face looked fierce, and he wasn't looking at me. Instead he was focused on the dark sky. "This is wrong," he said again, in a determined voice.

I pulled my shirt down and managed to sit up. I couldn't stand just yet. I'd been about to explode when Preston moved away and left me cold. My body was trying to process this. What had I done wrong, anyway?

"I'm so sorry, Manda. I shouldn't have touched you."

Confused, I slowly stood up, hoping my knees weren't too weak and could hold me. Once I was standing and sure I could do so without crumbling at his feet, I stared up at him. "Why?"

Preston shook his head and started stalking back to the Jeep. I watched him for a moment before jogging after him. He was being so weird. I was beginning to think he might just leave me here. He went to his side of the Jeep, climbed in, then slammed his door.

The state of dazed confusion I'd been in after he'd brought me to the brink of an orgasm was fading, and anger was taking its place real fast. Who did he think he was? Why was I the idiot who kept coming back and letting him hurt me? I didn't want to get in that stupid Jeep with him. I walked right past it and headed up the boardwalk that led to the street. My house was about two miles from here. I could walk it. No problem.

"Manda, what're you doing?" Preston's voice called out. I didn't look back. I just kept making my way to the road. He'd go away eventually. I didn't need this. I didn't want this. I hated how he made me feel when it was over. The few moments of heaven were not worth the hell he put me through when he was done.

"Please come back. I can't let you walk home. It's late."

He didn't get to decide what I did. He didn't get to decide anything about me. Preston Drake had done nothing to earn any privilege in my life.

"Manda, I'm sorry. I'm so damn sorry." The defeat in his voice had me slowing down.

I turned back and looked at him. He was outside his Jeep now, walking toward me. "I can't seem to control myself with you. I'm sorry. That was wrong back there. I had to stop it."

Chapter Eight

PRESTON

"If this is so wrong, then stop. Stop trying to get close to me. You run hot and cold, Preston. I am so sick of it. I can't keep up with you. I don't want to anymore." The angry glare she'd shot me when she walked past the Jeep was gone. Now Amanda just looked over it. She was tired of this. I couldn't blame her. I wasn't worth the hassle. I could never be what she wanted. She thought I was like Cage and the right girl could tame me. It wasn't about that. I didn't need taming. I needed fucking saving.

I wouldn't be free until I was out of college and got a job that would make me enough money to take care of my brothers and sister. Until then, I'd never be free to touch someone like Amanda. She wasn't like the other girls I messed around with. They knew the score. They meant nothing to me. Manda was different. She made me feel things. Things I'd prayed I'd never experience, because acting on them would be impossible.

"Just let me take you home. I promise this won't happen again. I shouldn't have brought you out here. Having you close like this makes me forget the reasons why this won't work. We will never work."

Amanda spun around and started stalking back toward the road. Her tight little ass swung teasingly in those shorts of hers that were always too short and drove me crazy. I'd been fantasizing about slipping my hand up a pair of her shorts for a couple of years now. Tonight that desire had taken over, and the craving to taste her.

"Manda, please don't do this. I said I was sorry. Just let me give you a ride. You don't even have to talk to me. Besides, you're barefoot. You can't walk home barefoot."

She stopped, but she didn't turn back around right away. Instead she placed both her hands on her hips and stood there in the darkness. She was thinking about it. I couldn't blame her. I'd hate me too. Toying with her like that was wrong. I could never do more than tease her. Because the cold hard fact was that the moment the call came in from a client, I'd have to leave her, and there was no way I'd be able to crawl out of her bed and into bed with someone else.

Finally Amanda turned around and walked slowly back to the Jeep. She didn't meet my eyes. She didn't even look my way.

She kept her eyes down as she passed me and opened the passenger side of the Jeep and climbed in.

I walked over to the driver's side and got in. Glancing over at her, I thought about explaining myself. Maybe just telling her the truth. I needed to tell someone. Would she understand?

"Don't, Preston. Just drive," she replied, as if she'd read my mind. I cranked the Jeep and pulled out onto the dark street. She was right. We'd said enough.

We rode in silence the two miles back to her house. I parked in her driveway, and she opened the door and got out, taking her sandals with her. She didn't look back at me or even tell me good-bye. The close of the door was hard and firm. That was her way of telling me that whatever we had been attempting was over.

Swallowing against the sudden lump in my throat, I turned my Jeep toward home. I wouldn't cry over her. I wouldn't. I'd never had her, not really. She didn't know me. She'd never accept the truth about me. It was better this way. Pretending like I could have her in any way was just a form of torture I didn't need. I had my family and my baseball career to focus on. Amanda Hardy was a distraction that could make me lose it all.

AMANDA

"What do you think of this one?" Willow asked as she stepped up onto the small platform in front of the wall of mirrors in another gorgeous white wedding dress. I thought she looked like every guy's fantasy. All her long red hair and her cleavage pouring out of the top of the sleeveless dress. She was the kind of girl who could make any guy change his ways. I was missing that sex appeal. I had the cute little girl-next-door thing going for me. I didn't have the sexy goddess thing Willow did. It was no wonder my brother had become like a panting dog at her feet the moment he met her.

"I love it. You're fabulous in it. However, I am still a fan of the one two dresses ago. I like the way it's short in front and shows off your legs but long in the back. It's a sexier dress. This one would make my mother very happy, but it covers up too much. You have the body. Flaunt it on your wedding day."

Willow blushed, and I was reminded of yet another reason my brother loved her. She was so completely blind to the fact that she was gorgeous. Every time you complemented her, she would get all red faced like she didn't believe you or know how to handle it.

"I liked that one too. I was just worried the short front was too much. Your mom wants us to get married in the church. Can I wear a short dress like that?"

My mom was having way too much input in this wedding. Willow had no mom to weigh in, and her older sister wasn't an option in helping her decide anything about the wedding. The fact that Tawny was living with my dad and their kid made it weird. Besides, Willow and her sister weren't very close.

"I thought you wanted to get married on the beach. I think that is the perfect dress for a beach wedding."

Willow twirled one of her long strands of hair around her finger. "Well, I do. But your mom really wants us married in a church. I didn't want to upset her. She's had so much to deal with already. And Marcus doesn't care. He just wants to get married."

Willow was going to have to learn to stand up to my mother, or Mom would run all over her. Mom loved to plan and be in charge. Willow was so eager to please her that she would let her. I wasn't going to let that happen.

"If you want a beach wedding, then have a beach wedding. This isn't my mother's wedding. She doesn't get to plan this. I'm not letting her plan mine, I can tell you that right now. You cannot let her start controlling your decisions. She'll do it about everything. Heck, she'll even name your kids for you. This is your life. Marcus is yours. Not hers. He's a big boy now, and he is yours. You make the choices. That dress was gorgeous on you. Marcus will love it. Have your beach wedding and wear your rocking-hot dress."

Willow smiled and bit down on her bottom lip, then nodded. "You're right. I shouldn't do what others want me to on my wedding day. It's about Marcus and me. No one else."

I felt a swell of pride in my chest that I'd convinced her to go with her heart. Do what she wanted. I nodded and sat back down in my chair, and I crossed my legs to wait while she went to put back on the dress we'd both loved.

My phone played the short tune to let me know I had a text message. I reached into my purse and pulled it out.

> Jason: Instead of me coming there this
> weekend, what would you say to dinner in
> NYC?

What was he talking about? Had he accidentally texted me when he'd meant to text someone else? I live nowhere near New York City.

> Me: I think you texted the wrong person. :)

That was awkward. Especially since he had mentioned coming to see me this weekend. He must have made plans with more than one girl.

> Jason: I'm positive that I texted exactly who I
> meant to text. I don't normally offer to ask my
> brother for his jet to take girls on dates. Only
> for the really special ones.

Oh. He wanted to fly me to New York City for dinner? Really? What did I say to this? I knew Sadie had done this kind of thing all the time last year while she was finishing up high school in Sea Breeze while Jax toured the states. But Jason and I had been on one date. This seemed kind of like a big deal for a second date.

Jason: The silence is not promising.
Me: I was just surprised. I don't know what to say.
Jason: "Yes" would be a really good option.

I laughed at his quick response. I really liked this guy.

"Who has you smiling down at the phone like that?" Willow asked with a grin on her face as she walked back out of the dressing room in the dress that I knew was meant for her.

"Jason Stone," I replied.

Willow wiggled her eyebrows. "Dating a celebrity."

"He isn't really a celebrity. Just the fact that he's related to Jax."

Willow laughed and stepped up onto the platform in front of the mirrors. "Yeah, I'd say being the brother of the world's favorite rock star makes him a celebrity."

Me: Can I think about it?

I wasn't ready to just say yes. Sure, I was mad at Preston about the other night at the beach. He and I hadn't crossed paths since then, but I just couldn't get him out of my head. Once the anger faded, I remembered his sad face. The hopelessness in his eyes. Those things had me wanting to hunt him down and ask him why.

Jason: Of course. Let me know when you're ready.
Me: Thank you.

"So what is it he's saying?" Willow asked.

"He wants me to go out with him again soon."

"And are you going?"

I shrugged. I wasn't sure. It all depended on Preston. Everything depended on him. If somehow I was missing something that I needed to know, I didn't want to just walk away without knowing the facts.

"Maybe. Not sure. I need to think about it."

Willow nodded. "Good idea. Dating him will put you in a spotlight. I imagine that isn't always fun."

I knew from Sadie's experience it wasn't fun at all. She was still getting used to it. But I wanted to change the subject. We weren't here to discuss my love life. We were here to find the perfect dress for Willow.

"That's it," I said, nodding to her image in the mirror.

Willow turned to look at herself. "Yes, I believe you're right."

"Marcus will be a puddle at your feet," I assured her.

Willow beamed at me. "Now. We still need to find you the perfect dress. Do you think Jason would want to come? Should I send him an invitation for you?"

I hadn't thought that far ahead. Would Jason and I still be talking then? It was very possible he would have moved on to another model by that point. I shrugged and straightened the train on the dress. It was covered in tiny pearls and weighed a ton. The fact that there wasn't much to the rest of the dress was made up for by the extravagance of the train.

"So do you or don't you?" Willow asked.

I realized I still hadn't answered the Jason and the wedding question. Sadie and Jax were coming, so why not invite Jax's brother? Even if we weren't dating then, I was sure we'd still be friends.

"Sure. Send him an invite."

Chapter Nine

PRESTON

Tonight Jackdown wasn't playing. It was a country night. Some country band from Tennessee was onstage. They were good with the cover songs they played, but their originals were pretty damn impressive.

Marcus sat back down with a beer. It was rare I got him without Willow these days. When he'd called and wanted me to meet him at Live Bay for drinks, I'd been surprised. Then he'd explained that Willow and Amanda were out shopping for the wedding dress. That explained it. Marcus was rarely anywhere without Willow.

"You seen Amanda around campus any?" Marcus asked before taking a swig of his beer.

"Yeah. We have calculus together." That was the only

response he was getting. I didn't want to talk about Amanda with him. He'd see through me real fast. Then he'd beat the shit out of me.

"I would never tell her this, but I am so glad she didn't go off to Auburn. I want to enjoy this wedding planning stuff with Low, and I would have been worried about Amanda all the time. Not knowing if some guy was taking advantage of her or if she was safe. This way I can enjoy this time with Low and keep my eye on Amanda in case she needs me." I almost choked on my beer.

I hadn't thought about it being unsafe for her to be so far away at college. I'd been so anxious to get her away from me, I hadn't considered Auburn might be dangerous for her. I was suddenly relieved she hadn't left. I might be bad for her, but I sure as hell wouldn't let anyone hurt her. Shit. Now I wasn't going to be able to watch her go off next year. Why'd he have to make me think about it?

"What are you scowling about?" Marcus asked, breaking into my thoughts.

"Sorry. Just thinking about homework. I got shitloads."

Marcus chuckled. "You haven't found a few girls to get that handled for you yet? Preston Drake is losing his touch? Say it ain't so."

Normally, I didn't do my homework. I got girls in my classes to do it. I'd flirt just enough to keep them happy, and maybe screw around with them toward the end of the semester. I'd been doing this since high school. The guys found endless entertainment in it. Especially when the semester ended and I had a hard time letting the girls down. It was drama I wasn't in the mood for this year. Ever since I'd had my hands and mouth on Amanda's body, my thoughts had centered on her. It was hard to concentrate on anyone else.

"Cutting back on the drama this year," I explained.

Marcus let out a low whistle. "Never thought I'd hear that from you."

I couldn't tell him all about the girl tying me up in knots. I'd listened to him go on and on about Willow when she'd come into his life. But now I had someone driving me crazy I couldn't talk about it. I couldn't get drunk in front of Marcus and spill my guts. Not if I wanted to live. He'd kill me. I had no doubt.

"Hey, Preston. It's been awhile. Where have you been hiding?" A blonde with a really big pair of fake boobs sidled up next to me and ran her hand up my chest. Yeah. I'd probably slept with this one. She had all the assets, and she was comfortable enough with me to touch me.

"Been busy," I said with a forced smile.

"Well, I've been missing you. Come dance with me," she purred in my ear.

I started to turn her down when I saw Marcus watching me. He was expecting me to say yes. That is what I would normally do. She'd be an easy lay. She was hot enough. If I told her no, then Marcus would start asking questions. I didn't want him asking questions. He knew me too well. If I said anything to tip him off that I was tied up in knots over his sister, he'd be furious. I had to dance with this girl. I didn't have to fuck her. Just dance with her. Act like my old self a little bit so no one questioned my sudden change. Besides, it wasn't like I had to be faithful to Amanda. I had no chance in hell of ever having a relationship with her. She would keep her distance now. I'd pushed her too far the other night.

I stood up and rested my hand on her lower back, and I led her out to the dance floor before Marcus could notice I wasn't interested at all.

AMANDA

I followed Willow into Live Bay. Marcus had texted her and told her to have me bring her here. He was waiting on her and having drinks with Preston. Which was why I was going inside too. I just needed to see his face again before I said yes or no to Jason's text.

Preston was like a drug I couldn't seem to walk away from.

"There's Marcus," Willow said, walking through the crowd toward the table they always occupied. No one was at the table other than Marcus, which was odd. Normally, one of the other guys was still here. I knew Preston was here. Marcus had just texted Willow. If he wasn't at the table or the bar, then he was with a girl. I refused to look out at the dance floor. Not yet. I needed to compose myself first.

"Hey, baby." Marcus beamed at Willow and stood up to pull her into his arms. The kissing immediately started. I didn't really want to watch my brother stick his tongue in someone's mouth, so I took a seat and mentally debated whether or not I should scan the room for Preston. What if he was dry humping a girl up against a wall? Could I handle that? I mean, I had no claim on him, but would it hurt too bad? Yes, probably.

"I missed you," Marcus said, pulling back from his attack on Willow's face.

"I missed you too but I have a dress I really think you're going to like," she replied, then glanced over at me. "I don't know how I would manage all this without Amanda. I'm so glad she didn't go off to school."

Marcus turned his attention to me and winked. "I'm glad she's here too."

"We, uh, talked about the wedding location today, and Amanda said I should have it where I wanted. Not to let your mother convince me otherwise."

Marcus frowned and turned back to stare down at Willow. "She's right. This is our wedding. I thought you liked Mom's idea of the church, but if you don't, then tell me. We'll get married wherever you want."

That was my brother. He was perfect. Guys like him were very hard to find.

"I really want to get married on the beach," she told him.

"Then it's done. I'll tell Mom to cancel the church, and we'll start looking at beach houses to rent."

Willow squealed and grabbed his face and began kissing him again. I turned my attention away from them and looked out at the dance floor. It didn't take long to find Preston. His blond hair always stood out. The almost naked girl he was dancing with also stood out. I knew I should look away, but I couldn't. I wanted to see him with someone else. I knew he treated me differently, but I wanted to see exactly how differently.

The girl ran her hands through his hair, and if he'd let her, I was pretty sure she'd hump his leg. They couldn't get any closer. When she pulled his head down to meet her lips, I jerked my gaze away. I would not watch that.

"You want a Coke, Amanda?" Marcus asked, and I looked over at him and realized he and Willow were both sitting now and no longer kissing. I was more in the mood to leave, but I decided staying and watching Preston all over another girl might be just what I needed to get him out of my system.

"Yes, thanks," I replied.

"Where is everyone else?" Willow asked.

Marcus nodded toward the dance floor. "Preston is danc-ing. Dewayne is on his way. Rock and Trisha are hanging out at home. Cage and Eva are probably locked up in Cage's apart-ment, where they always are lately."

Willow laughed. "Leave them alone. I love seeing Cage like this. He's so happy."

"Trust me, baby, I love seeing him obsessed with someone too. Makes me breathe easier."

Willow rolled her eyes.

As the song ended I glanced back up at the dance floor to see Preston walking toward us with the girl he'd been dancing with following close behind him. At least he wasn't touching her. Normally, Preston had his hands all over the girls he played around with.

His focus was on me, and I was extremely grateful that Marcus's back was turned to the dance floor. The waitress placed a coaster and my Coke down on the table in front of me. I dropped my eyes from Preston's and took a sip of the cold soda.

"Hey, Low," he said once he got to the table. "Manda."

I didn't lift my gaze to his. I simply replied with "Hello" and kept drinking.

"Hey, Preston," Willow said cheerily. "Haven't seen you on campus yet. We must have no classes together."

"Guess not," he replied.

"I want a beer," the girl said as she took the empty seat

beside me. "Hi, I'm Jill." It took all my restraint not to shove her off the stool.

"Amanda. It's nice to meet you," I replied. The politeness was trained into me. My mother had drilled it into my head. I could feel Preston's eyes on me. He was watching me. Did he think I would be rude to her? Just because he'd chosen her to screw tonight instead of me? I'd have to dislike the entire town if that was the case. He'd slept with most of the women in it.

"Oh, you're Marcus's little sister. I remember seeing you with Sadie White."

She knew Sadie? "How do you know Sadie?" Because she was not the kind of girl Sadie made friends with.

"I don't *know* her. I know *of* her. I'm a huge Jax Stone fan."

That made more sense.

"Amanda is dating Jax Stone's brother," Willow chimed in, smiling brightly.

"You are?" the girl asked in a disbelieving voice.

"No, not really," I replied, shaking my head and wishing to God that Willow would shut up.

"He is trying real hard. He was texting her today and making her smile awfully big."

This was my cue to leave. I reached for my purse and didn't make eye contact with anyone.

"Jason Stone is still contacting you? Didn't he leave with Sadie and Jax?" Marcus asked curiously.

Crud. I wasn't going to get away from this.

"You're still talking to Jason?" Preston asked, surprising me. I hadn't expected him to pipe up in this conversation. Not with Marcus sitting here. I looked at Marcus to answer. I would not look at Preston. This was not his business.

"Yeah, he's in LA. He just wants to see if we might could see each other again sometime."

Willow covered up a laugh with a cough. I shot her a pleading look to not say anything more. She understood and nodded.

"He wants to date you?" Jill said. "His picture is plastered all over the place with models and actresses." The disbelieving tone of her voice was grating on my nerves. I was well aware that I couldn't exactly compete with his normal choice in females, but surprisingly, Jason Stone liked something about me. Even if Preston Drake didn't want me.

"I need to go. I've got a paper to write, and I need to check in on Mom," I said, standing up.

"I'm sorry. I shouldn't have brought it up. Don't leave because of my big mouth." Willow sounded concerned.

I smiled at her reassuringly. "Really, I didn't mean to come in and stay. I just wanted to say hello to everyone. Now Preston can have my seat."

I didn't glance over at him.

"Thank you so much for today. You were so much help,

and I had so much fun with you," Willow said, standing up to hug me.

"I loved it," I replied, and hugged her, then stepped back and made one big sweep of the table, including Preston, who was still standing on the other side of Jill, watching me.

"Bye, y'all." I waved, then turned and headed for the door. I could not get out of here fast enough. This was a bad idea. I wouldn't be back here. Not for a while. Pretending like Preston wasn't a man whore was easier when I didn't have to witness it. Tonight was a reminder I needed but really wanted to forget.

"Manda," Preston's voice called out from behind me the moment I touched the handle on my car.

What was he *doing*?

I could act like I didn't hear him and open the door and get inside and drive away. Or I could see what had him running out here to talk to me. My decision making only gave him time to reach me. My escape plan was no longer possible.

"What do you want?" I asked, lifting my gaze to meet his.

He shook his head, and the sad, confused look was there in his eyes again. Dang it. I hated that look.

"Are you going to see him again?"

This was about Jason. Really?

"Probably," I replied, and jerked my door open.

"No, wait." Preston walked closer to me and blocked my entrance into the car.

"What are you doing?" I was growing impatient with him. He was back to his hot-and-cold thing again. I couldn't keep up.

"Do you want to see him?"

What was this? Did he want me to just want him? No one else? He liked having little innocent, stupid Amanda panting after him. Well, he could kiss my ass. I was over that. And I wasn't so innocent anymore, thanks to him.

"Yeah, Preston. I do. He likes me. He wants to be near me. He doesn't push me away."

Preston stepped closer to me, and his worried expression became a scowl. "How close has he got to you, Manda? Has he touched you?"

This was not happening. I was dreaming this insanity. Preston was not getting possessive of me when he didn't even want me.

"Move, Preston. I'm done with this. I can't do it anymore."

Preston grabbed my waist and pulled me up against him. "I'm sorry I can't be who you need me to be."

A few weeks ago I'd have wanted to prove to him he could change. I'd have believed I was the girl to change him. But I knew better now. He couldn't even enjoy touching me sober. I was not the one to change him.

"That's fine. I get it. Now move. I want to go home." I pushed at his chest, but he didn't budge.

"I want to change. You make me want to change everything. I just can't."

I let out a weary sigh before looking back up at him. "I know. One day someone will come along and you'll change for her. She'll be the one you can't live without, and she'll be more important than anyone or anything else. When that happens, you'll change. I'm just not her. Now please, just let me go home. We're done here."

Preston gritted his teeth and shook his head as if to keep from saying something, then let out one long breath before stepping away from my car door and letting me get inside. He stood there watching me as I closed the door. I backed out of my parking spot, and he was still standing there watching me. Once I pulled out onto the road, I glanced into my rearview mirror and he was still there. A week ago I'd have turned around and gone back to him. But I knew better now. He'd only send me packing after he tried to make it work with me and couldn't bring himself to do it.

Chapter Ten

PRESTON

Amanda was avoiding me, and I was going to let her. One of us needed to be strong enough to stop me from hurting her. She'd realized this and was putting a major halt to any interaction between us. I didn't see her after she'd left me standing there, watching her go at Live Bay, until calculus class the next week. When I'd walked into the room, I'd found her immediately. She'd surrounded herself with people and was sitting toward the back of the classroom instead of the seat close to the front where she'd sat last week.

Smart girl.

I took a seat in the front and didn't look back at her. She'd only distract me. The douchebag who'd been looking down her shirt last week was behind her today. I wanted to check and make sure he wasn't leaning up behind her. He needed to keep his eyes to himself.

I was battling with myself over turning around and checking on her or keeping my attention on the board, when my phone vibrated in my pocket. I slipped it out and saw Jimmy's name flashing on the screen. It was the emergency phone I'd given my brother. It was also after nine in the morning. He should be at school. Something was wrong. I grabbed my books and hurried out of the classroom.

"Jimmy?" I answered as I stepped into the hallway.

"Momma didn't come home last night, and Daisy has a real bad fever. She had one all night and I used cold rags on her head and gave her some Tylenol, but it keeps getting higher. She won't eat, and now she just cries real soft like."

Shit. I took off running for the parking lot.

"Okay, go get more cold rags and put them on her skin. Get her to sip on some ice water and tell her I'm on my way."

I hated my mother. She had no redeeming qualities. If something happened to Daisy because of her neglect, I was going to kill her.

"Brent, go get some ice water," Jimmy instructed. "I'm gonna get more cold rags."

"I'll be there soon. Take care of her. Call me if she gets worse."

"I will," Jimmy assured me, then hung up the phone.

I unlocked the Jeep and jerked the door open at the same time I heard Amanda calling my name. Glancing back, I saw her running after me.

"Preston, wait, what's wrong?" she asked in a panicked voice.

"Family stuff. I gotta go," I replied. I hated to run off on her when she was just being nice, but Daisy needed me.

I cranked up the Jeep, and the passenger-side door opened and Amanda jumped inside. Ah, hell.

"Manda, I don't have time for this. I gotta go."

She nodded. "Yes, you do," she agreed. "Go."

"Then get out of my Jeep," I replied, frustrated.

"No. You never get anxious or worried. Never. Something is wrong and you need help." She was right, but I was not taking her to my mother's trailer.

"Manda, please—" I was cut off by the ringing of my phone. Shit.

"What?" I asked, slamming the Jeep into reverse. I didn't have time to argue with a stubborn woman. My little sister needed me. This wasn't the time to worry about my pride. So what if Amanda saw where I grew up? Why did I care? It wasn't like I was trying to impress her.

"She sipped the water, then threw up," Jimmy said. The tightness in his voice told me he was scared. This was not something kids should have to deal with. Jimmy was having to be the adult at eleven, and it made me furious.

"Okay, keep the towels cold and keep them on her. I'll be there in five minutes."

"Okay, we will," he replied, and hung up.

I dropped the phone in my lap and pressed the gas as I pulled out onto the road. "Put on your seat belt, Manda."

I could see her buckle up out of the corner of my eye.

"What's wrong? Who was that?" She was starting to panic too.

"It was my brother. My other one. He's eleven. Daisy, my little sister, is sick, and my sorry-ass mother hasn't been home all night. Jimmy and Brent said she's really hot and she won't eat or drink. They just got her to sip some water and she threw up."

"Oh God," she replied. "Okay. She's going to be okay. We need to get her to the hospital. She's got a fever, so the vomiting sounds like a symptom of the high fever. Give me the phone," Amanda ordered, reaching for it before I could hand it over.

"What are you doing?" I asked.

"Calling your brother," she replied as she chewed at her nails nervously.

"Hey, Jimmy, this is Amanda. I'm a friend of your brother's. Listen, go to the freezer and get any ice you have. Go rub it across Daisy's forehead, her cheeks, her lips, and even up and down her arms. Cooling her down is real important."

I turned down the road that led to the trailer I hated so fiercely. The trailer barely anyone had seen. I didn't bring people here. But right now I was extremely grateful Amanda had come after me and jumped in my Jeep. I wasn't as scared with her here. She was nervous. I could tell by the tone of her voice and the way she was biting her nails, but she was keeping it together. I didn't feel alone. For the first time in my life, I didn't feel alone.

"Good job. Yes, it will melt fast 'cause she's hot. Keep it on her. No, it's okay, Jimmy. She's gonna be fine. We are almost there. We are going to get her to the hospital and get her the medicine she needs. Everything will be fine."

A tightness in my chest came out of nowhere. As I listened to Amanda reassure my brother, I wanted to pull her into my arms and cry. How damn crazy was that? This girl was making me a nutcase.

I pulled up to the trailer and reminded myself that getting Daisy to the hospital was all that mattered. Having Amanda see this place didn't matter. She could think whatever she wanted.

Amanda flung the door open before I'd put the Jeep in park and was running across the yard to the door of the trailer without waiting on me. I took off after her.

She didn't knock but went right in and called out Jimmy's name. He ran into the living room just as I got into the trailer. His eyes went from Amanda to me, then back to Amanda. "She's back here," he told her.

Amanda didn't look around the place in disgust like I'd expected. She didn't seem to notice anything other than Jimmy, who she hurried after.

"Hey, Amanda," Brent said as he looked up at us from his spot beside Daisy. He was icing her arms down just like Amanda had told them to.

"Hey, Brent. You're doing a really good job," she praised him, then walked over to the bed and touched Daisy's head. Daisy looked up at her with glassy eyes and whimpered.

"You're gonna be okay," Amanda assured her, and looked back at me.

"Get her. Let's go," she said, standing back.

I picked her up and cuddled her up against my chest. She curled into me instead of lying limply in my arms, and that small fact helped ease my fear. She wasn't lethargic. That was good.

"Come on, boys. You two go get in the Jeep," she instructed, and went ahead of me to open doors for us.

Once we got to the Jeep, Amanda moved Jimmy to the front. She crawled into the back, then held out her arms. "Give Daisy to me. I'll strap her in with me and hold her. You can drive this thing faster than I can."

"Okay," I agreed. I gave her Daisy, who went willingly. She didn't know Amanda, but like the boys, she was willing to trust her completely. It was that angel's face of hers. It was impossible for anyone to look like Amanda and be untrustworthy.

I ran around the Jeep and climbed in. We were speeding toward the hospital within seconds.

"How long has she had a fever, boys?" Amanda asked, looking back at them.

"Last night she felt warm and said her throat hurt. I gave her some Tylenol and put her to bed. Then all night she tossed and turned and cried. Her skin just got hotter and hotter," Jimmy explained.

I was waiting on Amanda to ask why my mother hadn't come home. Or if they had tried to call her. But she didn't. Instead she nodded. "Well, the two of you did a really good job taking care of her. No one else could have done a better job."

If my little sister wasn't sick and curled up in her lap, I'd grab Amanda's face and kiss her. She had no idea how much those boys needed someone to affirm them. They never got that from anyone but me. Her praising them meant more than she could know.

"I shoulda called Preston sooner," Jimmy said with a defeated sigh.

"You did exactly what you thought you should. You took care of her until you realized she needed a doctor. That's all anyone else woulda known to do," Amanda told him.

I pulled the Jeep up to the door of the emergency room and parked. They could tell me to move if they wanted to, but I was getting Daisy inside first.

Amanda handed her to me, and I took her straight through the doors.

The nurse at the reception desk gave me the usual annoyed look I got when I showed up with one of the kids. I'd been several times over the years.

"Sign in, please," she said.

"It's an emergency. Her fever is really high," I explained.

"It's the emergency room. Everyone in here has an emergency, I assure you. Now sign in please." The woman's bored tone infuriated me.

"She needs a doctor now. I can't put her down and sign her in—she's too sick to stand." I tried not to snarl, but this woman was pushing me.

"Sign in," she repeated.

My blood started to boil.

"What seems to be the problem?" Amanda's voice interrupted the next words out of my mouth, which was probably a good thing.

"Y'all need to sign in and take a seat. He can't seem to understand that."

Amanda's hand wrapped around my arm in a silent warning, and then she turned and walked over to the nurse coming out of a set of double doors.

"Hello, Diana. Could you please go tell Dr. Mike that I'm out here and I have a very sick little girl who needs to see him absolutely as soon as possible?"

"Yes, of course." The nurse glanced back at me holding

Daisy and motioned me toward her. "Y'all come on back with me."

Amanda flashed her a grateful smile. "Thank you so much, Diana. We're really worried about her. She's been running a high fever for the past few hours."

The nurse nodded and hurried to open back up the doors. Amanda walked over to me. "I'll be right behind you. I'm going to go check on the boys and get them settled in the waiting room, and then I'll head back."

"They aren't signed in or registered," the lady behind the counter, who was determined I was not getting back there, said as she stood up.

The nurse frowned at the woman. "That's okay. We'll be sure to get the information we need. Amanda is Dr. Mike's niece."

For once in my life, I was thankful for Amanda Hardy's social status in this town.

"Thank you," I told her before following the nurse back.

AMANDA

I don't think I'd ever been so scared in my life. Keeping my cool wasn't a strong point for me. I normally broke down in a fit of tears when things got tough. But seeing Preston's panicked face had made something in me click. He needed me to be strong, so I was suddenly strong. It was the oddest thing. I knew he needed me, and I wanted to be there for him. Then I'd seen Daisy and my own panic had risen, but I'd managed to remain calm. Knowing they all needed someone to help them had made me act like an adult.

I left Jimmy and Brent in front of the television with sodas and bags of chips I'd bought from the vending machine, then headed back to find Preston and Daisy.

Diana was waiting at the desk when I came by, signing some papers. I'd gotten lucky that she had walked out of the doors just when I needed someone to recognize me. I'd been going to church with Diana since I was a little girl. She'd also dated my mother's much younger half brother back when they were in high school. Now they worked together. I teased Uncle Mike about it whenever I had the chance.

"Come with me. We've got her hooked up to an IV, and we're running tests already. Mike stuck his head in and looked her over on his way to stitch up a head injury. He's coming back, but from his quick look, he believes it is strep. A pretty bad case, but she'll be fine. We are waiting for the results of the strep test now. As soon as we know, we'll start the antibiotics via IV."

We stepped behind the curtain and found Preston pacing at the foot of the bed while Daisy slept peacefully. He stopped and looked at me. "Hey."

"Hey," I replied. "Uncle Mike thinks it's strep. She's going to be fine. Sit down and stop pacing."

"I'll be back in a few minutes to check in. I need to go help set a bone," Diana said before disappearing behind the curtain that separated us from the rest of the patients.

"I don't know how to thank you enough. You just . . ." He paused and shook his head. "Took over. When I saw her there in that bed, so fragile, I was terrified. But you handled everything. Then we get here and you get her the best service possible."

"I'm glad I could help. Emergencies typically aren't something I deal with well, but today I just knew we had to get her to a doctor. Luckily, I'm related to one."

Preston stared at me a moment, and then a small smile touched his lips for the first time today. I was so happy to see that smile. "You're amazing, and you don't even know it."

My face grew warm and I ducked my head. I wasn't amazing, but hearing Preston say it like he meant it made me hope for something I knew I couldn't have. I'd been there when he needed someone. He was feeling grateful. He didn't suddenly find me attractive and want me. Those were two different things, and I needed to keep that in mind.

The curtain pulled back and Uncle Mike stepped inside. His dark brown hair was cut short but did that messy thing in the front that only guys who looked like him at thirty-four could get away with.

"There's my favorite Hardy." Uncle Mike beamed when he walked into the room. That was his favorite joke. Especially now that he hated my dad. He loved to tease Marcus about me being the favorite.

"Hey, Uncle Mike. Is she gonna be okay?" I asked.

"Yep. Kid's got strep. Bad case of it. Needs constant supervision and care. She'll be fine after about thirty-six hours of antibiotics, but it's real important to watch her and keep fluids in her, as well as make her eat small amounts once she starts to feel like it. She is contagious, so you need to keep her away from the other kids if possible. Biggest threat is if they eat or drink from the same dishes she used. Once she's had about twenty-four hours of antibiotics, she won't be contagious anymore."

I nodded, then reached over and squeezed Preston's hand. His fingers laced through mine, and he squeezed back. Uncle Mike's gaze fell to our joined hands before he went back to looking at the chart in front of him.

"I'm getting her prescriptions printed out right now. We want to keep her here a little bit longer to get the first round of antibiotics in her through IV before you leave."

"Yeah, of course. Thank you, Doctor," Preston replied.

Uncle Mike looked at Preston. "She yours?" he asked, shifting his eyes to me, then back to Preston.

He thought Preston had a kid. No wonder he was acting weird about us holding hands.

"No, sir. Well, yeah. Daisy is my little sister. I take care of her when my mom needs me to."

Uncle Mike seemed to relax a little. "That's awfully nice of you. Most guys your age wouldn't be so responsible with a younger sibling."

Preston didn't reply. This was making him uncomfortable. I didn't know a lot about Preston's mom, but I did know her trailer was filthy and she ran off and left her kids at home alone for days. That was enough to know that the kids relied on Preston a lot.

"Thank you for seeing her so fast. I owe you one," I told him, walking over to give him a quick hug.

He pulled me up tightly against him and whispered in my ear, "Watch out for that one," then dropped his arm and nodded one last time at Preston before walking outside our room and closing the curtain behind him.

I turned back to Preston. "She's going to be okay." This time I smiled in relief and walked over to wrap my arms around Preston. He might not want me to, but I needed to hug him. He'd been so upset, and now it was okay. I needed this hug.

Chapter Eleven

PRESTON

I stood in the doorway of my bedroom and looked at the two girls asleep on my bed. Amanda had fallen asleep reading to Daisy, and the book lay across her stomach. By the time we'd gotten Daisy back here and I'd tracked down my mom, Daisy was determined she was keeping Amanda. She'd begged Amanda to stay, and when Amanda had gazed over at me for help, I'd agreed that Amanda staying was a great idea. So Amanda had gone to pick up a few things, including several of her favorite childhood books, while Daisy took an afternoon nap.

It had given me time to call my mom and get the boys back to her while I kept Daisy. She hadn't even argued or come inside to check on her when she'd shown up to get the boys. I hated sending the boys back with her, but I couldn't keep them. I'd have to get a court order, and my mother was just vengeful enough to refuse me. Even if she allowed me to, the boys were better off separated from Daisy while she was sick. Besides, I couldn't do this on my own. Momma may be the suckiest mother ever, but she was home a lot more than I was. Then when baseball season started up, I'd be too busy to sleep, much less take care of kids. It was a no-win situation. I had to keep reminding myself that I'd lived through my life with my mom, and I hadn't had a big brother watching out for me.

Amanda's hands slipped and the book started to fall to the floor, causing her to wake up. She blinked several times, then turned her head to check on Daisy, who was curled up sleeping peacefully beside her. Amanda reached over and brushed the hair out of Daisy's face and checked her temperature with the back of her hand before slowly getting up. Her eyes found mine when she turned to walk to the door. She ran her hand through her hair in an attempt to tame whatever she'd messed up, then smiled at me.

"Guess I was tired too," she whispered as I stepped back and let her out of the room.

I closed the door behind her. "Yeah, Daisy kept you pretty busy."

Amanda chuckled softly. "She's a sweetie. I enjoyed spending time with her."

She had no idea how much it had meant to Daisy. Amanda

was the first adult female to give her any attention. "Thank you. I don't think I'd have made it today without your help. She's never been that sick before. It was scary as shit."

Amanda smiled up at me. "After what I witnessed with you today, I am convinced you'd have been just fine. Never would I have imagined that you'd be such a stellar big brother."

The teasing lilt to her voice was sexy. Everything about her was sexy. And she had a small bag packed with her things so she could sleep over. I wasn't going to be able to control myself. I needed something from her. The emotions swirling inside me were taking over. Everything from attraction to gratefulness to relief. We'd conquered something together today. I wanted to celebrate. With her.

"I'm going to go get a shower and go to bed, if that's okay. Where do you want me to sleep?"

Where I wanted her to sleep and where she was going to sleep were two different things.

"I'm gonna make myself a bed on the floor in the bedroom. You can take the couch. Unless, of course, you're up for sharing the couch. Then I'd be all in. I'm a really good bed buddy."

Amanda's eyes went wide before she let out a giggle. "As talented as I'm sure you are as a bed buddy, I think I'll pass. I can always take the floor in the bedroom if you want me to."

The one night of my life I get Amanda to stay the night in my apartment, she would not be sleeping on the floor. I wanted her on my couch. Actually, I wanted her in my bed, but Daisy was kind of occupying that at the moment. I was going to make sure Amanda used one of my pillows, though. That way, I'd have her scent for a while after she was gone.

"No, I insist. You're sleeping on the couch."

Amanda studied me a minute. I could see the concern and uncertainty in her eyes. She wanted to ask me something, and she couldn't decide if she was going to or not. I'd stand here and let her think about it as long as she wanted to.

"Did the boys get home okay?" she finally asked.

Not exactly what I wanted to talk about. I knew where this was headed. "Yeah, my mom came and got them."

"Are they, um, I mean, uh, do you think they're gonna be okay . . . there . . . I mean . . . ," she stammered nervously.

I walked over to the couch and sat down, then looked back at her. "They have a phone. If they need me, they'll call."

Amanda frowned and took a step in my direction. "Did your mom come up and check on Daisy?"

This was not a life that Amanda was going to be able to comprehend. Her dad may have screwed around and left them recently, but her life had been pretty damn privileged. "No, Manda. She didn't. She doesn't care. There is no one on this earth I hate more than my mother. Is that what you were curious about?"

My words had come out harder than I'd intended them to.

Amanda walked over to the couch and sat down beside me. "Preston, I am so sorry. I didn't mean to pry. I was just curious because Daisy never once asked about her mom or spoke of her today. That was odd to me. Growing up, when I was sick I always wanted my mom. I couldn't understand why she never asked for hers."

I laid my head back against the wall and tilted it so I could look at Amanda. She was worried and clearly upset. I was enlightening her about a world she didn't know existed, and that world wasn't even the worst part about me.

"You are the first woman to ever spend any time with Daisy. My mother is either drunk, asleep, or gone. Daisy is raised by Jimmy when they're home. I make sure the bills stay paid and the kids have food. Then, like you saw today, if someone gets sick, I handle it."

"Oh God, that makes my chest hurt," Amanda whispered, rubbing the ball of her hand over her heart. "I want to go cuddle up to Daisy and hold her. No wonder Jimmy acts twenty instead of eleven."

I reached over and pulled her hand away from her chest. "They'll be okay. I am, and I didn't have any older siblings to help me out. I made it without anyone. Don't get upset over it. They aren't the only kids growing up in this exact same situation."

Amanda's eyes held unshed tears as she tried real hard to

keep her bottom lip from quivering. Ah, hell. I'd made her cry. I hadn't told her all that to make her cry. I'd just answered her questions. I'd let her into my screwed-up life a little. More than I'd ever let anyone in.

"You're the only person I've ever told about the kids and my mom. I've never even told your brother."

Amanda pressed her lips together tightly and nodded. She didn't respond. She was still trying very hard not to cry. Her soft heart couldn't handle this. If she even knew a little bit of what my mom had done to those kids and me, she'd never be able to deal with it.

"Come here," I said gently as I reached for her arms and pulled her against my chest.

AMANDA

Going willingly into Preston's arms probably wasn't real smart, but at that moment, I just didn't care. I needed to hold him. I couldn't go hold Jimmy and Brent, but I could hold him. And tomorrow I would give Daisy every second of my attention when I wasn't in class. I might even skip them just so I could stay here. She'd be going back to her mom soon. The idea of her being neglected was painful.

"I'm sorry I told you all this," Preston whispered against my hair as he held me tightly to him. I wasn't sorry. He'd let me in.

It was something I'd wanted. However, when I'd wanted in, I'd had no idea I was going to find this out. Images of Preston over the years kept flashing through my mind. When I'd met him, he'd been a skinny kid with hair so long he kept it in a ponytail. Even in his faded jeans and worn-out T-shirt I couldn't help but think he was beautiful. But I'd wondered why his mother let him look like that.

"Thank you for telling me. For letting me help today. I know I'm reacting to this like the spoiled brat that I am, but I'm trying to process it. I want to go take them all away from your mom and keep them close. Take care of them. Make sure they have proper haircuts and clean clothes."

Preston's chest rumbled with laughter, and I looked up at him.

"Proper haircuts and clean clothes?" he asked, grinning down at me.

"I keep remembering the first time I saw you. Your hair was ridiculously long, and your clothes were so worn out. It didn't take away from the fact that you were the most gorgeous boy I'd ever seen, but still. . . ." Oh, crap. Had I really just said that?

Preston titled his head to the side and studied me a moment. "You thought I was gorgeous?"

Sighing, I started to pull back from his arms, but he held me firmly in place. "Answer me," he whispered, lowering his head so that his mouth was very close to my ear.

"Yes. You know you're gorgeous."

Preston slid a hand down my back until he had a firm grip on my waist, and then he pulled me up higher against his chest. "Maybe I don't know that," he replied, reaching with his other hand to cup my face and brush his thumb over my cheekbone. "Maybe I'm trying to figure out why you want anything to do with me."

Was he serious?

"I've had a crush on you since I was sixteen. Surely you know this. I wasn't very secretive about it. I've never missed one of your baseball games, not even the away ones. I found any reason I could think of to throw myself in your path. Then when I did get your attention, you were drunk, but I didn't care. I was willing to take what I could get. Maybe I didn't know you were as drunk as you were, but I was just glad you weren't treating me like a little girl anymore. I was tired of having to fantasize about you. I wanted the real thing."

Preston went very still. Dang it. I'd opened my mouth and said too much. He was going to shove me toward the bathroom now and go hide in his bedroom.

"You fantasized about me?"

Really? Was that all he got out of what I'd just said?

"Yes," I replied, rolling my eyes and trying to move away, only to be held in place with a tight squeeze of my waist from his hand.

Preston lowered his mouth until it was against my cheek. "Why don't you tell me about these fantasies? You know, so I understand better." His warm breath tickled my skin, and I shivered.

"That's a bad idea," I replied.

Preston's hand slipped under the hem of my shirt until his fingers were brushing up against my bare stomach. "I disagree. I'm thinking it's a real good idea," he said before trailing kisses against the tender skin behind my ear down to my neck.

Forming thoughts while Preston's hand was slowly moving up my stomach and his mouth was nuzzling and taking small nips at my neck wasn't exactly easy. I couldn't remember what it was we were talking about.

"See, Manda, it's a really good idea. So damn good," he said just before his hand cupped one of my breasts.

Focus. I needed to focus. There was a reason this was a bad idea. I just had to think really hard.

"Take this shirt off for me," Preston said in a harsh whisper. Then he pulled my shirt over my head and dropped it somewhere to the side of us. His eyelids were lowered, and it only made him sexier. I hadn't realized that was possible.

With one hand Preston reached around me and undid the hooks on my bra, then pulled it away. I'd been with him like this before, but it had been dark outside. We weren't in the dark now, and Preston's words "I know your boobs aren't that big" came back to haunt me. I didn't have the cup size most of the girls he dated did. He liked big boobs. Mine were nowhere near what he was used to. I glanced around frantically for my shirt.

"Manda, don't." Preston ran his hand through my hair and turned my head back toward him. Then his mouth covered mine. The soft warmth of his lips as they nipped and tasted me made my insides turn to butter. I slipped both my hands around his neck and held him there, afraid he'd realize I had small boobs or that he didn't want to do this again and push me away.

Letting out a low growl, Preston grabbed both my legs and pulled me completely onto his lap until I was straddling him. The pressure from his erection pressed against me sent shots of pleasure through my body.

I fisted my hands in his hair and continued to taste him and get lost in the connection I'd been denied before. His teeth caught my bottom lip, and he bit down gently with a small tug. I trembled and pressed down harder on his arousal, causing us both to moan from the sensation.

Preston's hands ran up my thighs, and then they both went up to cup my breasts. Once again I was reminded how lacking I was in that department. I tensed and started to move back.

"What's wrong?" Preston asked, pulling me closer even as I tried to pull away.

"Nothing. But . . . can I just wear my shirt?"

Preston lowered his head, keeping his eyes locked with

mine until his tongue darted out and licked over one of my nipples. Then he pulled it into his mouth, and my body betrayed me by shooting off fireworks. I grabbed his shoulders and held on as he continued to lavish attention on one breast, then the other one. The cries of pleasure coming from my mouth couldn't be helped. Preston's tongue had complete control of my body.

When the warmth from his talented administrations stopped, I opened my mouth to beg for more, but the snap on my blue jean shorts stopped me. Looking down, I watched as Preston unzipped my shorts, then ran his hand over the pink satin of my panties.

"Why did you want to put your shirt on, Manda?" he asked, raising his eyes to meet mine.

My shirt? What? I was confused. . . .

"What?" I asked, mesmerized by the way his long lashes brushed his cheeks as he stared at me with this hungry, intense gleam in his eyes.

"You wanted your shirt on. Why?"

Oh yeah . . . my shirt. I'd forgotten.

"Um, my, uh, it was just that . . ." I didn't want to say this. I didn't want to bring it up. I just wanted him to keep slipping his hand farther down my shorts. If I reminded him that my boobs were too small for his taste, this may not happen.

He cupped one of my breasts and ran his thumb over my

nipple. "They taste as sweet as they look," he whispered in a husky voice.

"Oh," I breathed, watching him touch me.

"So why would you want to cover them up?"

He wasn't going to let this go. Sighing, I tried to will his hands to slip farther down my shorts. It didn't work. He wasn't going to do anything else until I answered him.

"Because they're smaller than you like," I mumbled, ducking my head to hide the humiliation on my face from having to actually say that out loud.

Preston froze, and I mentally cursed. I knew it. He'd stop now.

"Stand up, Amanda." It wasn't a request. It was a command.

He was sending me to take a cold shower. I crawled off his lap and stood up, crossing my arms over my chest. I would look for my shirt later. Turning, I started to head to the shower, when Preston grabbed my hips and pulled me back. "Where do you think you're going?" he asked.

I glanced back at him. "The bathroom, to cool down."

Preston lowered his eyebrows and shook his head. "No, you're not."

Did he want me to leave instead?

"Turn around, Manda." The deep, authoritative voice sounded sexy, but I didn't want to turn around. I wanted to go hide in the bathroom. "Please, baby. Turn back around," he whispered in my ear.

He knew how to work me. That was for sure. Slowly I turned back around, keeping my arms crossed over my bare chest. Preston reached down and tugged on my unzipped shorts until they were sliding down my legs. "Step out of them," he told me, and I did without question.

He reached up from his relaxed position on the couch and tugged at my arms until they uncrossed and fell to my side. He cupped each breast with his hands and held them as if they were precious before looking back up at me. "You're fucking perfect. Everything about you. Your smile. Your laugh can brighten up my whole damn day. The way you care about people so much that you drop everything to help them. These sexy-as-hell legs of yours that have been giving me raging hard-ons for years. These perfect, round, soft tits with nipples that I swear taste like candy. And then there is this." He slipped a hand between my legs and ran his middle finger across the wet silk of my panties. "Fuck, baby. It doesn't get any better than this." He groaned before covering my mouth with his and kissing me hard and fast. Each thrust of his tongue made my knees weak. I knew what he wanted. I knew what I wanted, and the wild kiss only heightened my desire.

I reached for his shirt, grabbing handfuls of material, and pulled it up and over his head. I needed him naked too. I pulled back from our kiss and ran my hands over his chest so I could feel each defined muscle. The small jump in his pecs made me smile.

"You've got about three seconds left of exploring, Manda. I can't take much more."

I ran my fingers down to the button on his jeans and undid it, then slowly unzipped them. Just as I started to tug on them, Preston picked me up and kissed me hard on the mouth, then threw me down on the couch. "Time's up," he growled as he covered me with his body.

I opened my legs. I could feel his erection pressed against me. Now we had only one layer of jeans between us. Preston ran his hand down my stomach and then slid his fingers inside my panties. When his fingertips reached their destination, I grabbed him and bucked against his hand. "Ohmygod, Preston." I panted.

He dropped his head to the curve of my neck and began sliding his fingers in and out of me. Each time they reentered me, I moved against the pressure. My body was taking over, and all I cared about was the pleasure.

"That's it," he breathed against my skin. "Let me make it feel good. I want you to come against my hand so I can feel it."

The naughty words sent me over the edge. I screamed out his name, but his mouth covered mine to muffle the sound. The pulsing had erupted into ecstasy, and my body was trembling underneath him. His fingers slid back out, and his body left me. Opening my eyes in a panic, I started to beg him to come back. But he wasn't leaving. He was taking off his jeans.

Watching Preston Drake strip was one of those things a girl would never, ever forget. His boxer briefs fell to the ground along with his jeans, and I swallowed . . . hard. Although we'd had sex before, I'd never actually seen him naked. I'd never seen any guy naked. It was amazing.

Preston took both sides of my panties and pulled them down, then threw them to the floor with the rest of our discarded clothing.

"You're so beautiful," he breathed in an awed voice as he stared down at me.

"So are you," I replied, because it was the truth.

Preston smirked. "You're gonna have to stop calling me things like 'gorgeous' and 'beautiful.' I'm gonna get a complex. Why can't I be 'sexy,' or maybe 'irresistible'?"

"You're those things too. Trust me." I smiled up at him.

Preston held himself over my body while he looked down at me. "That night. In the storage shed. I'll never forgive myself for that. It'll never be like that again with us."

I reached up and tucked the hair that was hanging over his eyes behind his ear. "But it felt good. Really, really good. Better than any of the times I'd fantasized about."

Preston froze. "When you say 'fantasized' . . . do you mean you thought about me when you touched yourself?"

My face was instantly hot, and I knew he'd seen my blush and knew the answer. There was no use in denying it. I nodded.

"Holy shit," he breathed. "I'm not gonna be able to get that image out of my head."

He bent his head and kissed me softly on the lips. "I want inside you so bad. But if you want us to stop here, we will."

No stopping. I was desperate enough that I might tie him up this time if he tried to escape. "I want you inside me too."

Preston bit his bottom lip and closed his eyes tightly. "Baby, between you telling me you touch yourself while thinking about me and you saying you want me inside you, I may fucking blow before I even get inside you."

Giggling, I shifted my hips underneath his, wanting to feel him with nothing between us. "Mmmm, not yet," he said, and bent his head to kiss my lips. Then he went lower to kiss each nipple. He pulled each one into his mouth before kissing a trail down my stomach. When his hands touched the insides of my thighs and pushed them open farther, I stopped breathing. At the first flick of Preston's tongue against my clit, I had to bite down hard on my bottom lip to keep from screaming out his name.

I reached down and grabbed handfuls of his hair as he continued to taste and lick. Knowing he was completely sober and doing this made it even better. My body began to tremble, and I knew I was close. I wouldn't be able to stop myself from crying out.

Preston's mouth left me, and I was about ready to beg him when I heard the rip of foil and looked down to see him slipping a condom on. Oh . . . never mind. I wanted that more.

His eyes lifted to meet mine. "That was incredible. Nothing has ever tasted as good as you do."

The naughty talk was something he excelled at, I'd decided. I was pretty sure he could bring me to an orgasm just by talking dirty in my ear. I wondered if he'd try that sometime.

Preston lowering himself over me stopped my train of thought. He closed his eyes tightly as the tip of his erection met my entrance. "I don't want to hurt you," he breathed out in a ragged whisper.

"You won't. Please," I begged, and lifted my hips.

Preston eased inside me slowly. "So tight. Fucking heaven."

When he was completely inside, we both let out moans. He was inside me. I wanted to keep him there. I'd never felt this close before with anyone. I knew now how disconnected he'd been the first time we'd done this. This time was so different. He was right here with me. Feeling everything I was.

"You're so warm and tight. I want to stay right here," he said before covering my mouth with his. His tongue thrust into my mouth, and I sucked on it hard.

Preston started to move. My hips moved with him as he slid in and out of me. He kissed me and whispered words of approval as his movements grew faster and harder. I was climbing with him. I needed more. I knew what was coming this time, and I wanted it.

Just as my orgasm hit me, Preston grabbed my hips and thrust hard one last time, calling out my name. It was perfect.

Chapter Twelve

PRESTON

After waking up several times during the night to find Amanda still tucked tightly against my chest, it was a major letdown when I woke up alone.

I stretched and sat up, searching for the pieces of clothing we'd thrown around the room. Amanda's were gone, and mine were neatly folded on the chair. When had she left? Standing up, I reached for my jeans and slipped them on before going to find my phone so I could call her and find out where the hell she was.

If she thought last night hadn't changed things, then she was so very wrong. It had changed everything. My life was fucked up and there wasn't anything I could do about it, but I wasn't about to let Amanda go. Not now.

Whispering and giggling came from my bedroom. She was still here, or Daisy was talking to herself. I opened the door slowly to find Amanda sitting on the bed with Daisy. They were talking quietly, but whatever they were talking about was making Daisy laugh. Amanda was dressed in a short skirt, so almost every golden inch of her legs was in clear view. I'd had those legs wrapped around me last night. I closed my eyes and forced the images away. Daisy was here. I had to keep my hands off Amanda in front of Daisy. This was going to be hard.

"Pweston!" Daisy squealed as her eyes met mine, and she clapped happily. I'd been spotted. Daisy's cheeks were a healthy pink today, and she was feeling much better. The happy glow on her face made my heart swell. Amanda had put that look there.

"Hey, my Daisy May. Looks like you're feeling better this morning," I told her as I walked into the room. I fought hard to keep my eyes off Amanda. I wasn't sure just yet how to explain to her how I felt. I sure as hell couldn't tell her what I did that paid for this apartment and also took care of my mom's place and the kids. I'd lose her, and after last night I knew that wasn't an option. I couldn't lose Amanda.

"I'm feeling bettah," she replied. "And Amanda is gonna cuwal my hayah today."

"She is? You got a big date I don't know about?" I teased, sitting down beside her. She giggled and shook her head.

"I just like cuwals," she replied.

Amanda started to move, and I couldn't keep from looking at her anymore. I turned my head in her direction and watched as she got off the bed and straightened her incredibly short skirt. She needed to change. That was too short.

"Where you going?" I asked her.

She shrugged and twisted a lock of her hair around her finger nervously. "I thought I'd give y'all some time to visit. I have a class in thirty minutes. I could come back after, if that's okay. I told Daisy I'd curl her hair. . . ." She trailed off and looked down at the floor.

I hadn't been awake when she'd woken up, to talk to her about anything. There was no telling what was going through her head right now. But I knew I needed to clear a few things up before I let her walk out of my apartment with that damn skirt on.

"Daisy May, why don't you watch a little television while I go fix you some breakfast and see Amanda off to school. Okay?" I told her as I stood up.

Daisy nodded, and I handed her the remote to the flat-screen on my wall that I'd won last month in a poker game.

I looked back at Amanda and nodded toward the door. She walked toward it and I followed her out. Yeah, that skirt was way too short in the back. If she bent over, someone would see her sweet little ass. She was going to have to change. No question.

Closing the door behind me, I moved quickly and grabbed

her waist, then turned her around to face me and pressed her up against the fridge.

"You were gone when I woke up," I whispered before kissing the corner of her mouth.

"I woke up early," she replied.

"I missed getting to see you all rumpled from sleep, touching you while that sexy, sleepy haze was still in your eyes." I slipped my hand up her thigh and easily cupped her almost bare butt, thanks to the barely there panties she was wearing. "Manda."

"Yeah," she replied a little breathlessly.

"You're gonna have to go change."

She went still in my arms.

"I can't let you go out like this. It'll drive me crazy. This skirt's too short, sweetheart. Guys will be looking, and I don't want them looking."

A slow smile spread across her full red lips. Thank God. She wasn't going to get all pissy about this, because I really didn't want to force her to do anything.

"You're jealous?" she asked, almost as if she didn't believe it as she said it.

"Hell yeah, I'm jealous," I replied, running my hand over the soft skin of her bottom. "I'm not sharing this. I don't want to think about other guys looking at you in this."

Amanda's smile got bigger, and I was real close to ripping these panties off and taking her against the fridge. The fact that my little sister was in the other room was the only reason I wasn't inside her right this minute.

"I'll change," she replied, reaching up to touch my face. She kissed my cheek, then took in a deep breath as if she was smelling me. "So last night . . . it wasn't just a onetime thing?"

I would question how she could think that, if it wasn't for the fact that I'd had sex with her before and walked away. She had every right to think I was going to walk again. She didn't realize that I was incapable of pushing her away anymore. We'd gone too far.

"Last night changed everything," I assured her before kissing the corner of her mouth. "I'll never be able to get you out of my system. I don't want to. I need you, Manda." I covered her mouth with mine and slipped inside to taste her. This connection with her was the first thing in my life I was scared of. I'd never feared anything else—I could handle it. My brothers and sister I knew I'd be there. I could take care of them. I'd do whatever I had to, and I knew they'd love me. But this thing with Amanda—if I lost it, if I lost her, I would lose it all. In the screwed-up life I'd been dealt, she was my only source of comfort. Just being with her made everything else seem like it would be okay.

I'd always be honest with her about everything . . . except the one thing that could take her from me. She'd never understand. Even if she did, she'd never be able to accept it. If she knew I slept with wealthy women for money, she'd leave me. She could never know.

AMANDA

> Jason: Have you thought about that dinner in
> NYC yet?

The text from Jason came during my literature class. I stared down at my phone and tried to think of what I was going to tell him. If the decision was between him and Preston, then it was Preston. I liked Jason, and he was probably the safer of the two guys when it came to protecting my heart. But that was just it. I wasn't worried about Jason hurting me, because I knew he didn't have that power. We'd only gone out one time, and that was to my brother's engagement party. It wasn't like I'd led him on.

Tucking my phone back into my backpack, I decided I'd deal with him later. I needed to think about the proper response. The professor dismissed class, and I hurried back outside to my car to get back to Preston's. I had promised to do Daisy's hair, and if I was completely honest with myself, I was anxious to see Preston again. Last night and this morning almost seemed like I'd walked into one of my dreams.

Having Preston look at me with emotion in his eyes was amazing. And him telling me I had to change may have been a little barbaric, but honestly, I'd put on a pair of sweats if he asked me to. The fact that he was possessive of me and didn't want other guys to look at me made my silly heart soar.

The bad thing was, I kept waiting for my alarm clock to

wake me up. This didn't seem real just yet. My phone started ringing, and I reached into my backpack to get it out. Preston's number lit up the screen.

Smiling, I answered and put the phone to my ear. "Hey."

"Hey. You out of class yet?"

Was he checking up on me? Really?

"Yeah, just got out."

"You coming back here?"

"Um, I was planning on it. I promised to do Daisy's hair, remember?"

He paused and sighed. Oh no, it was already ending. Time to wake up.

"That's right. I just wanted to make sure your plans hadn't changed. I need to run up to the gym and meet with Coach. I can't leave Daisy here alone."

Oh . . . he wasn't trying to get rid of me.

"I just hate to ask you to come here and stay with her while I'm out."

Smiling, I opened my car door and got inside. "I'm glad I can watch her for you. I was planning on spending the rest of the day with Daisy, so it's no problem. I'll be there in a few minutes."

Another pause. What was wrong with him?

"Okay. Thank you, Manda."

Was he really this unused to people helping him out with

the kids? "No need to thank me. See ya in a sec." I clicked off and turned the car toward Preston's.

The door to Preston's apartment opened before I could knock. Preston reached out, grabbed my hand, and pulled me inside. His mouth was on mine immediately. It was different this time than it had been the other times. Something about it was desperate. Like he was trying to hold on to me. Was he worried that I was going to change my mind? After the way I'd chased him for months? I let my backpack fall to the floor, and I slid my hands into his hair. He needed some kind of reassurance from me. I was sure of that. So I gave it to him.

"I don't want to leave you," he said against my mouth as he closed the door behind me, then pressed me up against it.

"I'll be here when you get back," I assured him, then took a nip at his bottom lip before stroking the inside of his mouth again with my tongue.

"But I don't want to leave," he repeated. His voice was a little panicked sounding as his hands ran up the inside of my shirt and cupped my boobs. "I want you, Manda. Just you."

I couldn't help but smile. That sounded so good. "It's just a workout, Preston. I'll even give you a massage when you get back."

His arms tightened around me, and I felt his phone vibrate in his pocket. He muttered a curse and then pulled away from me. He ran the pad of his thumb over my bottom lip. "I gotta go. I wish I didn't."

This clingy Preston was something new. I liked it, but then, it also bothered me a little. I didn't want him to worry every time he left me that things would be different when he got back. Was he insecure? I'd never pegged Preston as insecure.

"The sooner you go, the sooner you get back," I told him, biting down on his thumb that was still touching my lip. "Now go."

Preston nodded and dropped his hand from my mouth. He started to say something more and stopped. I moved away from the door and watched as he opened it. He glanced back at me one more time before he left. I gave him a reassuring smile, and a slow, sexy smile touched his lips. I liked it when he was smiling. I didn't want him worried or anxious. When he closed the door, I realized he hadn't taken a bag with him. That was odd. Maybe he kept a change of clothes in his locker at the gym.

Chapter Thirteen

PRESTON

I couldn't do it. Cassandra Gregory was one of my biggest clients. She'd sent many more wealthy women my way too. But damn if I could leave Amanda at my apartment and walk into this woman's beach house and screw her. It would be a fucking miracle if I could even get it up. The guilt of having lied to Amanda and left her there taking care of Daisy was bad enough. Remembering how good it felt to be inside Amanda and having her cling to me and call out my name while she found release was a whole other issue. No one else was going to measure up to that. I'd see her and feel wrong. I couldn't do this.

I pulled my Jeep into the parking lot of Cassandra's beach house. I was going to have to tell her something. Anything to put this off. I needed the money. Jimmy had another orthodontist appointment for his braces next week, and I needed at least a thousand dollars for that. Then I needed to get new windows put in the kids' rooms. Two of them were cracked. Jimmy had said water was wetting the wall and floor when it rained. The last thing I needed was for the trailer to get a rotten floor.

My phone rang. I glanced down to see my mom's name light up the screen.

Shit. Not who I wanted to talk to right now. But if I ignored her, she could go over to the apartment while I was gone and Amanda was there.

"What?" I said angrily into the phone. It was all her fault I was even in this predicament.

"Bring Daisy home. She's better by now. And my car's got a flat tire. I need new tires."

"I'll bring Daisy home tonight if I think she is okay. And if you want new tires, get a damn job."

Stupid bitch hated for me to pay the bills, but she sure didn't mind asking me for money.

"You want me driving around on those bad tires of mine with your brothers and sister? Fine. I'll drive 'em to school. They hate the bus anyhow."

It was a threat she'd keep because she was just that vicious.

I glanced up at the house in front of me. I needed the money. I always needed more money. I should have forced the prick who Dewayne had invited to the poker game to pay me cash and not taken that damn flat-screen. It wouldn't have been enough cash, but it would have helped.

"I'll get your tires. But you better not drive the kids anywhere until I do."

I hung up the phone and threw it in the passenger seat. Shutting off all emotion and locking any feelings I had for Amanda deep inside, I opened the door to my Jeep and stepped outside. I'd been doing this for three years now. I could do this. I had to.

Three hours later I parked my Jeep back at my apartment and got out, slamming the door behind me. I'd had enough time on the drive home to get very worked up. I kicked at my tire and slammed both hands down on the hood. Deep breaths. I needed to take deep breaths. My chest hurt, my stomach was twisted in knots, and the fuck money in my pocket was heavier than it had ever been. Before I'd let Amanda in, this had been easy. Now it was sick. I was a screwed-up son of a bitch, literally. I needed to feel whole again. I needed to be near Amanda. I stalked across the parking lot and made my way up the stairs, taking them two at a time. Seeing her and holding her would make it better.

The woman I'd just been paid well to entertain flashed in my mind, and I froze. I couldn't touch Amanda right now. I had to get clean. I needed a shower. The hottest fucking shower I could stand. Amanda didn't need to be close to the cheap, meaningless sex I'd just had.

I opened the door and walked in. The television in my room was on, and I could hear the girls talking. Before either of them realized I was home, I headed for the bathroom.

AMANDA

I heard the click of the front door closing and watched the bedroom doorway for Preston to appear. He didn't. Glancing over at Daisy, who was now watching the television again after explaining to me that this girl was a bunch of kids' nanny and a couple of them were adopted, I eased off the bed.

"I'll be back," I assured her when she turned her head full of curls to look at me. She smiled and went back to watching her show.

I closed the bedroom door on my way out and walked into the living room. The sound of the shower answered my question. Preston had come home from the gym all sweaty, and he wanted to get clean first. That was a shame. I'd have liked to see him sweaty.

I went over to the fridge and pulled out the fried chicken and biscuits that Daisy had helped me make earlier. Preston was sure to be hungry after being at the gym for three hours. I turned on the oven and put a chicken breast and a leg along with a couple of biscuits on a cookie sheet, then slid it inside. I wasn't a fan of the microwave. I was more than positive it was the cause of all kinds of health problems.

The water in the shower turned off, and the butterflies in my stomach started up as I waited anxiously to see him again. It was ridiculous that I was so excited about it. He'd only been gone three hours.

When the bathroom door opened, Preston stepped out with nothing but a towel around his waist. There were no words for this. Nothing compared. His eyes met mine and a smile touched his lips.

"Hey, you," he said as he walked over to me. I was cemented to my spot in the kitchen.

"Hey," I managed to reply. Keeping my eyes off his body and on his face was another problem.

"Something smells good." He looked over at the oven, then back at me. "Did you cook?"

"Maybe."

Preston lowered his head until his mouth hovered above mine. "Sexy as hell and she cooks. Dayum, baby, it don't get no better."

Giggling, I stood on my tiptoes to kiss his mouth before stepping back and checking on his chicken.

"Daisy helped me," I told him.

"Is that so? I think you need to check on it again," he said with a wicked grin on his face as I stood back up.

"It needs a few more minutes," I explained.

"I was just admiring the view."

I let my gaze travel down his damp, barely covered body, then back up again. "I could say the same," I told him.

Preston's eyes went dark and smoldering instantly. "You look at me like that again, and I'll haul you off to the bathroom and take you up against the sink."

I took a step toward him. "Is that a threat or a promise?"

Preston reached for my waist and jerked me against him, when the bedroom door opened. Daisy came skipping out, smiling.

"Pweston," she called out in greeting, and then a small frown touched her forehead. "Wheyah is youwah clothes?"

I covered my mouth to stifle my laugh and reached for a pot holder to get Preston's food out of the oven.

"Well, Daisy May, I need to go get some. I just took a shower to get the nasty off me."

"We cooked you dinnah," she said happily, pointing to the food I was putting onto a plate for him.

"And it looks delicious. Thank you, girls, for taking care of me. I'll go get some clothes on, then come eat."

"Good idea," Daisy agreed.

I watched Preston walk toward the door to his room, and the view of him in his towel was just as nice from the back. I needed a fan.

"Did you tell him about the peanut buttah pie yet?" Daisy asked in a whisper after Preston closed the door.

"Nope. I thought I'd let you surprise him with it. Since you did all the hard work on it."

Daisy clapped her hands and did a little happy dance. There was no way she was going to be able to let him eat all his meal before she pulled that pie out of the fridge.

"Why don't you help me fix him a drink?"

Daisy ran to the dishwasher and got out a clean glass. She handed it up to me. "He likes to dwink root beeah, I think. 'Cause Jimmy said he dwinks beeah, but I don't think it's the kind my momma dwinks. He don't like it when she dwinks that stuff."

Bless her heart. She was so little and knew so much already. I wasn't about to be the one to tell her that Preston did in fact drink beer. But I also knew there was not going to be any root beer in this kitchen.

"How about the sweet tea I made earlier? You think he'd like that?" I hoped so, because that was what he was getting. I opened the fridge and shoved the Bud Lights to the back of the fridge and moved the orange juice in front of them before Daisy noticed.

"It's yummy sweet tea. I think he will," she replied.

I finished pouring his tea and fixed him a plate at the table with Daisy's help just in time for him to come strutting out of his room in a fitted light-blue T-shirt that matched his eyes, and a pair of low-slung jeans. That look should be illegal.

His feet were bare and tanned. I hadn't paid much attention to them before, but now I knew even his feet were sexy.

"Should I stand still until you're done?" Preston teased. I snapped my head up and met his amused gaze. "Don't let me stop you. I was enjoying it. Please continue."

I couldn't help it. I laughed. He'd caught me ogling him.

"You dress like that, and it's hard not to look," I replied, and turned away from him to unload the dishwasher.

"What's wong with his clothes?" Daisy asked, confused.

I opened my mouth to tell her nothing, but Preston beat me to it.

"Nothing, Daisy May. I just think Manda may like the way I look in my clothes."

My head shot up and his twinkling eyes met mine.

"If she does, then you should weah them all the time. She's sweet and fun and pwetty, and you can bwing hewah with you when you come see us."

The excited little voice made me want to go hug her tightly and assure her she'd see me again. She still hadn't said a thing about her mother or even mentioned going home. That said more than any words she could have said. It broke my heart.

"That's a good idea, Daisy May. Maybe I should wear this every day. Might get Manda to stick around a little while. She and I could come get you and the boys and take you to get a burger sometime."

Daisy jumped up excitedly on the balls of her feet. "Yes, yes, please." She turned back to me. "Do you like him in otha clothes, owah just those?" The sincerity of her question made me smile. She was really going to campaign to get Preston to wear that outfit every day just so she could see me again. If she hadn't already edged her way into my heart, she'd have done so then.

"Actually, Daisy, I think he looks nice all the time. He just caught me looking this time."

Daisy's eyes went big, and a grin broke out on her face when she looked back at Preston. "She likes you, and she's weally, weally pwetty and fun."

Daisy was selling me to Preston. That might have been the sweetest thing ever.

"She smells real nice too, and I have a thing for that pretty blond hair of hers," Preston added, leaning back in his chair and studying me.

"She does smell good," Daisy agreed. "And hewah sweet tea is yummy."

Preston nodded. "Yeah, she has all kinds of stuff that is yummy."

I pressed my lips together to keep from laughing, and leaned a hip against the counter to watch the two of them study me.

"And she can sing, too. She singed me all kinds of songs."

Preston's eyes went wide at Daisy's statement. Dang it. I hadn't meant for her to tell Preston

I'd sung to her. She'd asked me to, and I figured no one had ever sung to her before. I'd let her crawl up into my lap, and I'd sung her every song she'd asked me to.

"Really?" Preston asked with a mischievous smile on his face. "Hmm. I didn't know that. I guess that will be the deciding factor for me. Amanda will have to sing for me before I decide if I want to keep her around."

Daisy seemed pleased with this. "Yay! You will keep hewah. She sings weal pwetty."

I already dreaded the moment he got me alone.

Preston's phone rang, and he tensed up immediately. The playful look on his face was gone. Who was he expecting?

He reached into his pocket and pulled out his phone, then let out a sigh. "I'm bringing her home in a little while. Let me eat first."

Oh no. It was his mom. I wasn't ready to give Daisy back to that woman.

"Thirty minutes."

He put the phone down and looked over at Daisy. "Momma is ready for you to come home, Daisy May. Why don't you go get your stuff together while I finish up?"

Daisy's little face fell, but she didn't argue. She nodded and went to the bedroom.

I watched her until she was out of sight, then looked back at Preston. "Does she have to go?" I asked in a low voice.

Preston frowned and nodded. "Yeah." He didn't like it either.

"You think she'll be okay? Will your mom remember to give her the antibiotics every day? Because it is real important that she take them until they're gone."

"Jimmy will make sure she gets all of it. He's good with stuff like that."

Tears stung my eyes, and I had to walk away before I started crying and Daisy saw me. I went to the bathroom and turned on the faucet to mask my sniffling. The idea of sending Daisy back to that old, dirty trailer with a momma who didn't care was horrible.

"Hey." Preston opened the door to the bathroom and stepped inside. "Come here." He pulled me into a hug and rested his chin on my head. "I know this sucks, but I promise you, she'll be fine. I'm going to make sure you get to see her again. Heck, if you'll stop crying, I'll get her a phone too so you two can talk."

I nodded. I liked that idea. "Okay."

"Okay you want me to get her a phone?" he asked.

"Yes."

Preston chuckled. "Done. Now stop crying. I check on them more than once a week."

I didn't want to make him feel like he was failing them when it was obvious he was doing everything he could to take care of them. If he had a real job, I didn't know what it was. He had school and baseball. Over the years he'd had some side jobs, but nothing that stuck around long. Somehow he got money. I'd started to ask him about it when the bathroom door opened and Daisy stood there frowning up at us.

"What's wong?"

I couldn't let her know why I'd been crying. I smiled and stepped out of Preston's arms. "Nothing. I just got something in my eye and came in here to get it out." I reached back and turned the water off.

"Why was Pweston hugging you?"

The kid didn't miss anything.

"I was getting it out for her," Preston replied.

Daisy seemed to be okay with this answer, so she nodded. "I got my stuff weady to go."

"All right, my Daisy May, let me finish eating, and then we will go."

"But what about his supwise?" Daisy asked me, looking at the refrigerator hopefully.

"I think now would be an awesome time for his surprise," I replied, and she dropped her bag and ran over to retrieve the peanut butter pie out of the fridge. Preston shot me a questioning look and I just grinned.

"I did all the hawd stuff. Just ask Manda," Daisy informed him as she held out the peanut butter pie toward him with pride.

"You made me a pie?" Preston asked with awe in his voice as he bent down to her level.

"Yep, I did. Peanut Buttah."

Preston bent over and kissed her cheek. "I bet that's gonna be the best peanut butter pie I've ever had."

Daisy beamed up at him, and at that moment, Preston Drake was absolutely perfect.

Chapter Fourteen

PRESTON

I was restless. Amanda had left when I went to take Daisy home. She said she needed to go eat dinner with her mother. Last night she'd told her mom she was staying over at a friend's. She said her mom would get curious if she didn't show up tonight. The whole apartment smelled like Amanda. I hadn't been alone with her since work today. I needed to be alone with her. The fear inside me was eating me alive. If she ever found out . . . That couldn't happen.

My phone rang, and I stalked over to the counter and jerked it up. It was the wrong Hardy.

"Hey," I said, trying not to be irritated that it was Marcus and not Amanda.

"Hey, what're you up to tonight?"

Waiting by the phone for your sister to call me wasn't exactly something I could tell him. "Nothing. Just at home."

"Low is studying for an test, and she needs me to get out of her hair. Feel like meeting me at Live Bay? Rock will be there. Jackdown's playing, and you know Trisha won't miss it."

No. I wanted to stay here and wait on Amanda. But then if she didn't call, I might go a little crazy. I needed a distraction.

"Okay, yeah. I'll meet you there."

"Sounds good," he replied, and we hung up.

I slipped on my boots and grabbed my keys. I'd go hang out with my friends until Amanda called.

The place was already crawling when I walked in. I stopped by the bar and grabbed a beer before making my way over to our table. Marcus was already here. Rock and Trisha were taking up only one stool since she was in his lap. Dewayne wasn't around.

"There he is," Marcus said as I pulled out the stool beside him and sat down.

"But for how long? Soon as a girl comes over here sniffing, we'll lose him for the night," Rock drawled.

Marcus laughed.

I tried not to tense up. They'd notice if I acted different. Then they'd all start asking questions. And there was no way in hell I was answering those questions. Marcus was like my brother, but if he tried to keep me from Amanda, there was gonna be a problem. No one was stopping this.

"I'm taking a night off," I replied.

"Someone wear you out last night?" Rock asked.

Wasn't going there with them either. This was hard. I'd always been able to talk about girls with them. But then, I'd never talk about Amanda the way I talked about those other girls.

"I'm just not in the mood," I explained, and took a long swig.

A phone rang, and Marcus pulled his out. "Is she okay? . . . Yeah, I checked on her today. . . . Sorry, I'm at Live Bay. Can you hear me now? . . . If she's sleeping fine, then you should be good if you want to leave. . . . Uh, no. Preston, Rock, and Trisha are here. You wanna come see me? . . . *Ha!* Sure you do. I'll see you in a sec."

He hung up the phone. "My mom is going to wear Amanda out. As much as I'd have missed her, I don't like the idea of her staying here to take care of Mom. She needs a life."

That had been Amanda. My phone vibrated in my pocket. I pulled it out and looked down.

Amanda: Is it okay with you if I come to Live Bay? If not I'll just go to bed and see you later.

Hell, no. I needed to see her tonight.

Me: Your brother thinks you're coming here.
Come ease his mind. Then we'll figure out a
way to leave.

"Is Preston texting?" Rock asked. "When the hell did he start texting?"

Amanda: Okay. See ya in a few.

I slipped my phone back into my pocket and looked up to see the entire table staring at me with incredulous expressions on their faces. So I didn't text that often. What was the big deal?

"What?" I asked, reaching for my beer.

"You were texting someone," Marcus replied.

"Intensely," Trisha added.

With Amanda headed up here, I did not need them watching my every move.

"Actually, it's called sexting. You get them worked up enough, and they'll start sending sexy little videos via text." I winked and leaned back in my seat.

That was what they expected of me. Marcus laughed and shook his head. Rock raised his eyebrows and looked at Trisha. "If I get you that new iPhone, will you send me sexy little videos?"

Trisha giggled and whispered in his ear.

I turned my attention off them and watched the door.

I managed to stay in the conversation at the table without appearing like I was as disconnected as I was.

Then the door opened, and Amanda finally walked in.

Motherfucking hell.

She was wearing a short little red dress and cowboy boots. I was going to end up in a fight.

AMANDA

I wasn't sure this was such a good idea. Every time I'd ever been in Live Bay, Preston had been drunk and there were girls with centerfold bodies wrapped all over him. I'd changed clothes three times trying to find something that made me look sexy enough to compete with the girls I'd be up against in here. Unfortunately, nothing I owned made my boobs look any bigger than they were. So I decided to play up my strengths. Preston liked my legs. So I went with that.

I looked over at their table, and Preston's eyes were already locked on me. He looked . . . mad. Why was he mad? Maybe mad wasn't the word. Maybe he looked fierce. I wasn't sure. The good thing was, the only girl at their table was Trisha. I had been prepared to walk into something much worse.

As I headed toward the table, someone stepped in front of me. I looked up to see Dameon Wallace's smiling face. I'd thought he was gorgeous in high school. But now he didn't seem so perfect anymore.

"Hello, Dameon," I replied, taking a step to the side to get around him.

"Hey, Amanda. Haven't seen you since graduation. How are things?"

I smiled. "Good, thank you, and you?"

Suddenly, Preston's hand grabbed mine, and he pulled me close to his side. "What are you wearing?" he whispered in my ear as he pulled me away from Dameon.

"A dress," I replied, trying to figure out why he was asking me such a ludicrous question and why he was making a scene in front of my brother.

"I'm gonna end up beating someone's ass tonight because of this dress," he growled, and let go of my hand. "Go to the table. I'll handle this with Marcus."

I nodded and hurried to the table, trying to look casual while Marcus studied me carefully.

"You made it," Marcus said, looking over my shoulder at Preston, who was right behind me.

"Yep" was the best reply I could come up with. I smiled over at Rock and Trisha, who also seemed to be studying me, then Preston, curiously.

"Want to tell me what that was about?" Marcus asked, his gaze locked on Preston instead of me.

I was almost afraid to look at Preston, but I couldn't help it. I needed to make sure he was okay.

"That douche was all over her, and you were just gonna sit here and let it happen. Someone had to go get her," Preston explained in an annoyed tone.

"That was mighty chivalrous of you." Trisha sounded amused and not at all fooled.

Marcus turned back to look at me. "Did that guy touch you?" The edge to his voice meant he was buying Preston's excuse. That was good. But I still didn't want him going and roughing up Dameon for just saying hello.

"He's a friend from high school. We did the flirting thing in school but never anything more. Preston misunderstood."

The tension in Marcus's shoulders eased, and he nodded.

I chanced a glance at Preston, who hadn't relaxed at all. He was even more tightly wound now than he had been before. This was a really bad idea. My coming here was going to be an issue.

"Did I take your seat, Preston?" I asked, trying to distract him.

He shifted his gaze to me. "No. You're fine. I'm gonna go grab another beer and I'll get a stool. You want something?"

"A Coke, please," I replied.

He nodded and headed toward the bar.

"Amanda" Marcus called, and I tore my eyes off of Preston's retreating form and looked at him.

"Yes?"

"Why do I feel like I'm missing something here?" he asked, studying my face closely.

I shrugged. "I don't know."

He looked back at Preston at the bar. Preston was getting our drinks and blowing off a girl at the same time. He looked very uninterested, which made me smile. Preston's eyes met mine and a knowing grin tugged at his lips. His eyes shifted to my brother's and the smile vanished.

I decided to study the stage. Jackdown had just come back on the stage, and Trisha was doing her normal cheering.

"Here's your Coke," Preston said, sliding a mug of ice and a can in front of me, then pulling up a stool on the other side of Marcus. He wasn't sitting beside me. This was so frustrating. I just wanted to tell Marcus and let him get over it. How bad could it be?

The music was too loud to hear anything else, so no one talked while Krit's voice filled the room. He had a smooth sound with a little raspy touch to it that made girls go crazy. I had to admit, the guy was hot. I'd never really been into him like a lot of my friends, but then, deep down I'd always had a thing for Preston. It was hard to focus my attention on anyone else. I had liked Dameon in high school, but it was never anything very serious.

A girl walked up to Preston and started whispering in his

ear. She wrapped her arms around his neck, and his eyes shot directly to me. This was what I was afraid of when I'd decided to come tonight. Girls knew Preston as a player. They loved him for it. Preston moved forward away from her mouth, which was entirely too close to his body.

His eyes never left mine. I dropped my gaze to my soda and contemplated just leaving. This was too hard. I couldn't get upset about the girl because of Marcus. Preston couldn't act like he was taken because of Marcus. If I was going to be anything more than just a blip on Preston's radar, we were going to have to tell Marcus.

I couldn't just keep going this way. Preston's reputation would require he act a certain way to keep Marcus from questioning things. I reached for my purse and stood up. I'd tell Marcus bye and go back home. It was where I should have stayed.

Preston was up and out of his seat before I could say anything. I stopped and watched as he pushed the girl away and walked over to me. "Dance with me," he said in my ear, taking my purse and laying it back down on the table, then pulling me out to the dance floor.

Chapter Fifteen

PRESTON

I'd be fighting tonight, but it wouldn't be with some guy who was getting too close to Amanda. It would be with her brother. He'd been watching me closely, and I'd just given him a very good reason to suspect something. But it had been a choice between letting the girl paw all over me in front of Amanda and watching her face fall, or having my best friend take a swing at me, so I was going with the ass kicking.

I couldn't let her walk out of here like that. She'd been upset and about to bolt. I wasn't going to let that happen.

"What are you doing?" she asked as I pulled her into my arms once we were in the mass of moving bodies. Hopefully, far enough in that Marcus couldn't see us. Although there was a good chance he was right behind us.

"Dancing with you," I replied, slipping my hands down over the curve of her hips.

She smiled. "That's not what I meant, and you know it."

I glanced back over my shoulder to see if Marcus was barreling down on us. Coast was still clear. I turned back to Amanda. "You were about to leave," I told her.

Her face pinched into a frown. "Yeah, well, I'd seen more than I could stomach."

I pulled her closer to me and bent my head to whisper in her ear. "I'm only interested in you. If you'd left, I'd have chased your sexy ass down."

She laughed, slipped a hand up my chest, then twined it behind my neck. "I'd have let you catch me. You wouldn't have had to try real hard."

I was ready to haul her out of here and get her alone. But that wasn't going to happen until I faced one big hurdle.

"I'm gonna have to talk to Marcus about this."

Her smile fell. "I know."

I wanted to kiss her and reassure her, but I'd pushed it far enough. There was a good chance Marcus, me, or both of us could end up in the emergency room if I gave in to that urge.

"He's gonna be upset," she said.

I laughed. "No, baby. He's gonna be pissed. So damn pissed he's gonna go for my throat."

Her hands fisted in my hair. What was she going to do, try to hold me here?

"Maybe we don't have to tell him. I can learn to deal with the girls."

No, she couldn't, and I sure as hell couldn't deal with the guys. There was no hiding that. When that dickwad had stepped in front of her, I'd been one-track-minded. I didn't care who saw me or what they thought. I just wanted him to move. If he'd touched her, it would have been a lot worse.

"I want guys to know you're with me. I don't like them getting close."

She giggled and pressed against me again. "Well, at least no one was hanging all over me. You had a girl making out with your back."

I eased both my hands down over her butt and squeezed it gently, causing her to laugh louder. "If he'd touched you, things would have gone down a lot differently."

"Oh, really? How so?"

She was teasing me. It was easy to forget we weren't alone when she looked up at me like that.

"I'd have beat. His. Ass."

A hand gripped my shoulder. It was too big to be a female's, and the hold it had on me meant Marcus had finally come after me. Amanda's eyes went wide, and she started shaking her head at him.

"I got this. It'll be okay," I assured her. She dropped her hands from my neck and grabbed on to my arm tightly.

"Outside. Now," Marcus said in a loud, angry snarl. Oh yeah. He was pissed. "Let him go, Amanda," Marcus snapped at her.

"Don't talk to her that way." I raised my voice and got right back in his face. I understood he was mad, but he sure as hell wasn't going to take it out on her.

"Outside. Now," he repeated.

I looked back at Amanda as Marcus stalked toward the door. She was holding on to me so tight her fingernails were digging into my arm. "Stay here," I told her, and she shook her head.

"No way!" she yelled. I started moving over the crowd with her holding on to my arm. She was going to have to let me go. Marcus was only going to get more furious if she kept holding on to me like this.

"Ah, fuck. What the hell have you done?" Rock said as he stepped in front of us just before we reached the door.

"Move, Rock," I said, pushing past him.

"Please, God, tell me you didn't"—he paused and looked over at Amanda—"do what I think you did," he finished.

"This isn't your business. Just let me go talk to Marcus," I replied.

Rock let out a hard laugh. "He ain't planning on talking to you. He's planning on whooping your ass and then locking his sister up in her bedroom for the rest of her life. I just hope he ain't got a gun on him."

Amanda's grip on me tightened. I wasn't sure if it was because she was worried about Marcus hurting me or keeping us apart. I'd never fought with Marcus before, so I wasn't real sure who was gonna come out of this one on top, but I sure as hell wasn't gonna let him keep Amanda from me.

"Manda, girl, you need to stay inside with Trisha," Rock said, reaching out to get Amanda's arm. "Ain't no reason for you to go out there. Let go of Preston before Marcus sees you clinging to him and blows up."

"Don't. Touch. Her." I clipped out, trying real hard not to jerk her away from him.

"Chill the fuck out. I'm trying to keep her from seeing you and Marcus beat each other's heads in. Ain't something she needs to see."

I took a deep breath and looked down at her. "You want to go with Trisha, Manda?"

She shook her head and squeezed me tighter.

"I'm not making her leave me. Besides, neither one of us will let her get hurt."

Rock shook his head and sighed. "What were you *thinking*?" he asked. "She's Marcus's little sister. You could screw around with anyone else. Why did you mess with his sister?"

I didn't care that Rock was the size of a bear and built like a brick wall. He wasn't going to lump Amanda in with any other girl I'd ever slept with. I stepped up until I was in his face. "Never talk about her like that again. She is not someone I'm screwing around with."

I swung the door open and walked outside with Amanda still attached to me.

"Maybe you should have been nicer to Rock and brought him out here with you," she said, walking as closely to me as possible.

"I don't need Rock. It's gonna be okay. But he's right. You need to let go of me. This ain't gonna help Marcus's temper."

She shook her head, and I gave up.

Marcus was pacing in front of his truck. When he saw us, he stopped and his hands fisted at his sides.

"Let go of him, Amanda," he ordered as we approached him.

"No, Marcus. Listen to me. You don't understand. You need to calm down and let me explain."

"I don't need an explanation. I've known Preston since we were kids. I've seen it all from him. Enough to know that he isn't the kind of guy a girl like you needs to be hanging on to and defending. You don't know him, Amanda. I do."

"Yes, I do! I know a lot about him, and you have no idea what is going on here. I started this. He ran from me for months. He pushed me away, and I just kept on coming back. And he is not treating me the way you seem to think he is."

"She didn't chase me," I said. I couldn't stand to listen to her tell him she'd come after me so hard and I'd just given in. That wasn't the way this had happened at all.

"I didn't think she did," Marcus replied in a deadly calm voice.

"Yes, I did! I even took advantage of him when he was drunk one night," Amanda said, stepping in front of me.

"Manda, don't—"

"He was completely drunk, and I came on to him. He doesn't even remember it. He tried so hard to keep me at arm's length. He was nice to me, but he kept telling me no. Then his sister got sick and I ran after him to his Jeep and went with him. She is so sweet and little, Marcus. We took care of her together, and then things just happened. I finally got past his walls. He let me in. Don't ruin this for me. I'm in love with him."

What?

Marcus reached for Amanda and jerked her away from in front of me. His fist was planted firmly in my face before I could wrap my head around the fact that she'd just said she loved me.

"You sorry-ass motherfucker!" Marcus roared, and jerked me up by my collar before his fist connected with my face again.

I could hear Amanda's screams in the distance. But my eyesight was blurry and my head felt foggy. I shook it and raised my hands to block any more attacks while I tried to stop my world from spinning.

"Marcus, NO!" Amanda was crying. My head cleared up

real fast. This was making her cry. I didn't want her to cry.

When his fist came at me this time, I blocked it and shoved him hard in the chest to get him to back off me. Hitting him would upset Amanda more, but I couldn't let him beat the shit out of me either.

"I trusted you. You're my best friend. How could you screw around with my little sister? She thinks she loves you," Marcus roared. "She doesn't even know you. Tell her, Preston. Tell her the shit you've done."

"Shut up!" I yelled. "You got your hits in. She's upset. I'm not going to hit you and upset her more." I reached up with my arm to wipe the blood that was trickling out of my nose. Amanda ran past her brother and barreled into my chest.

"Dammit!" Marcus growled.

"I'm so sorry, I'm so sorry." Amanda cried against my chest. Seeing her like this was making me crazy. Could he not see what he was doing to her?

"Give me a minute," I barked at him. "Let me calm her down first. She needs reassurance we aren't gonna kill each other. Can't you see that?"

I bent my head and cupped Amanda's face so I could look down at her. My left eye was swelling closed, but I could still see her tear-streaked face. I hated seeing her like this. If it wouldn't make things worse, I'd take a few swings at her stupid-ass brother for making her cry.

"I'm okay. I won't let him hit me anymore. He caught me off guard."

She loved me. Her words replayed in my head again. How could someone as fucking sweet as Amanda Hardy love me?

"I just want to go. I need to get you some ice, and you're bleeding." She hiccupped.

"I know. I'll let you do both those things, but first let me deal with him, okay?"

She wrapped both her arms around my chest and held on tight. This was her way of protecting me. No one had ever protected me.

"Okay, I've seen enough," came Rock's voice from behind me. "Back off, Marcus."

"It's my sister he's screwing with, Rock. Don't tell me to back off."

"Yeah, that's why I let you beat his face in. I thought the same thing." Rock stepped in between us. He looked back at me. His gaze dropped to Amanda, then lifted back up to my face. "This is different."

"He doesn't do different," Marcus spat out. "She's my little sister. I'm supposed to protect her. I've always protected her. I can't let him near her. He isn't good enough."

The pain at hearing words I already knew were true thrown in my face by one of the only people who I had thought accepted me, flaws and all, was hard.

Amanda turned her head around to face her brother. "Don't you dare say that. Just SHUT UP, Marcus."

Rock waved his hand in our direction. "You see that? You ever seen him hold on to someone like that? He didn't fight back—not because he couldn't, because if it was a real fight between the two of you, my money'd be on Preston. He's been fighting his whole life. He didn't hit you because he didn't like upsetting your sister. He was protecting her."

Marcus took fast, angry breaths as he looked down at Amanda holding on to me, then back up at me. He ran his hands through his hair. *"Shit."*

"But she said she loves him," Marcus told Rock. Then he looked back at me. "She loves you. Do you even know what to do with that?"

I kissed the top of her head. "Cherish it like it's the most precious thing on the face of the earth," I replied with all sincerity.

"Well, hell. He's gone and got all poetic," Rock said, grinning and shaking his head. "Never thought I'd see the day."

Marcus leaned back on the hood of his truck and crossed his arms over his chest, then hung his head. We'd won. He was conceding.

"Your eye's gonna completely close up if you don't go get ice on it. Y'all go on. I'll deal with Marcus," Rock said, nodding toward my Jeep for us to leave.

I wanted to promise Marcus I'd never hurt her, or to tell him

I loved her too. But I couldn't do those things. If she ever found out about what I did to take care of my family, she'd be hurt. I wanted her. I needed her. But did I love her? Could I love her if I couldn't be completely honest with her?

AMANDA

I fixed an ice pack while Preston took a shower and cleaned all the blood off his face. I cringed thinking about his beat-up face. It was going to be hard to forgive Marcus. He'd just kept hitting Preston, who wasn't even defending himself. I'd known Marcus would be upset, but I didn't know he would be so violent. I'd never seen Marcus fight anyone, and I'd hardly ever heard him curse. He'd done both tonight.

Why he couldn't have just listened to me and let me explain, I didn't understand. He just lost it. If I hadn't let go of Preston's arm, he wouldn't have hit him. It was my fault. The only thing I could have done to protect him was stay in the line of fire, and I'd moved thinking I could get Marcus to talk about it. To listen to me.

The bathroom door opened, and Preston came walking out in nothing but a towel again. I could get used to that. The bruises on his face and his swollen eye, however, had my complete attention at the moment.

"Sit down. We need to put ice on your eye," I informed him before pushing him toward the couch.

"You not gonna let me put on clothes first?" he asked in an amused tone.

"Nope. We've waited too long already to ice your eye. Sit."

He didn't argue. He adjusted the towel to keep it from gaping open when he sat down, and leaned back. I handed him the ice pack. "You do it. I don't want to hurt you."

"Wish I had a steak. It would work better," he said, taking the pack and holding it to his eye and wincing.

"I'm so sorry," I said again. I couldn't help it. Every time I looked at his face, I felt guilty.

"Stop it, Manda." He reached for me. "Come here."

I went willingly. I needed to feel him and know he was okay. Besides, his chest was naked, and snuggling up to it was something I wanted to do very much.

"I expected Marcus to come at me. He was mad. I can't blame him."

I ran my fingers over the ripples in his stomach. "He was an asshole. I can't believe he acted that way."

Preston chuckled. "Yeah, well, baby, there's a lot about me you don't know. Marcus knows most of it. He knows enough to not want his little sister anywhere near me."

What did that mean? Was *he* now saying I was an idiot too?

I started to pull away, and Preston's arms tightened on me. "Where are you going?" he asked.

I'd told my brother I loved Preston tonight. Heck, I'd told

anyone in the parking lot who was around to hear me yell it. But Preston hadn't said the same. I hadn't really expected him to. I knew he didn't love me. But I guess I expected more of an affirmation from him. Something more than him agreeing that Marcus being mad was warranted. It was like he was agreeing that I was making a mistake.

"Manda, tell me what's wrong." I could hear the concern in his voice.

Tears stung my eyes, and I blinked them away. I was not going to cry. I was tired of crying about everything. No wonder Marcus treated me like a baby. I acted like one.

"You just sound like you're agreeing with Marcus. Like you think my wanting to be with you is a bad thing."

Preston's body stiffened, and then the ice bag dropped beside him. His hands were on my waist, pulling me into his lap.

"Look at me, Manda," he said gently.

I did as he asked, and the emotions I could see in his eyes were enough. He might not love me, but he felt something really close. I could see it.

"Nothing about this thing we have is a bad thing. I'm not gonna lie about it: I don't deserve you. I'm sure as hell not good enough for you, but as long as you want me, I'm all yours."

That wasn't a proclamation of love, but it was as close as I would ever get with Preston. I knew enough about his past to know he'd never been serious about any girl.

"Is this thing with us going to be exclusive? Or is it just a thing . . ." I trailed off, not sure how to word this. I didn't want to say "just sex," because it wasn't about the sex. We were more than that, or at least I thought so.

"Hell yes, it's exclusive. You can't date anyone else, Manda. I can't deal with it. I was ready to rip a guy's arms off for talking to you tonight."

This was a two-way street.

"Um, and you . . . is it exclusive for you?" I asked tentatively. I knew if he couldn't tell me yes, I wouldn't be able to do this. I was in too deep emotionally.

Preston grinned. He ran his hand through my hair and cupped the back of my head. "Baby, all I see is you. It's something I've never experienced, but I can't see anyone else anymore. Just you."

My heart slammed against my chest. Preston pulled my head close enough that his lips could touch mine. I knew his face was sore, so I kissed him back softly. I didn't want to hurt him.

"Manda, I want you," he whispered against my lips.

Those weren't the three words I wanted to hear from him. but they were a very close second. I eased off his lap and stood in front of him while I reached back and unzipped my sundress and let it fall to the floor.

"Sweet Jesus," Preston whispered.

I hadn't worn a bra with my sundress, and I'd worn a pair of the skimpiest panties I had. I was bending down to take off my boots when Preston leaned forward and grabbed my arm.

"Leave the boots on."

"How am I going to get my panties off?"

He flashed me a wicked grin, then grabbed both my legs and pulled me in between his. Running his hands up my legs, he slipped both hands under the thin strings holding my panties up, and with one hard jerk they fell off me.

"I don't even want to know how you knew how to do that."

"I'll replace them. I'll buy you a bunch just like them," he promised, pulling me down onto his lap as he removed the towel he was wearing.

Chapter Sixteen

PRESTON

"Can we do it this way?" Amanda asked nervously as she straddled my lap.

God, she was so damn innocent. Knowing I'd been the only one ever to touch her, to be inside her, to taste her, made my insane possessiveness worse. I wanted to keep her close. Away from everyone else.

"Yes, sweetheart, it feels real good this way," I assured her as I held her hips. "You'll have all the control."

I leaned forward and pulled one of her nipples into my mouth. They were right there, teasing me. I couldn't ignore them. I was pretty damn sure I was addicted to them. She arched her back and let out a soft moan.

"I want it in," she pleaded.

I smiled up at her. "Then put it in."

Her eyes went wide with surprise, and then she slowly lowered her body until the tip of my erection touched the entrance we both wanted it in so badly.

"Do I just go down?" she asked, looking back up at me.

If I wasn't so incredibly turned on, I would have laughed. "Yeah, just go down on it." I liked the way that sounded.

She bit her bottom lip as she eased down on it.

"Ah, that's so good," I groaned as she teased us both by going slow.

"Yeah," she panted, "it is."

She paused, and I wanted so badly to thrust up, but I held back. This was going to be all her. "Do I keep going?" She was breathing fast and hard, making her tits bounce gently in my face. God, it didn't get any better than this.

"All the way down," I assured her.

She sank down all the way, and my hips bucked on their own accord, causing her to cry out.

"Fuck, baby," I growled as her muscles inside squeezed my dick.

"Ohgod. It feels so good," she said, throwing her head back and giving me complete access to her pretty neck. I leaned forward and kissed and licked several soft spots before she started to move. Lifting her hips, she said, "I wanna move."

"Up and down, baby. As fast or slow as you want to. It's your ride."

"Oh," she breathed, her eyes going wider at my words.

She eased up, and I had to fist my hands at my sides to keep from taking over. This was making me fucking crazy. Flipping her on her back and pumping in and out of her until we both screamed out in release was very tempting. But then, watching her experience this for the first time was something I'd never forget.

"Preston," she breathed.

"Yeah, baby?"

"Can I go faster? I think I wanna go faster."

Ah, hell yeah. "You ride me as fast and hard as you want to. If it feels good to you, it feels just as amazing to me. I promise. You can't do this wrong."

She nodded and placed both her hands on my shoulders, then eased up off me and sank back down quickly. "AH!"

She did it again, harder this time. It was the most amazing thing I'd ever felt. It was hotter inside than before, and softer. . . .

SHIT!

I wasn't wearing a condom. Shit, shit, *shit*.

I grabbed her waist as she started getting her rhythm and stopped her.

"No, please," she begged, sinking back down on me. "Yes, oh God, Preston."

Fuck me. How was I going to stop this?

She lifted her hips and sank back down on me hard, then

cried out again. She was so close. If I wasn't positive I'd shoot off like a damn cannon when she came, I'd let her finish first.

"Manda, I gotta put on a condom."

She didn't stop like I'd expected. She lifted her hips faster and rocked back and forth this time while making sexy little moans that were gonna push me over the edge.

"Manda, a condom, baby. I forgot a condom."

"S'okay. I'm on the pill," she said before pressing down harder and rocking her hips back and forth.

Why the fuck was she on the pill?

"Preston, AH! Preston," she cried out, grabbing my shoulder and leaning forward as she began trembling in my lap.

I couldn't hold back. I wrapped both my arms around her and buried my head in her shoulder as I shot off my release inside her.

AMANDA

I didn't want to move. Ever. Preston was inside me. I was completely satisfied, and his mouth was nibbling at my neck. No wonder girls in high school liked sex so much. Nothing I'd ever done under the covers in my bed felt like this.

"Why are you on the pill?" Preston asked against my neck.

Smiling, I arched my neck a little more so he could cover more skin.

"Irregular, really bad periods. I've been on the pill since I was sixteen."

I'd never thought the fact that I took that little pill every day would come in so handy.

"I've never had sex without a condom before," he said, tilting his head back to look at me. "Being inside you with nothing between us was the best experience of my life."

My body felt warm all over. Knowing he'd enjoyed it as much as I had made it even better.

Preston leaned forward and kissed me. "It isn't safe though. As good as that felt we can't do that again. We need to protect you. I have protection. Can we do this again?"

"If you're a very good boy," I teased.

His hands slipped down my back until they were caressing my bottom. "I can be real good. So damn good you'll want to strip for me all the time."

Giggling, I shifted my hips and felt him still semi-hard inside me. Oh.

"Manda, if you don't get off me, we are gonna have to have a round two real soon."

I wiggled a little more on his lap, and this time he laughed. "You're going to kill me. Death by sex with the hottest woman on the planet. That's one helluva way to go."

A knock at the door startled me, and Preston tensed underneath me. I looked from the door to him, and he lifted me off his lap. Then handed me a towel. "Go on in the bathroom and take a shower."

I was worried it could be Marcus. I didn't want him hurting Preston any more. I wrapped the towel around me and stood there.

Preston pointed to the bathroom, and I shook my head. "It could be Marcus."

Preston laughed. "Well, you standing there like that ain't gonna help matters if it is."

"You can't answer the door naked," I pointed out.

He looked down at himself and smirked. "No, I can't." Then he headed for the bedroom. Another knock and a "I know you're in there. Open the damn door" told us it was Dewayne.

Preston came walking out of the bedroom in a pair of sweats and pointed to the bathroom. "It's Dewayne, and we both know he ain't here to kick my ass. Go take a shower, and don't come out in a towel."

Smiling, I walked into the bathroom and closed the door behind me.

Pressing my ear to the door, I listened to see what Dewayne wanted before I turned the water on. He could be here to warn us Marcus was on the way.

"She in here?" Dewayne asked.

"Word travels fast."

Dewayne let out a bark of laughter. "Hell yeah, it does.

You messing around with Marcus's sister, that's screwed up. Even for you."

"Shut up, D. What do you want, other than to see if Amanda is here?"

"Ah, you know, the usual. You got Marcus ready to pound in anyone's head who looks at him the wrong way. Rock and I have to keep him from getting thrown in jail. So I need to know, are you just fucking her, or is this more than that?"

"It's Amanda, D. Don't say that. Ever."

There was a pause. "So Rock was right. For you to mess around with Manda, it has to be for a bigger reason. She got to you."

"I've been attracted to her for a couple of years now, but she was too young. She's not anymore, and I . . . It's different with her. Everything is different."

Hearing him admit that it was different with me eased the worry that he might never love me. Just to know he felt something.

"I'd say it was your business, but since we were kids if something goes wrong with one of us, then it is everyone's business. Just be careful. I know shit you probably don't know I know. It ain't the kind of thing relationships are built on. And Manda ain't the kind of girl you just use for a little while."

"I *know* that. Don't you think I fucking know that?"

Another moment of silence, and then the front door opened and closed. I stepped back and took a deep breath.

226

The bathroom door swung open, and Preston walked inside with a wicked grin on his face. "Since you waited on me while you listened in on that conversation, I think I'll help get you clean and you can show off those singing abilities of yours in the shower. I've been waiting all damn day to hear them."

Chapter Seventeen

PRESTON

Letting Amanda go home was hard. I wanted to keep her here. Every time she walked out my door, I worried that she wouldn't come back. That she'd find out the truth about me. Tonight was family dinner at her house. She said her brother had told her that he didn't want her to tell their mom. She wasn't emotionally stable enough to deal with it.

I didn't expect her mother to accept me. She knew I was from the wrong side of town. She knew I'd gotten in trouble all through high school and Marcus had helped bail me out. I was Marcus's charity case in her eyes. I'd never be good enough for her daughter.

My phone vibrated in my pocket, reminding me of my appointment. Every time I had to go work, I loathed it more. I'd started looking in the paper every day for a job that could pay me enough to take care of the kids and fit into my schedule with classes and baseball season when it started up. So far there was nothing. I wasn't qualified for anything. But I wasn't giving up. I had to find a way out of this. I wanted to be worthy of Amanda, and I knew I never would be as long as I continued doing what I was doing.

I reached over and picked up my keys. I had to go do this. If I wanted to keep my scholarship and feed the kids, I had to do this.

I walked up the back steps to the three-story brick house that belonged to our illustrious mayor. He was shagging his secretary and his wife was paying me for the same service. She had been for over a year now.

I had to park half a mile down the road and walk up from the back of the house and use the back door. She'd leave it unlocked.

Opening the door, I went inside and headed for the stairs. Sometimes she waited on me in some ridiculous piece of lingerie, and sometimes she was just upstairs in bed naked, drinking wine. Depended on her mood.

I reached the first step and heard voices. That couldn't be good. She was always alone when she called me. I froze and listened. It was another woman. I recognized the voice, but I couldn't put my finger on who it was. Surely she hadn't invited over another one of my clients for a threesome. I charged extra for that, and right now I wasn't sure I could pull it off. Getting up for just her was going to be hard enough. I was having to close my eyes and pretend lately. It was the only thing that worked.

"I'll see you at the committee meeting next week, then. Thank you, Janice, for offering to help. Having your name behind it will always drive more volunteers." Janice was the mayor's wife. This was an impromptu visit she was dealing with, and they were coming around the corner. Shit.

I'd started to make a run for it when Mrs. Hardy turned the corner and our eyes met. *Fucking hell.*

Janice's eyes found me, and they went wide with surprise. She hadn't been expecting us to get caught either.

I stood there unable to move from this train wreck. How did I explain this? I didn't need this woman to know what I did. I was going to find another job, and when I did, I was going to make myself worthy of Amanda. Her mother knowing this dirty secret of mine would ruin everything. She'd tell Amanda. If she ever found out about Amanda and me, she'd tell her.

"Oh, Preston. I'm so glad you're here. The uh, toilet that is broken is upstairs to the left. It just keeps running over." Janice's forced smile and high-pitched voice weren't very convincing. "Run along now and get it fixed." She waved her hand and smiled back at Amanda's mom.

Mrs. Hardy's eyes were still locked on mine. She was connecting the dots, dammit.

"Yes, ma'am. I thought you mentioned that your washing machine was broken too." I was a hell of a lot more convincing.

She nodded nervously. "Yes, yes it is. But go on and get that toilet fixed."

I nodded and headed up the stairs, praying Mrs. Hardy believed this bullshit.

"Sweet kid. He can fix anything," Janice said in the same nervous, high-pitched tone.

"Is that so?" Mrs. Hardy asked. The tone of her voice made my stomach knot up. She knew.

Fuck it all to hell. She knew.

AMANDA

Preston had gone to work out again today. He got a call from his coach and had to leave unexpectedly. I'd been on my way over here. We were going to go down to the beach. We only had a few weeks of heat left before the fall air started making it impossible to enjoy it.

I scrolled through my text messages to kill time, and I saw Jason's unanswered one. It had been two weeks since he'd sent it. He hadn't sent another one. I'd been so wrapped up in Preston I'd forgotten about it.

Me: I am so sorry I haven't responded. With
school starting back up and everything, I've
been busy.

I might need to call him. Two weeks was beyond rude.
Jason's response popped up on the screen.

Jason: That's okay. I've talked to Sadie. I know
you are seeing someone. Lucky guy.

Sadie hadn't mentioned Jason when we'd talked the other
day. She was happy for me, but she'd sounded worried too.

Me: Yeah. That too. I should have responded,
though. I'm really sorry.
Jason: Don't worry about it. Just promise me
if things don't work out that you will give me a
call. Keep this number.

He was really sweet. If things didn't work out, I'd be crushed.
There would be no calling someone else.

Me: I'll remember that. Thank you again for
the offer. Flying to NYC for dinner would be
amazing.

Jason: Offer stands. Just say the word.

The door to the apartment opened, and Preston walked in with a scowl on his face. He'd only been gone an hour and a half. He wasn't very sweaty, either.

"Hey," I said, laying my phone down to get up and go to him.

He held up his hands to hold me off. "I'm nasty. Let me get a shower first." He didn't say anything else. He just stalked to the bathroom and closed the door. Loudly.

Was he mad that I was still here?

My phone played the text song, and I reached down to get it.

Jason: I got an invitation to your brother's wedding.

Willow must have sent it when she'd thought there was something going on between us.

Me: Are you going to come?

Please, God, no. Preston wouldn't be nice to him. I wouldn't be able to talk to him if I wanted to keep Preston calm.

Jason: I want to.

What did I say to that? I couldn't be rude. Sadie and Jax were coming.

The bathroom door swung open.

"I'm sorry I was in such a bad mood when I got back," Preston said, walking out of the bathroom.

I looked up from my phone. "It's okay. I was worried you wanted me to leave. I can if you have things to do."

Preston frowned and closed the distance between us. "God, no. I want you with me. I just had a bad afternoon. I hated having to leave you."

"You weren't gone that long. We have plenty of time to spend on the beach before the sun goes down."

Preston bent down and kissed me.

My text alert went off.

Oh crap.

Preston pulled back and looked down at my phone.

> Jason: You didn't tell me no. I'm taking that as your approval.

I didn't move. Preston had read it. Trashing it now wouldn't change that. I wasn't even sure if this was going to be a big deal. So I waited for a reaction.

"Jason? Jason Stone?"

I nodded.

The angry snarl in his voice told me this would be a very big deal. He took the phone out of my hands, and I let him. I hadn't said anything wrong.

He scrolled up and read through our texts. When he got back to the last one, he lifted his eyes to meet mine.

"That's what you want, Manda? Private jet rides to NYC?" He threw my phone onto the table and stormed into his room. I jumped when his door slammed behind him.

My eyes filled with tears. He hadn't even let me explain. He'd just stormed off. I hadn't said that was what I wanted. I was being polite.

The door opened, and I backed up, not sure if I should leave or if I should plead my case. I wasn't used to having a man mad at me. It was scary. My dad had never yelled at me, and until the night Marcus found out about Preston and me, neither had Marcus. My heart was racing in my chest, and I felt like I was going to throw up.

Preston pointed at my phone. "You talk to him often? Hmm?"

I shook my head. "No-o-o," I stammered.

"Sure as hell sounds like it. He's got money. Your brother sure as hell approves if he's sending him a wedding invitation."

"I didn't know about the invitation until just now."

Preston let out a hard, angry laugh. "You knew about the jet ride to New York City, though, didn't you? Looks like you were the one texting him today too."

"I had forgotten to text him back the last time he texted me. I was trying to be polite. He's Jax's brother," I explained.

Preston turned around and slammed his fist into the wall. "Fuck that, Manda. You texted him. You wanted to talk to him."

A tear trickled down my face, and I couldn't think of the right thing to say to make him understand. He was so angry. For the first time ever, I wanted to leave his apartment. I wanted to go somewhere alone and cry.

I walked over and got my phone off the couch, then picked up my beach bag and headed for the door. I didn't look back at him. I couldn't or I'd break down crying right now.

I didn't want him to see me cry. I wanted to be mad at him and yell at him and tell him how stupid he was being, but the lump in my throat was stopping me.

I hurried out the door and down the steps. When my foot hit the bottom step, I burst into tears. I hadn't been able to make it to my car. Wiping at my face, I slipped on my sunglasses, which had been on top of my head, and started out toward my car.

The sound of heavy steps running down the stairs startled me, and I turned around to see Preston running after me.

"Manda, wait. I'm sorry. Please don't leave."

A smart person would've kept walking. I wasn't a smart person.

Preston's panicked face as he begged me not to leave was more powerful than common sense.

"I'm an asshole. God, baby. I'm so sorry. I was upset when I came in, and then I saw the text and it set me off. I'm not going to lie, I'm jealous as hell. You're mine, and he's after you. He has money and your family's approval. Two things I don't have. I want to be able to fly you to New York City on a damn jet, and anywhere else you want to go, but I can't."

That was the only explanation I needed. I understood. I took the few steps separating us, and I grabbed his face and kissed him fiercely on the mouth. I was possessive with it. I wanted him to understand that all I wanted was him. Not a ride in a jet and a fancy dinner. He moaned and ran his hands through my hair and pulled me closer to him. I controlled the kiss. I bit his lip and pulled his tongue into my mouth, and I sucked hard before plunging back into the warmth of his. When I finally broke the kiss, we were both breathing heavily.

"Day-um," he whispered.

"No one compares to you. No one. Get that through your head," I told him, and slipped my hand up his chest. "I don't need jets and fancy locations. I just need you."

237

Chapter Eighteen

PRESTON

Amanda had fallen asleep on her stomach. After we'd played around in the water until we were both very satisfied, we'd come back up to lie out on the towels she'd brought with us. I'd coated her back with sunscreen, and she'd dozed off while I was rubbing it in.

I'd lain here and watched her sleep for the past thirty minutes. I'd also fought the urge to throw a towel over her ass. Every time I felt eyes directed this way, I made sure to stare them down until they looked away.

After having to leave her to go work, I'd come back pissed off. I was still looking for a job that could pay me what I needed. I was even looking into working night shifts somewhere. Anything to get me out of this hell I was in.

Seeing the text from Jason Stone had been all I'd needed to push home the fact that Amanda deserved more than what she was getting. I couldn't even tell her I loved her. She hadn't said those three words to me again. That one time she'd told her brother, and that was it.

I knew she was waiting on me to say them, but how could I? Did I want her? Yes. Did I need her to breathe? Yes. Could I imagine life without her? No. But could I be in love with her, truly in love with her, and deceive her at the same time? I wasn't sure. Love was honest. It was pure. I was neither of those things. So how could I love?

Her eyelashes fluttered, and opened slowly. Sleeping beauty was waking up. My chest hurt just looking at her. She was amazing. Everything about her.

"Were you watching me sleep?" she asked, smiling up at me.

"It's fascinating," I replied.

She buried her face into the towel, but I could see the pleased grin on her face. She never asked for affirmation, but she needed it. That surprised me. I'd have thought she'd had enough of it growing up and didn't need it, but now I wondered if she had gone without it. She had a dad who worked all the time and mother who was on every committee in town. Had she been the rich little girl in the big house with no one around but her brother to tell her that she was beautiful, that she was smart, that she deserved more than a sorry-ass loser like me?

She sat up and stretched. Almost every golden inch of her body was on display.

"I have another family dinner tonight. So I'm going to have to head home soon," she said with a frown on her face.

She had family dinner every week. Since her dad had left them, she never missed it. I could tell it was important to her mother and she didn't want her mother upset.

"Okay. I'll stay home and do homework and wait on you to crawl into bed and send me a naughty text message."

She giggled and pulled her hair up into a knot on her head. I loved watching her do little things like that. I could sit and watch her all damn day and never get bored.

"Naughty text message, huh? I thought that was called sexting," she replied.

I reached over, grabbed her arm, and pulled her on top of me. "Oh yeah, we can sext all you want to. You can tell me all the things you want me to do to you, and I'll tell you just how I'm gonna do it," I whispered in her ear, then took a nibble.

"Mmmm, okay. I like that idea," she replied.

Smiling, I slipped my knee up between her legs. "You just have to promise to play with that pretty little pussy for me."

Amanda gasped and slapped at my arm. "You are so bad, Preston Drake."

"Only with you, baby. Only with you."

Her phone started playing that country song about cowboys and angels. It was her ringtone. She needed a new one. I was beginning to get jealous of any guy in a cowboy hat.

"It's Willow," she said, looking over at me. "She doesn't know about us. Marcus isn't telling her because he's afraid she'll make him tell Mom, and he wants to wait and tell Mom after the wedding. No more added drama and all."

Shit. I'd assumed he'd never tell their mother. Or at least I'd hoped by the time he did I'd have another job and I'd be able to deny it. Mrs. Hardy didn't really have any proof. As far as she was told, I was there to do the plumbing. I had to find another job. Before this damn wedding.

"Hello," she said, pressing the phone to her ear. "Yep. I'll be there. Did you bring the dress home? . . . Yay! Now let's hope it fits. I feel like I've gained five pounds lately. . . . If it doesn't, I'll go on a diet. Promise. . . . See ya in a little bit." Amanda clicked her phone off and smiled before crawling off me and standing up. "I've got to get home and take a shower before dinner. Low is bringing my bridesmaid dress over." I didn't want her to leave me, but I also needed to spend some time finding a job.

"I'll be waiting on my sext."

AMANDA

Mom had been acting weird all night. She was normally very happy on family dinner night. She adored Willow and getting to assist in planning the wedding—which was now on the beach instead of the church where Mom had wanted it— something she looked forward to when we were all together.

She'd said very little about my dress, which fit perfectly, much to my relief. While we'd all discussed the wedding cake colors and if the groom's cake should be cheesecake or chocolate cake, Mom had stared out the window.

When the door closed behind Marcus and Willow, I turned to go up the stairs.

"We need to talk."

I stopped and looked back at Mom. She was standing at the bottom of the stairs with her arms crossed, staring up at me. Something was definitely wrong.

"Okay," I said, walking back down the steps and following her as she made her way into the living room.

"Sit down, Amanda."

I was suddenly very nervous. The serious tone of her voice wasn't something I was used to hearing. I couldn't figure out what in the world this could be about. Unless . . . she knew about Preston. That could be bad, but at least we were about to clear the air and I wouldn't have to hide it from her anymore. Besides, I was positive once she got to know him she'd like him. She'd just never really spent any time with him.

"I received an interesting call today from a friend of mine. It was someone who saw you today. On the beach."

It was about Preston.

"So you know who I was with, then?"

She nodded. "Preston Drake."

"Listen, Mom. I know you don't approve of him. But all you know about him is that his mother is low class and he grew up rough. He has gotten into some trouble growing up, but he's different now. If you'd just—"

"He sleeps with women for money. He's a gigolo, Amanda. A very well-paid one."

I busted into a fit of laughter. Where in the world had she heard that? It was ridiculous. How had she come up with something this insane?

"This isn't a joke, Amanda. I saw him."

She *saw* him? What the heck did that mean? How did she see him?

"Mom, whatever it is you think you saw, you didn't. Preston doesn't sleep with women for money."

Mom walked over to the chair across from me. "I went to visit Janice. She had volunteered to do some work on the Sea Festival committee. She hadn't been expecting me, and I noticed she seemed a little nervous. We talked over everything for about thirty minutes. When we stood up to leave and walked to the door, Preston Drake was sneaking up her staircase. He stopped and looked at me like a deer caught in the headlights. Janice got all flustered and made up something about Preston coming to fix her toilet. That boy was not there to fix her plumbing."

There had to be a better explanation. He wasn't going up to the mayor's bedroom to sleep with his wife for money. This was Sea Breeze, Alabama. Not Los Angeles. What had gotten into my mom?

"You mean to tell me you think Preston was there to service Janice? That's crazy, Mom. It is very likely he was there to help her fix her toilet. He does odd jobs sometimes."

My mother let out a weary sigh, and her face pinched into a frown. "I stood outside long after she closed the door, and I watched the window in her bedroom. Preston Drake was in there. He closed the curtain, and soon Janice's shadow joined him."

"It was a shadow, Mom—"

"I told Blanche about this the next day. I figured if anyone knew, she would. Blanche pays Preston for sex. She has been since she and Ken divorced. Apparently, he has a small, discreet client list among the wealthy women in this town. Preston is a high-priced gigolo who services attractive older women. He doesn't do odd jobs, Amanda."

I was dreaming. I had to be dreaming. This was a nightmare, and I was about to wake up. I shook my head and stood up. I couldn't sit here and listen to this. I didn't believe it. Preston was too good. He would never lie to me about something this big.

"I was worried you wouldn't believe me. You fell for those pretty-boy looks of his. Why don't you ask him? See what he says. Watch his reaction. Then you come back and tell me this is a lie."

I grabbed my keys off the hook beside the door and ran outside. Preston could explain this. Because this couldn't be true.

Chapter Nineteen

PRESTON

I'd been watching my phone for the past hour, waiting on Amanda to text me. After once again searching the job listings online, I'd come up empty handed. If I had taken welding in school, I'd have a job, that was for damn sure. If I didn't need money right now, I'd go to school for welding. That way I could work hours that fit into my schedule and make more than enough money to cover our needs.

A knock at the door interrupted my thoughts, and I put my phone down and grabbed a pair of discarded sweats. I jerked them on quickly and went to the door. It was after eleven. Who the hell was coming to see me so late?

When I opened it, Amanda walked inside, pushing past me. "I have to ask you a question. It is going to sound ludicrous, but I need you to listen to me, and then you can explain how very wrong my mother is."

Her mother. No. God, no. I couldn't say anything. My voice left me. This was not happening. Not now. I hadn't had enough time to fix it.

"Preston, you've gone pale."

I couldn't look at her. She knew. She didn't believe it, but she knew.

"You're scaring me. Preston, look at me."

I needed her to say it. "What did your mother tell you?"

I was going to lie. I needed a lie to get out of this. I couldn't lose her.

"She said . . ." Amanda let out a frustrated sigh. "I can't even believe I'm about to say this out loud."

She didn't believe it. I could convince her it wasn't true. I could tell her something else. The women I worked for wouldn't want the truth out. They'd never back up her mother's story.

"Just tell me," I urged, finally making eye contact with her.

She ran her hand through her hair and looked over at the couch. "You want to sit down? It's kind of unbelievable, and it may take a while to explain."

Getting her farther away from the exit for her to go running out of was a good idea. "Sure."

I followed her over to the couch and sat down in the chair across from her. I wasn't sure how this was going to play out, and sitting too close to her might be a bad idea. I also wanted to see her face.

"My mom found out that you and I are seeing each other. Apparently, someone saw us at the beach today. She was upset, which I'd expected. But why she was upset was not at all something I'd expected."

She twirled a strand of hair around her finger nervously. "Mom saw you at the mayor's house. Going upstairs . . ." She trailed off. She wanted me to say something. What could I say? There was no denying I'd been there. This was my chance to lie. To cover this mess up. But my mouth wouldn't open. I couldn't come up with one thing to say to ease her mind.

"She said you were sneaking upstairs and that Janice was really nervous. Then after she left, she saw you through the bedroom window closing the curtains, and then she saw Janice's shadow join you."

Again, it was my chance to lie to her. But I couldn't. The lies wouldn't come.

"Preston, say something."

I realized, sitting there looking at her, that I loved her. I'd been right. When you love someone, you can't lie to them. It hurts too much. It's a deception that goes too deep.

"I remember seeing her," I finally replied.

Amanda raised her eyebrows. "And? Were you in Janice's bedroom?"

The truth was going to rip my heart out, but it was what she deserved. What she'd always deserved.

"Yes, I was."

Amanda didn't say anything. She just sat there staring at me in shock. I knew she was waiting on some reason as to why I was in Janice's bedroom other than what her mother had told her. I wished like hell I had a reason other than the truth.

"My mom said Blanche Turner told her that she pays you to sleep with her. That many women do. Tell me that isn't true, Preston. I don't believe you'd do something like that."

I stood up because sitting down was impossible. This was the moment I'd feared since I'd let Amanda in. "I have classes and baseball, and three other mouths to feed, and a whole other house's bills to pay. Three kids aren't cheap. I have to make sure they're fed and still keep my scholarship, which means I don't miss baseball and I don't fail classes. It's more responsibility than most adults have, Manda."

Amanda stood up. "Are you telling me this is true? All this time, you've been leaving me to go screw other women for *money*?"

"They mean nothing to me. They know it. There is no emotion. Just sex. It's more money than I could make doing anything else. It keeps the kids taken care of, and I don't have to worry about how I'm going to keep their electricity on or how I'm going to pay for braces or for new tires for my mom."

Amanda shook her head. The disbelief in her eyes sliced through me. "You never thought to tell me about this? How long have you been doing this?"

"Three years."

"Three years? So you just started dating me and let me promise to be exclusive and that I wouldn't be with anyone else, while you left me regularly to screw other women?"

"*No!* It was just sex. I felt nothing for them. Ever. They were a job. That's all they've ever been."

"But you didn't tell me—"

"I didn't tell anyone, Manda. It's not something I'm proud of. I tried to push you away. I tried to tell you I wasn't good for you, but you wouldn't stop. You kept getting close, and I wanted you so bad."

"You let me fall in love with you," Amanda said as a sob escaped her.

And I'd fallen in love with her. I couldn't tell her that now. Not like this. She'd think I was saying it to keep her. I didn't want her to ever doubt it. If I told her now, she'd never believe it.

"I'm looking for another job. I'm trying to find something else to do. I don't want to do this anymore. I want to be worthy of you. Of your love. I just need some more time."

Amanda covered her mouth as another sob broke free. She shook her head. "No. It doesn't work like that. You should have told me. You made a fool out of me. I thought what we had was special to you. I knew you didn't love me, but I thought you cared for me. But all this time, you were leaving me to go have sex with other women. I don't care that they paid you. It's that you did it. That you could do it. I could never have let another guy touch my body. Not when I was with you. I wouldn't have been able to stomach it." She wiped at the tears streaming down her face.

"I had to have the money—"

"No, Preston. That isn't a good enough excuse for me. You should have told me in the beginning. Before I fell foolishly in love with you. You should never have asked me to be exclusive and led me to believe you were doing the same thing." She turned and headed for the door. This was it.

No!

I ran after her and wrapped my arms around her from behind. It was time to beg. "I swear to you that I will find another way to make money. I never cared about any of them. Just you, Manda. It's always just been you. Don't walk out of here. I can't lose you."

She was stiff in my arms. "When you chose to sleep with other women and lie to me about it, then you decided that you could lose me. You knew all along that if I ever found out I'd be gone, but you did it anyway. Let me go, Preston."

I deserved this. Every moment of agony and pain that followed, I deserved it. Letting my arms fall away, I watched helplessly as Amanda opened the door and walked out without a backward glance.

She wouldn't be back. This was it for us. Just as I'd realized that I couldn't keep lying to her because I was in love with her, she'd realized that you can't love a lie.

AMANDA

When I opened the door to my house, my mother was standing there waiting on me. Any anger I'd felt was gone. It was replaced by a cold, numbing pain.

"Well?" she asked.

"I won't ever see him again, if you agree to never tell Marcus about any of this. I don't want him to know. If you tell Marcus, I will go back to Preston Drake. You won't be able to stop me. But I can promise you I'll never speak to him again if you promise me you'll never breathe a word of this to anyone. Especially my brother. He doesn't need to know."

Mom frowned. "Does he know about you and Preston?"

"Yes. He knows."

She didn't like that. "What am I supposed to say to him if he asks about your breakup?"

I shrugged. "Tell him I changed my mind and realized Preston wasn't good enough for me after all. Or tell him I'm seeing Jason Stone now. Just don't tell him the truth."

Might as well lie about how it all ended. The entire relationship was one big fat lie. It seemed fitting. I walked past my mom and up the stairs. I wouldn't get much sleep tonight, but I wanted to be alone. My broken heart needed privacy to grieve. Hearts don't realize they've been lied to. They still love anyway.

Chapter Twenty

PRESTON

Rock was leaning up against my Jeep when I walked out of the gym. His arms were crossed over his chest, and he was wearing black aviators. I hadn't seen him in more than a week. Other than going to classes, to the gym, and to my mom's to check on the kids, I hadn't seen anyone. I hadn't worked and I was almost out of money, but I'd never be able to go back to what I'd been doing.

"You hunting me down?" I asked, throwing my gym bag into the back of the Jeep.

"Seeing as how you're hiding out, I had to come find you."

I jerked open the door. "Well, you found me."

Rock opened the passenger-side door and sat down. He wasn't about to let me drive off. What did he know? I had been expecting Marcus to barge into my apartment and beat the shit out of me all week. But other than a text from him saying my tux fitting was next Thursday, that was all I'd heard from him.

"Heard Manda broke it off with you," he said, studying me to see my reaction.

"You heard right."

"The thing is, I don't believe the reason why. Doesn't make sense to me. Marcus believes it, and it's probably good he does, but I'm not buying it."

I wasn't sure what the reason she'd given Marcus was. Obviously, it wasn't the truth.

"I can't help what you believe."

"It just seems to me that the guy I saw so fiercely determined to take a stand against his best friend over a girl wouldn't just stand by so casually while she up and moves on to another guy."

I gripped the steering wheel tightly. That hadn't been what I was expecting. Manda was seeing someone else already? That didn't sound like her.

"I'd expect you to go hunt down Jason Stone and beat the shit out of him like you wanted to do to Marcus. I'm finding it real hard to believe you're okay to just let him have her without a fight."

Jason Stone? Fuck.

"Guess she wanted things I couldn't give her," I clipped out, and cranked the Jeep. I didn't want to listen to any more of this.

"Or maybe that ain't what is really going on. Maybe she found out about your job, and she couldn't handle it."

How did he know?

"What do you mean?"

Rock shrugged. "You know, the job that allowed you to take care of your brothers and sister and pay your bills too. The one you kept a secret. The one I had to do some serious badass detective work to figure out."

He'd followed me. Bastard.

"Why didn't you tell this to Marcus?"

"Marcus ain't my only friend. I don't got favorites."

I let my head fall back on the headrest and sighed. "How long have you known?"

"Since the Friday after the engagement party. I was sure you were dealing drugs, and I was tailing you."

"So you knew before I started dating Manda?"

Rock nodded. "Yep."

'Then why the hell did you let me get away with it? I couldn't stay away from her. Someone needed to stop me."

"Because I was pretty damn sure you were in love with her. I'd never seen you in love. And Manda is a sweet girl. I figured if anyone could make you walk the straight and narrow, she could. But you never stopped working. I couldn't figure that out."

"I have mouths to feed."

"There are other jobs out there that don't require illegal activity."

I let out a hard laugh. "Nothing pays me enough. The ones that do I'm not qualified for."

'That's 'cause you're looking in the wrong place."

I turned my head to look at him. "Where do you suggest I look?"

"You're looking in the right place now." He smirked. "Drive to Pensacola. I got a guy I want you to meet."

"In Pensacola?"

"Yep. He owns a club. I used to work for him. Bouncers get paid real well. Late hours and good money."

A bouncer?

"How good is the money?"

Rock closed his door and buckled his seat belt. "The nicer the club, the better the pay. The place I'm taking you to pays more than most at fifty dollars an hour, and you'll get six hours a night. As many nights as you can handle."

Three hundred dollars a night. I could work Thursday through Sunday nights and make twelve hundred dollars a week.

"You think you can get me this job?"

Rock laughed. "I already got you the job. I'm just taking you to meet your new boss and get your paperwork done. You start this weekend."

AMANDA

After two weeks of dreading calculus because I'd have to see Preston, and then arriving and him not being there, I had come to the conclusion that he'd dropped the class. This was a good thing. I didn't want to see him. I wasn't sure yet how I'd react to seeing him.

My phone started playing my ringtone, and I reached into my backpack and pulled it out as I walked across campus to the coffee shop. I needed caffeine if I was going to make it through the study group I was headed to next.

"Hello."

"Good morning," Jason's voice greeted me.

"Good morning to you, too," I replied.

"You sound better this week."

Jason had made the mistake of calling me the day after my breakup with Preston. When he'd asked me how I was doing, I'd starting sobbing and telling him about my breakup. Of course I left out the actual reason why we broke up. Preston didn't deserve my protection, but I couldn't stop myself. I loved him. He'd shattered my heart, but I still loved him.

"I think it works that way. Each week you get a little better. Maybe by next month I'll be out dancing in clubs."

Jason chuckled. "Yeah. Well, let's not get carried away. Clubs aren't real safe for a single girl. I, of course, could escort you."

I hadn't led Jason on at all. I'd been painfully honest with him. I was still in love with Preston. I probably always would be. But if Jason wanted to be friends, then I'd like that. I needed friends right now.

"I'll keep that offer in mind."

"How's wedding planning coming in the Hardy household? Only two more weeks."

The wedding had taken over our lives. There were flowers everywhere, and candles and several different china patterns covering the dining room table. It was insane. Willow was the most laid-back bride I'd ever met. She just smiled and agreed to things. My mother, on the other hand, was a freaking bridezilla, and she was just the mother of the groom.

"I think I may borrow that jet of yours and fly to the Keys until it's over. That or kill my mom."

Jason laughed. "I'll let you borrow the jet, but I don't think Jax has enough influence to get you off the hook for murder. Running away sounds like a safer plan."

"You're probably right. I'll stick with plan A."

"I'm still planning on kicking your butt on the Go Kart track. After the wedding, the race is on."

We had gotten into a conversation about the Go Kart track in town and how I knew which one was the fastest and I couldn't be beat. He disagreed that he couldn't beat me. We made plans to go race after the wedding.

"I haven't forgotten. I'm currently in training, Hollywood. You're out of your league."

My phone beeped, and I pulled it back to see Jimmy's number flashing across the screen. Why would Preston's little brother be calling me?

"Um, Jason, I gotta go. I've got a call on the other line I need to take."

"All right, Bama. I'll talk to you later."

"Bye," I replied before clicking over.

"Jimmy?"

"It's Brent."

"Brent, are you okay?"

"I'm okay, but Momma's been asleep for a real long time, and we can't wake her up. I called Preston and he didn't answer. Jimmy isn't home yet from school, and I don't know if I should call 911."

I ran back toward the parking lot for my car. "How long has she been asleep?" I asked.

"Since yesterday morning."

Oh no.

"Weren't you at school yesterday and today? Could she have gotten up while you were at school?"

That had to be it.

"No, she hasn't moved. At all."

"Okay, Brent. I'm on my way right now. I want you to call 911 when we hang up, and tell them this exact same thing, okay? Then you and Daisy sit together in the living room. I'll be there in about five minutes. Be waiting on me."

"She's dead, ain't she?"

How did I tell this little boy his mother was very likely dead? That or in a coma.

"We don't know that. She could just be sleeping a long time. You call 911. I'm on my way. Is Daisy okay?"

"Yeah, she's sitting here beside me."

"Good. You keep her right there with you. See you in a minute."

"Okay, bye."

He disconnected the line, and I dialed Preston's number. It rang three times, then went to voice mail.

"It's Preston. You know what to do."

"Preston, it's Amanda. Brent just called me. Your mother hasn't woken up in two days. They're worried. I had him call 911, and I'm on my way over there. Call me as soon as you get this."

I ended the call and gunned the engine.

Chapter Twenty-One

PRESTON

A loud banging sound interrupted my dreams. I tried to block it out. I wasn't ready for this dream to end. Amanda was laughing and running down the beach while I chased her. She didn't hate me. She still loved me. The banging was joined with a ringing noise and some yelling. I peeled open my eyes and glanced over at the clock. It was four in the afternoon. I'd slept all day. I hadn't gotten home from work until almost four this morning. Then I'd been too jacked up on coffee to sleep. It had been almost seven before I crashed. I had to go back to work at eight tonight.

The banging reminded me of why I was awake. I stumbled out of bed and made my way to the door before whoever was on the other side beat it down.

I jerked it open to see Marcus standing on the other side. "Shit, man, I was getting ready to break the door down. I've been calling you, and then banging on this door for over ten minutes when that didn't work."

"I was sleeping. I'm working nights now, you know."

"That's right. I forgot you worked last night. Listen, I need to tell you something, and I don't know how you're gonna take it, so you might want to sit down."

This was not something you wanted to wake up to. "What is it?" I demanded. I didn't need to sit down, I just needed to know.

"It's your mom. She overdosed." He paused and waited for a reaction from me.

"Did it kill her this time?" This wasn't her first overdose.

Marcus placed his hand on my shoulder and let out a heavy sigh. "Yeah, man. It did."

I turned and headed for my room to put on some clothes. The kids would need me. I slipped on some jeans and tried to figure out how I could fit all three kids in here and take care of them when I was working nights. Without my mom's rent and utilities I'd have a little extra to hire a sitter.

"You okay?" Marcus asked from the doorway of my room.

"She was junkie, Marcus. It was bound to happen. I just need to get to the kids. They're probably scared."

The tightness in my chest surprised me. I wouldn't grieve for this woman. She'd done nothing for me in my life. I swallowed the weak emotion from the little boy deep inside who had wanted his mother to love him. Even a little. I'd figured out long ago she never would. I wouldn't shed a tear for her now.

"The kids are fine. Amanda has all three of them. They're getting ice cream, then going to the park. She sent me to find you. There are custody issues you have to deal with."

Amanda had the kids? How? Why? No matter how much they liked her, they would have called me first.

"How did Amanda know to get the kids?"

"Your younger brother called her. Told her your mom hadn't woken up in two days, and Amanda left school and rushed over there. She also had him call 911 while he waited on her to arrive. They couldn't reach you, so they called her."

Brent had called Amanda. My chest hurt. All three kids had been upset when I'd had to tell them I wouldn't be bringing Amanda around anymore. Daisy had even cried. But they'd known they could count on her when they couldn't get me on the phone. A lump formed in my throat, and I grabbed my keys and headed for the door.

"I know she left you for the Stone guy, and I'm sorry about that, man."

So that was what she had told him. She'd left me for Jason Stone. Was she even dating him, or had it just been her way to cover up the truth?

"You were right. I wasn't good enough for her. She finally

wised up and saw it too." I opened the door and headed down the stairs. I couldn't talk about this with Marcus. Not right now.

"For what it's worth, she still cares about you. She was really upset about this, and she was worried sick over those kids."

"The kids love her" was the only reply I had.

"But you don't?"

I stopped and looked back at him. I'd told enough lies. I wasn't going to keep on telling them just to make everyone feel better. "I'll always love her. Always." I jerked open the door to my Jeep and jumped inside. "Where am I going?" I asked.

"DHR is waiting on you at the trailer."

I shifted into drive and took off.

I wouldn't have to fight Momma for the kids now. She'd made it easy. I wasn't exactly the best option as a parent, but anything was better than her. And I didn't want them separated. I couldn't let them go. I'd figure this out somehow.

AMANDA

I held Daisy's cotton candy ice-cream cone while she ran over to the slide to go down it another time. She alternated between taking a lick of her ice cream and sliding. The ice cream wasn't going to last too much longer. The sun was getting the best of it.

"Has Preston called you yet?" Jimmy asked, taking the seat beside me.

"No, but my brother did find him, and he is at the trailer talking to the people who determine where you go. He's an adult and your closest relative, so he should have no problem getting custody," I assured him. Brent and Daisy were too young to think about the legal issues. But it was bothering Jimmy. He understood the courts had rules.

"What if he doesn't want us full-time?" Jimmy asked.

"He will."

"He never tried to take us from Mom."

"Because she would have fought him on it, and he'd have lost. He was also afraid that he'd draw attention to the situation and they'd take all of you away from him and each other."

Jimmy nodded. "Yeah, he explained that to me. I'm just worried that they will do it now."

My daddy was buddies with two of the three judges who could possibly hear this case. They played golf every Saturday morning and had since I was a little girl. If I had to go to my daddy and beg and plead with him for their help, I would.

"I promise you this will be okay."

Jimmy sighed. "I hope so. You know, Daisy really misses you."

"I miss her, too. I've missed all three of you."

Daisy came running back to me with a big grin on her face to take another few licks of her melting ice cream.

"You better stop and eat it, Daisy, before it just melts away," Jimmy told her.

"It gives me headaches if I eat it too fast," she replied.

Jimmy just smiled and kicked at a rock down by his feet.

"Amanda, is my momma in heaven?" Daisy asked.

I looked down at her little face. She was the first one to say anything about her momma's death. The boys had acted like nothing important had happened. Brent was swinging by himself, and I was giving him his space. But he hadn't brought up the fact that his mother was dead.

"I don't know a lot about heaven, Daisy. I'd like to think that because she brought such amazing kids into this world, there was someplace nice she got to go once her life was over."

I was pretty sure the woman was rotting in hell, but I wasn't about to tell that to her seven-year-old daughter.

"I don't know much about heaven eithaw. I just been to Sunday school a few times with my next-dowah neighbow."

I'd grown up in church, and I still didn't know a lot about heaven. "Church doesn't have all the answers, Daisy. Sometimes the answer we need is in our heart. We just have to listen to it."

Daisy looked down at her chest and frowned, then looked back up at me. "I've nevah heawed my hawt befowah."

Jimmy chuckled beside me, and I smiled over at him.

"Listen real close, and you'll finally hear something one day," I told her.

She nodded, then spun around and ran back toward the slide.

267

Once she was far enough away, Jimmy looked at me. "Thanks for not telling her the truth."

I felt tears sting my eyes. He was so young to know so much. "I happen to think that was the truth."

Jimmy shook his head. "No, that ain't the truth. I believe there's a heaven for the good and a hell for the bad. And we both know my momma wasn't good."

How did I argue with him? He knew more about how cruel his mother was than I did. I couldn't sit here and tell him his mother was in heaven when I knew she wasn't. He was right. She'd probably split hell wide open.

"Jimmy." Preston's voice interrupted my thoughts, and I lifted my eyes to see him walking up to us. His eyes were full of concern as he looked at his brother.

Jimmy stood up and walked to meet him halfway. Preston pulled him into a tight hug and whispered something in his ear. Jimmy nodded and looked back at me. "Thanks, Amanda. For everything," Jimmy said.

The lump in my throat was painful. I nodded. I wasn't sure I could talk. This was the first time I'd seen Preston since I'd walked out of his apartment. Knowing he'd just become the guardian of three kids, that the world was on his shoulders, and how alone he must feel was killing me. Dammit, why did I have to love him so much?

"Pweston!" Daisy came running from the slide when she

spotted her big brother. Preston bent down and opened his arms wide, letting her run into them.

"Hey, my Daisy May. You been havin' fun?"

Daisy nodded and pointed back at me still holding her ice cream. "Amanda came and took us away from all those people. She got me ice cweam and bwought us hewah to play."

Preston didn't look up at me. He kept his gaze on Daisy. "Sounds like she saved the day. You ready to go to my place now?"

Daisy nodded enthusiastically, then broke free of Preston to run back to me.

She wrapped her arms around my waist and squeezed me tightly. "Thank you for getting us and the ice cweam."

I bent down and kissed the top of her head. "You're very welcome."

"Will you come see me?" she asked, pulling away and looking up at me pleadingly.

"Yes. I'll talk to your brother about that. We'll have another ice cream date, okay?"

Daisy beamed at me. "Okay. I'll see you soon," she called out as she ran back to Preston, who was standing a good distance away from me with his hands tucked in his pockets.

"Go get Brent, and y'all go on out to the Jeep," he said to Jimmy, and then he turned to look at me.

I stood up and walked over to throw away the ice cream

and close some of the distance he had left between us.

"Thanks for going after them when they called you today. And sending your brother to wake me up. It means a lot." The flat tone of his voice was so unlike him. It was as if all emotion was gone. He sounded hollow. I wanted to wrap my arms around him and tell him it would be okay. That I'd help him, that I loved him. But I couldn't. He'd never loved me. He'd lied to me. As much as I wanted to ease his pain right now, I wasn't the one to do it.

"If they ever need me, all they have to do is call. I'll help however I can."

Preston nodded and looked away from me. Holding my gaze wasn't something he wanted to do, apparently. I hated that. I missed him so much.

"Thanks," he replied.

He started to turn to walk away. I didn't want him to leave yet. I wasn't done looking at him. Being near him. I wanted to say more. For him to say more. This was just so wrong.

"Wait, Preston," I called out before I could stop myself.

He paused, then looked back at me. I had to say something. I didn't know what to say. I couldn't tell him I was sorry about his mom, because I knew he wasn't. I couldn't tell him I missed him, because what good would that do?

"Don't do this, Manda. You made the right choice. You've got your dinners in New York and rides in a jet now. It's what you deserve. And I've become the guardian of three kids. I love them. It'll completely change my world. And it's what I deserve." He didn't wait for me to process his words. He just walked away. And I let him.

Chapter Twenty-Two

PRESTON

Trisha had been a lifesaver this past weekend. She had come to the apartment and stayed with the kids while I worked. Rock had even come the last two nights. She'd made cookies for the kids and let them each make their own homemade pizzas. It was like she was having as much fun as they were. And she was refusing to let me pay her for watching them.

She'd even shown up at six on Monday morning to help me get them ready for school, and she'd brought them all a lunch box packed with food. They had all looked at the lunch boxes like they didn't know what to do with them. I knew for a fact that they'd been eating free lunches in the lunchroom since day one of kindergarten, and not once had my momma packed them a lunch.

Jimmy had looked up at me when Trisha handed him the solid black Igloo lunch box, and smiled. "She packed me lunch," he'd said in an awed voice. If I hadn't been worried about Rock knocking me on my ass, I'd have grabbed her face and kissed her. She had no idea how much her thoughtfulness meant to them.

I'd gotten them safely on the school bus and was now wide awake. My days of sleeping in were over. By the time I got to my ten o'clock class, I'd be wired on caffeine.

I'd poured my first cup of coffee when a knock sounded at the door. Who the hell was it now? I set my cup down and walked over to open the door. Trisha stood outside, with Rock behind her. She looked anxious.

"Hey, y'all. Did you forget something?" I asked, stepping back to let them in.

Trisha came in, followed by Rock, who closed the door behind him.

"No. We want to talk to you about something," Trisha said, glancing up at Rock.

"Okay, uh, y'all want some coffee?" I asked.

"No, thank you. Can we sit down?" Trisha asked.

Typically, I'd be less patient this early in the morning, but after all they'd done for me over the past few days, I'd open a vein and give them a pint of blood if that was what they wanted.

"Sure. Have a seat." I waved them over to the couch.

I sat in the chair across from them and took a drink of my

coffee while I waited on them to say whatever it was they had come here to say.

Trisha took a deep breath. "I don't know if you've noticed that we haven't been around as much lately. Like at Live Bay, we aren't there as often and we haven't been leaving the house much."

I had been too wrapped up in my world with Amanda to notice anyone else. I just nodded instead of explaining how unaware I'd been.

"Well, Rock and I've been trying for over six months to get pregnant. Last month we went to a specialist, and I was told there was a one percent chance that I'd ever conceive. He said we could try different procedures they had, but it would cost thousands of dollars up front." She paused and looked back at Rock again. He'd wrapped his arm around her shoulders and tucked her up against his side.

I didn't know if she wanted me to comment on this, or how in the hell this had anything to do with me. So I waited for more.

"We checked into adoption, but it also costs thousands of dollars to adopt a baby, and you are put on waiting lists. It isn't easy, and we don't have thousands of dollars. We'd have to get a loan, and we might not be approved for a loan even then. It would be unsecured. Anyway, we started talking about adopting an older child. One in the state system who needs a home. I want a little girl." She teared up as she said the words "little girl."

"My momma was a lot like yours. She didn't want to have much to do with me. Then she ran off with one of her boyfriends when I was eight, and I never saw her again. I remember lying in bed at night and pretending that there was a momma out there who wanted me. She was going to come get me one day, and she would love me." Trisha stopped and reached up to wipe a tear that was rolling down her cheek.

"I saw Daisy, and I wanted her immediately. She was just what I wanted. A little girl I could love and raise as my own. I knew you'd never split the kids up. I understood that. So this weekend I offered to stay with them because I wanted to spend time with them."

She took a deep breath and blinked back the tears filling her eyes again.

"I want them all. Jimmy and his sweet, caring nature—he reminds me so much of you. And Brent is so funny and charming when he opens up. They don't expect anything, and that breaks my heart. I want to give them everything. I want to love them and reassure them that they have a home. I begged Rock to come with me Saturday night to stay with them. I wanted him to get to know them. He fell in love." She sniffed and smiled up at him.

"Daisy wrapped him around her little finger in minutes, and he agrees that Jimmy is you made over, so of course he loved him. Then Brent just gets to you. You can't help it. I know you just lost your mother and things are unsettled for y'all. I don't want to come into your life and disrupt everything. I just want to know if there is any chance that you would consider letting Rock and me have the kids. We have the room. You've seen the new house we're renting. I'd make them lunches and go on field trips. We'd bake cookies and go cut down our own Christmas tree every year. They'd never be left alone. I'd love them. We both would."

When I lifted my eyes from Trisha's hopeful, tear-streaked face to see the unshed tears in Rock's eyes, I knew my answer. They wanted to give them what I wouldn't be able to. I'd be the big brother who wouldn't remember to pack their lunches. I'd be gone to school and games and work all the time. They'd know I loved them, but they'd be fending for themselves a lot of the time.

With Rock and Trisha, they'd have parents. The kind of parents I never got to have. The ones who gave them a happy, secure life. This wasn't an opportunity most kids in their situation were given. There was even a real good chance the judge wouldn't give the kids to me. He'd take them away and split them up into foster care.

"They'd be the luckiest kids I know to have you two as parents," I replied.

Trisha let out a sob and covered her mouth with her hand.

"I'll call their social worker, and we'll go from there."

AMANDA

It was the last family dinner before the wedding. I'd thought Mom was in such a tizzy planning that she'd cancel it, but she didn't. Instead she ordered a fancy cake from the bakery in town and lit candles on the table. We were making this last one count, apparently.

Marcus and Willow walked into the kitchen holding hands. Marcus was whispering in her ear, and she was giggling. They made me want to vomit, they were so sweet. Romance just made me angry these days. I hadn't heard from Daisy or the boys since the day in the park. I'd hoped Daisy would call me, but I knew they were settling in with Preston and dealing with things.

"Whoa, Mom. You went all out," Marcus said as he took in the fancy cake and candles that decorated the table.

"It is the last family dinner before this family goes from three to four, and I wanted to celebrate the wonderful new changes to come," she said with a smile.

She had left Dad out of that count. She pretended like he didn't exist. Marcus respected that. To the point that Dad wasn't even invited to the wedding. Neither was Willow's sister, Tawny. Only Larissa was coming. She would be the flower girl.

"You didn't have to do all this," Willow told my mother. "You've been working on the wedding nonstop for weeks. But thank you. It means so much."

Willow had a way with people. My mom was a tough nut to

crack, and she had adored Willow since she'd first met her at a family dinner. I had been charmed by her immediately too, so I understood her effect on people.

Then again, Willow scored big points just for making Marcus so happy. Anyone who made my brother smile like she did had to be perfect in every way.

"I want everything to be special for the two of you," Mom replied, waving us toward the table. "Everyone have a seat. I'll bring the food to the table."

"I'll help you, Mom," Marcus said, pulling Willow's chair out for her, then turning to follow Mom into the kitchen.

Willow looked across the table at me. "Can you believe I'm going to be Mrs. Marcus Hardy by this time Saturday night?"

Smiling, I nodded. "Yes, I can. I expected it after I saw my brother with you the first time. He was hooked. It was all over his face."

"I'm the luckiest woman in the world," she replied.

The pain in my chest was something I was getting used to. Seeing other couples in love and happy hurt because I wanted that. Not with just anyone, either. I wanted it with a guy who didn't want it with me in return. Seeing the way my brother looked at Willow, I yearned to be looked at that way. By a guy who had never told me he loved me. Who had lied to me and betrayed me. Yet I still wanted him. Would my heart ever stop wanting him?

"Are you okay? You seem down." The concern in Willow's voice was obvious.

I knew Marcus hadn't told her about Preston and me. She didn't even know we had dated. I couldn't exactly tell her that my heart was damaged beyond repair and I was dying inside. She thought I was interested in Jason Stone.

"I'm just tired. I'm sorry. I'll try not to be such a downer."

She frowned and started to say something else, when Marcus and Mom walked back into the room carrying the trays of food that had been catered. Mom hadn't had time to cook this week. She'd been too busy worrying over things like what ribbon to tie on what chair.

"This smells amazing," Marcus said as he set the pan full of fried crab claws and hush puppies down on the table.

"I thought we'd do seafood tonight. Since it's a beach-themed wedding."

That made no sense, but my mother was obsessive, so I ignored it.

Marcus reached for some food and started putting it on Willow's plate. He always did things like that for her. He made her breakfast in the morning and brought her coffee. My brother had been raised to be a southern gentleman. My mom had accomplished that and then some.

"Guess what I found out today," Marcus said as he started to fix his own plate.

"What?" Mom asked.

Marcus looked over at me. "Looks like Trisha and Rock are gonna adopt Preston's brothers and sister."

"What?" I couldn't act like I didn't care. Because I did.

Marcus raised his eyebrows and nodded. "Yep. Trisha found out awhile back she can't get pregnant. They wanted to adopt. Then she met the kids, and she and Rock want them. Preston's already got the ball rolling. The kids' social worker doesn't see that this is going to be a problem. The court will find it a perfect solution. Preston wouldn't have gotten to keep those kids. He has his job as a bouncer four nights a week, and then he has school and baseball. He has no time to raise kids."

Trisha and Rock would be amazing parents. And the kids would still be in town close to Preston. He could get them whenever he wanted. Trisha would love Daisy. She'd be the momma that Daisy deserved.

Wait . . . Preston's job as a bouncer at a club? Was this something he'd made up to cover the truth, or had he really found himself a new job?

"They'll make wonderful parents. I'm so happy for them and those kids," I replied, trying to keep the emotion off my face. My mother was watching me. I could feel her eyes studying my every move. I could not let her see any weakness.

"Yeah. Preston is pretty pumped about it. He has been worried about losing the kids because he's so young. He didn't want them split up and put in the foster care system. This removes that possibility."

I nodded and picked up a crab claw. "When did Preston start working as a bouncer?" I asked, trying to sound casual about it. I put the crab claw in my mouth and pulled the meat off with my teeth while I waited on Preston to answer. I would not look over at my mother.

"A couple of weeks ago. Rock hooked him up with a great gig. He works four nights a week and gets paid some serious jack. He sleeps most of the daylight hours during the weekend, though. It was why no one could get him on his phone the day his mom died."

Marcus was being careful too. He could sense the tension coming from Mom. I hadn't told him that she knew about Preston, but I was pretty sure he was able to figure it out by the major vibes she was putting off.

"Makes sense. Well, I'm glad things are working out for him," I replied.

Marcus shifted in his seat, and the questions in his eyes as he looked at me were clear. He wanted to know if Mom knew. He also was questioning her involvement in our sudden breakup. I couldn't have him asking her anything. She'd tell him about Preston. I didn't want Marcus to know. I needed him to think this was my choice and I'd moved on.

"So change of subject, but Jason is flying in tomorrow. He

wanted to come early so we could spend some time together. If you need me for anything, give me advance notice, because I have plans with him too," I told my mother.

Mom's tension eased and she smiled. "Oh, that's good to hear. I'm sure I'll need you some, but you can always bring Jason with you. We can find some use for his muscles."

"He doesn't have muscles, Mom. He has people lift everything, from his luggage to his damn fork. The kid hasn't ever done any type of manual labor." Marcus sounded annoyed.

"He has a gym in his home, where he works out daily. I can assure you he has very nice muscles," I said sweetly, meeting my brother's gaze across the table.

"If that's what you want, Manda. Then be my guest."

It wasn't what I wanted. But nothing was about what I wanted. It rarely was.

Chapter Twenty-Three

PRESTON

I hadn't had a drink in weeks. But right now I needed at least four straight shots of tequila. All week I'd been worried about tonight. Being the best man in Marcus's wedding was something I'd always expected. But now that it meant walking down the aisle with the maid of honor, who also happened to be the one girl I was in love with and could never have, it was going to be pure hell.

I'd been busy all week helping Rock and Trisha get their house ready for inspection. We'd painted the boys' room blue and bought them bunk beds, along with a television and an Xbox. Then we'd painted Daisy's room a pale yellow, and Trisha had insisted she have a canopy bed. Daisy called it her princess room. There was a little pink-and-purple table with two chairs sitting in the corner with a tiny little tea set on it. Then there was a dollhouse that had more rooms than any doll could need, with everything from a high chair to working ceiling fans in it.

I was exhausted, but I was also positive that the inspection was going to be a success. Now, tonight, instead of working I was here trying like hell not to look over at Amanda. I'd gotten a glimpse of her when she'd walked into the beach house the Hardys were renting for the reception. She was wearing some slinky little pink dress and matching heels that made her legs look even longer. I'd jerked my gaze off her quickly. My intention was to pretend like she wasn't here. It was the only way I could do this.

"Preston." Her soft voice called my name, and I turned around to see she'd walked over to me. Her hair was left down instead of up like the other girls'. It hung in perfect silky golden curls down her back. Her very bare back. There was hardly anything to that dress she was wearing. I tore my eyes off her dress before I caved and checked to see if she was wearing a bra, and I met her gaze.

"Manda," I replied. Wishing the bar was open already. I needed it for the rehearsal, not after the rehearsal.

"I heard about Trisha and Rock getting the kids. I wanted to tell you how happy I was for y'all."

Dammit. She was going to be all nice and friendly. Did she not understand that she tied me up in knots? I was trying to find a way to live without her. This was going to fuck up every-thing. I'd made a little progress. It was shot to hell now.

"Thanks. The kids are real happy about it," I replied, and looked away from her. Anywhere but at those green eyes that I'd seen darken during an orgasm and twinkle with laughter when I'd said something funny.

"Are you doing okay?" she asked.

What kind of question was that? Did it look like I was doing okay?

"I'm always doing okay, Manda."

I could hear her swift intake of breath. What had she expected me to say? The truth? She couldn't handle the truth.

"That's good. I'm glad to hear that. I'll, uh, see you later," she stammered, and I looked down at her as she walked away. The back of her dress scooped down all the way to her lower back. Any farther and her perfect little ass would be showing. Dammit, did her brother not require her to wear more clothes than that?

She stopped walking, and I tore my gaze off her ass to see who she'd stopped to talk to. Jason Stone. His arms wrapped around her in a hug, and the blood in my head started pound-ing furiously against my temple. He was touching her bare back. Had he touched her other places? Had he touched her places only I'd touched her?

Fuck.

I stormed for the doors leading outside to the beach. I needed some fresh air, and I needed space. Why had she brought him here? I'd thought the story that she was seeing him was a lie to cover up the truth. But maybe it hadn't been a lie. Maybe she had run straight to him and his fucking jet. I slammed both hands, palms down, on the wooden railing outside and let out a stream of curse words. I'd known this day would come. Seeing her with someone else. I just didn't know it would be so damn soon.

"You okay out here? We kinda need that railing for the wedding. If you could refrain from destroying it, that would be much appreciated."

I turned my head to look at Marcus. He had walked up beside me.

"By any chance is this random act of violence over the fact that my sister is here with Jason Stone?"

No use in denying it. "I wasn't ready to see her with someone else so soon."

Marcus leaned on the railing with his elbows. "I was kind of surprised too. I mean, one day she is telling me she loves you, and then the next thing I know, you two are broken up and she's dating Jason. Just don't seem right. Amanda isn't fickle."

Why hadn't she told him? Was she protecting me, or was she protecting her pride? I wanted to believe it was me she was protecting. She'd been the only person to ever protect me. To want to protect me.

"She wised up. I wasn't good enough for her. You said so yourself."

Marcus let out a heavy sigh. "I shouldn't have said that. You're my best friend. I love you like a brother. I just had seen you over the years go through girls faster than you did underwear, and I didn't want my little sister to be one of those girls. I didn't want her hurt. You're not a bad guy. You're a great guy. You're loyal to a fault. You can cheer up a whole damn room. You've always had my back. If you were in love with a girl, then she'd be one lucky woman." He paused and turned his head to look at me. "But you never said you loved Amanda. I knew for you to be faithful, you had to be in love with her. Even after she claimed to love you, you never said you loved her."

I hadn't told anyone how I felt about her. I was tired of keeping it to myself. Amanda didn't want to hear it now. She'd never believe me, anyway. But I could tell Marcus.

"I love her. I'll love her until the day I die. No one else is ever going to take her place. It's impossible. I don't want to even try. The weeks I spent with her were the best ones of my life. Having her love me was amazing. But I screwed up. I always screw up. It's what I'm good at."

Marcus stood back up and put his hand on my back. "No, it's not what you're good at. You're good at a lot of things, but screwing up isn't one of them. We all make mistakes. God knows I did with Low back when I found out about her sister and my dad. But when we find that one person who completes us, we don't give up. No matter how bad we screwed up. We make it right."

I stood there looking out at the water as Marcus's footsteps faded away. He had no idea what he was saying. If he knew I'd been screwing women for money while with his sister, he'd kill me. When he thought Willow had betrayed him, he'd reacted the way any man would. Amanda had done nothing but love me and trust me. What I'd done to her was so much worse.

AMANDA

"Do I need to be worried about my life being in danger?" Jason whispered as I led him to the room where he could wait while we rehearsed. Mom had football playing on the massive flatscreen and appetizers and drinks set out.

"No. Why?" I asked.

Jason laughed. "Either you are completely blind, or you're just really good at ignoring things. But Preston just stormed out of this house after shooting me a death glare."

I stopped walking and looked back at the double doors that were standing open and led out onto the beach. "Preston went outside?"

"Yeah. When we hugged. He saw it, and what could only be

described as rage lit up his face before he tore out of here like a man being chased."

Really? He had seemed so uninterested in talking to me. I was still trying to deal with the fact that I annoyed him now. My presence was something he truly despised.

"I don't think he left because of you. He can't stand to be near me. He probably left because he was afraid I'd try to talk to him again. This weekend is going to be oh so much fun. I have to walk down the aisle with him. Sit by him at the reception, and we both have to make toasts."

Jason reached out, took my hand, and squeezed it. "Amanda, that guy doesn't dislike you. I don't know what he has said to you, but I can promise you what I just saw was not disinterest or annoyance. He was ready to take me apart for touching you. I know guys. I am one. Trust me."

I wanted to believe him. I really did, but it was hard. I knew Preston well, and I could see the blank, empty emotion in his eyes when he looked at me. I was dead to him. I couldn't let myself hope for anything more. It already hurt too much. I didn't need to add to the pain. Not if I was going to find a way to move on from this and live again.

"I'd like to, but I can't. I know him too well." I walked over to the table. "You can get anything you like to drink here, or snacks are over there. I hope you like SEC football, because that's all we watch around here. The other teams aren't really important in the grand scheme of things."

Jason laughed. "So you SEC people really are as obnoxious as I've heard."

"Not obnoxious. Just being honest. The facts are the facts," I replied, and winked at him.

"The facts, huh?"

"We can go over the last ten NCAA national championship winners if you want to clear up any confusion," Rock drawled as he walked into the room.

"Case in point. If you want to make friends, don't dis the SEC," I said, nodding toward Rock.

"Got it," Jason replied.

"Hey, Amanda," Brent said, following Rock into the room.

"Hey, you! I didn't know I was going to get to see you tonight," I said, going over to hug him.

He wrapped his arms around me, then nodded toward Rock. "I'm here with Rock and Trisha. They're gonna let us go live with them. Jimmy and I even got bunk beds and an Xbox. Preston keeps beating us at the football game he bought us, though. I'm practicing. I'm gonna take him out next time."

I would not get all weepy over this. I was just so happy for them. Hearing the joy in his little voice was wonderful.

"I have no doubt you'll be beating your brother in no time. I have complete faith."

Brent nodded and looked over at the table of food curiously.

"You want something to eat? Help yourself. I need to go see who has the flower girl. We're about to start soon."

Brent hurried over to the table.

"Bring me one of them cookies," Rock told Brent as I walked out of the room

PRESTON

Rehearsal had been difficult for reasons much different from those I'd come here dreading. Being near her was hard, but seeing her with *him* was harder. I'd had to keep myself in check while walking down the aisle beside Amanda. She wasn't wearing a bra. She needed to wear a bra, dammit.

The rehearsal dinner had assigned seating, and Amanda's was beside Jason. Mine was directly across from them, since I was the best man. I got to witness their joking around and flirting. I didn't even pretend that it didn't bother me. I spent my entire meal glaring at him. The next time he called her "Bama" I was going to come across the table and pummel his face in. He didn't get to give her nicknames. She wasn't his. Or was she?

I managed to make it through the meal without causing anyone bodily harm. The moment it was finished, I bolted for the door. I had to do this shit all over again tomorrow. I was never going to make it.

Chapter Twenty-Four

PRESTON

The Hardys were putting the wedding party and out-of-town guests up at a hotel across the street from the beach house where the wedding was being held. I'd gone downstairs this morning for some breakfast just in time to see Amanda walking out the front door on the arm of Jason Stone. His rock-star brother and Sadie White were with her. I lost my appetite.

I wasn't going to be able to make it through today if I didn't get a grip. I had to control my emotions. I'd been keeping them in check until I'd seen Amanda again last night. She'd tried to talk to me and I'd been rude. I'd protected myself. A lot of good it had done me.

I'd go talk to Marcus. He'd make me feel better. I was heading for the elevator when it opened and Marcus came barreling out. His eyes looked panicked. "Have you seen Low?" he asked, looking past me to the lobby.

"No, I haven't. Why?"

Marcus swore and gritted his teeth. "Because she's missing. We had an argument, but it was over. I thought we were good. Then I went to get her, and she wasn't in her room. I've called Mom, and she's not at the beach house. I can't find her any-where."

She was probably off somewhere taking a breather. "Calm down, dude. The girl ain't going anywhere. She's here some-where. You just got wedding nerves."

Marcus took a deep breath and nodded. "Yeah, you're right. I'll find her."

He took off for the front door. I didn't follow him. Instead I headed back up the elevator to my room.

I stopped outside the door I'd seen Cage go into last night. I could talk to Cage. I needed to talk to someone. I knocked on the door.

It opened up, and Eva was standing there in her robe look-ing like she just got out of bed.

"Hey, Eva, sorry if I woke you up," I said, and walked into the room before she could turn me away. I was running out of friends to talk to. Cage was a last resort.

"Preston?" she replied. It sounded more like a question.

"She's here. I mean, I knew she would be, but *fuck me*, I

hadn't been prepared to see her with him. What the hell does she see in him? He's a prick." I stalked over to a chair and gripped the back tightly. I wanted to hit something. Anything.

"Who is *she*?" Eva asked.

"Where's Cage?" I asked her instead. I wasn't here to talk to her. I needed a guy to rant to.

"I don't know," she said sadly.

What the hell did that mean?

"He just left?"

"He was gone when I woke up," she replied.

Low was missing. Cage was missing. "Fuck. Marcus can't find Low, either," I told her. I didn't want to assume anything, but that was the truth.

The door swung open and Cage walked inside. His eyes swung from his upset girlfriend to me, and the fury that lit them told me he had the wrong idea.

"*What the hell* are you doing with my girl in my hotel room?" Cage asked in a cold, even voice.

"I came looking for you. Wipe that stupid-ass alpha snarl off your face. I'm not here to make a play for Eva," I replied, annoyed that he was acting the same way I would.

Cage walked over to stand by Eva, who shifted away from him.

"I'll talk to you later. You got your own set of problems," I said, and headed out the door.

AMANDA

Breakfast with Sadie was nice. I'd missed her. Seeing her again would have made this day perfect, if it wasn't for the fact that my heart was broken and every time I saw Preston's face and he looked past me it shattered all over again. The wedding pictures would be starting soon. I needed to put on my bridesmaid dress and fix my hair.

I started to walk to the stairs, where I knew Willow was going over things with the wedding director, when I saw Preston's blond hair out on the beach. He was alone. His hands were tucked into his pockets, and he was watching the waves crash against the shore.

I slipped off my heels and headed out there after him.

He couldn't hear me approaching, thanks to the wind and waves.

"You out here hiding?" I asked when I was close enough for him to hear me.

His shoulders tensed. That was the only clue I had that he had heard me.

"Is this the way it's always going to be between us? Can we not even go back to being friends?"

Preston's shoulders rose and fell as he sighed. "I can never be your friend, Manda."

"Why? I didn't do anything wrong. You did. If I can forgive you, then why can't you forgive me? Why do you have to hate me so much you can't stand to be around me?"

Preston turned his head to look at me. "Hate you? You think I hate you?"

I shrugged. Yeah, that was what I thought. He sure acted like it.

"I don't hate you, Manda. I could never hate you."

"Then why are you treating me this way? Why can't you at least look at me? Talk to me? I'm not asking for—"

Preston grabbed me and slammed his mouth against mine violently. His tongue plunged into my mouth, wrapping around mine while his hands grabbed my butt and pulled me hard up against his body. I'd barely had time to respond, when he was suddenly gone. I opened my eyes, and he was standing in front of me breathing hard. "That is why I am acting the way I am. Because every time you get near me, I want to grab you and hold on so damn tight you can't go anywhere again. I want to kiss you until you forget what a sorry-ass bastard I am. But I can't. You want to move on, and I am trying to let you."

He wasn't over me. He wanted me. But he didn't love me. Could I live without love? I wanted what Marcus and Willow had. But I also wanted Preston. Did I let go of the dream of a fairy-tale romance so I could have my dream of Preston?

"You show up here with him," he growled. "How the fuck do I handle that? All I can think about is, has he touched you? It's killing me. It is literally eating me up inside. Knowing he may be touching you in places only I had touched you.

Places that were *mine*. Mine! And I fucked it up and lost it."

I took two steps, closing enough distance between us so that I could touch him. I'd made my decision. Preston wasn't raised like my brother. He hadn't been given love. How did I expect him to know how to love if no one had ever shown him? Marcus could love easily. He'd been loved all his life.

I'd show Preston how to love. Maybe one day he'd love me too. He just needed someone to teach him how love works. How it feels. That it isn't built on lies. I loved him more than my fantasy of what I thought romance was. I would never be happy with anyone but him.

I reached out and placed my hand on his heart. His pec muscle jumped underneath my hand. "I'm not dating Jason. We are friends. Only friends. Never even kissed him. He knows my heart is unavailable. I've explained it to him, and he is okay with that. He isn't looking for anything more with me. This weekend he knew was going to be tough on me, so he flew in to be supportive. Nothing more."

Preston was breathing hard. "He hasn't touched you anywhere? Because he sure as hell hugs you too tightly."

I grinned and shook my head. "He has hugged me twice. That is all."

"He's got money. He's got fame. He's got that damn jet. Why don't you want him?"

I rubbed my thumb over his heart. "Because I love you."

The hard mask on his face fell away, and his eyes swam with emotion.

"How? Why?" he asked, reaching up to cover my hand with his. "I don't deserve it."

"I disagree. You're special, Preston Drake. I think I've been in love with you since my sixteenth birthday and you came to my bonfire party on the beach with Marcus. You winked at me and called me beautiful. From that moment on I watched you. I was fascinated by you. Then as I got older, I wanted you. Once I got you, I realized I was in love with you."

Preston slid his other hand around my waist and rested it against my lower back. "The night you walked out on me and you knew the truth, there were no more lies standing between us, and I realized this crazy, wild, intense feeling I had for you was love. I'd never had this before. Sure, I loved my brothers and sister, but nothing like this out-of-control emotion I couldn't name. I had been scared to tell you I loved you because I couldn't believe that what I was feeling was love if I wasn't telling you the truth about me. I lied to you because I knew you'd leave me if you found out. I didn't want to lose you."

My breathing stopped.

I'm more than positive my heart did too. "You love me?"

He smiled and lowered his head until his lips hovered over mine. "I love you with a scary, insane, wild, amazing love. I always will. No one else could ever make me feel this way."

I pressed my lips against his and wrapped my arms around his neck. Both his hands locked on my waist, and he picked me up. I wrapped my legs around him while I kissed him with all the emotion pouring through me. His hands slipped under my dress and cupped my bottom so he could hold me up.

"Come on, guys. Really? This is my freaking wedding day. Can y'all save that crap until it's over?" Marcus's voice carried out over the wind, and we broke apart to see him grinning at us a few feet away.

"She's hard to resist," Preston called back out to him.

"Well, try. Please. Everyone is getting ready inside. We need the best man and maid of honor. If y'all could try not to make out during the wedding pictures, I'd appreciate it."

Preston laughed and set me back down on the sand. "I take it you're not going to bash my face in this time?"

Marcus shook his head. "No, but if the two of you had continued to look at each other and sulk like babies, I was going to bash your face in for being an idiot."

"I take it you found the bride," Preston said.

What did that mean? Had he lost her?

Marcus shrugged. "Yeah. She'd gone to eat fries."

"Fries?" we both asked in unison.

Marcus rolled his eyes. "Yeah, fries. It's one of those Cage and Low things I'm still learning to deal with."

Preston squeezed my butt and then patted it. "You go on ahead with your brother. I'll follow behind. Tonight isn't the time to deal with your mother's reaction."

I'd forgotten about her. Crap.

Chapter Twenty-Five

PRESTON

I wasn't sure if the wedding was as beautiful as everyone said it was. All I'd been able to see was Amanda. I could attest to the fact that she was gorgeous. It was hard to see anyone else around her. She commanded my complete attention.

The wedding dinner, however, was another thing. Once again she was seated beside Jason, since he was her plus one, and I was across the table getting to witness it.

She'd smiled at me reassuringly throughout the meal. I knew she was trying to get me to stop staring Jason down, but it couldn't be helped. I was pissed, and I wanted him to leave.

When the longest meal I'd ever sat through was over, Jason had stood up and congratulated Marcus and Low, then explained he had a plane waiting on him. Amanda said she'd walk him out.

I didn't want them alone. I trusted her, but I couldn't say the same for Jason. Once they stepped out of the dining room, I started to stand up and follow them. Marcus's hand gripped my arm tightly. "Don't," he whispered.

"Let go of me," I warned.

"Listen to me. She doesn't want him. She is being polite. He was her guest. Don't make a scene. She'll be right back." Marcus was talking under his breath so no one could hear him but me. I knew he was right, but I didn't like sitting here waiting.

"What if he tries to kiss her?"

"She'll stop it. Trust her."

I did trust her, dammit.

Amanda walked back into the room, and she immediately looked toward me. She mouthed, *Let's go.* Then she turned to go say her good-byes to her mother and some guests.

"I'm hoping you two find the time to see us off later," Marcus said before I could even stand up. He'd read her lips too.

I nodded. "Wouldn't miss it, and thank you for trusting me with her."

Marcus smiled. "You *are* my best man. Who better to trust her with?"

I grinned and headed out the door. Amanda was already out here somewhere waiting on me, and I was more than anxious to get her alone.

Two hands reached out of the shadows and wrapped around my arm, tugging me into the darkness.

"You weren't very nice in there," Amanda scolded before kissing my neck and running her hands up my chest.

"I was on my best behavior," I replied, grabbing the bottom of this ridiculous excuse for a dress and pulling it up so I could run my hands over her ass again. She was wearing a fucking thong. I'd made that discovery on the beach earlier, and it had driven me crazy every time I looked down at her ass in this dress.

"No, you were a bad boy. I'm surprised Jason toughed it out as long as he did." She bit down on my earlobe and raised her bare leg up my side. I grabbed her under the knee and pulled it higher.

"He was too close to you, and you don't have on a bra. Manda, you have got to start wearing a bra, baby. I'm gonna get arrested if you don't."

She giggled and reached up to pull the straps of her dress down until her breasts were bare.

"Fuck, baby. I've got to get you back to my apartment. Now. Real fast." I bent down to flick her erect nipples with my tongue.

"Mmmmm, I can't wait that long, and we have to be here to see them off," she moaned, pressing my head closer to her nipple until I pulled it into my mouth and sucked.

I wasn't going to be able to wait that long either at this

rate. It had been too long since I'd touched her. I was ready to be buried up in her, and this time I might not ever come out.

"Preston," she panted.

"Yes, baby?"

"Go down the beach that way. There are no houses, and it's dark and empty. I need you right now." She was pointing off into the darkness.

She wanted to have sex on a beach? Hell, yes.

I slipped the straps of her dress back up her arms and covered her tits back up, then grabbed her hand and led her out deeper into the darkness. We walked until the music and laughter from the house had faded away and there was no sound other than the waves.

Amanda pushed at my chest when I tried to pull her against me, and she reached for the button on my pants. There was a wicked gleam in her eyes as she looked up at me. She got the button undone and unzipped them, then pulled down my pants and my boxer briefs. I slipped off my shoes and stepped out of them. My girl wanted me naked, so I was going to oblige her.

She placed both her hands on my thighs and stuck out her tongue and took a swipe at my dick. Holy shit.

"Manda, baby . . . Ohgod." She wrapped a hand around the base of my cock, then covered it with her mouth.

"Baby, AH, you . . . OH, Manda, God, that feels incredible."

I gave up trying to stop her. I couldn't form words. I reached down and buried my hands in her hair, and watched in delirious pleasure as she slid my dick in and out of her mouth like it was a damn Popsicle and she couldn't get enough.

"Holy . . . fuck. UH, yeah. That's it. So good." She sucked harder when I praised her. If I wasn't about to explode, I'd keep on talking, but I needed to get her sweet, hot little mouth off my cock and get inside her.

I reached down and pulled her up. The popping noise her mouth made when my dick sprang free might go down as one of the hottest sounds ever.

"I don't want to stop," she said with a pout, trying to go back down on her knees.

"I was about to lose it right there in your sexy-as-hell mouth, and I didn't want to do that. I wanted to lose it in you."

Amanda made a cute little O with her mouth, and I reached under her dress to rid her of her panties. I threw them aside, and she laughed at yet another torn pair of her little sexy underwear. I was going to go buy her some more tomorrow. We were gonna need them.

I slipped a finger into her, thinking I needed to get her ready, when my hand met wet heat. "You liked giving me head, didn't you?" I asked in wonder as she trembled against my hand, more than wet enough for me. "That's so damn hot," I whispered, lowering my mouth to capture hers. She was turned on and ready for me just by sucking my damn cock. Shit. This woman owned me. I'd be her slave for life. I just couldn't lose her again.

AMANDA

Preston unzipped my dress and let it drop to the sand below us, and I kicked it aside. He reached for his pants and pulled out his wallet and a small foil packet. I watched as he tore it open with his teeth then slid the condom down over himself. His white teeth bit into his bottom lip as he worked to get the protection in place.

"I'm gonna lie down, and I want you to get on top of me. Just like you rode me on the couch." He pulled his shirt off, then lay down on the sand, and I stepped over him and lowered myself on him.

"Ah, damn, I'm not gonna last," he breathed as I placed my hands on his chest and let him guide his erection into me. I was more than ready for him. As soon as he had it in place, I sank down on him and we both cried out from the pleasure of it. I'd missed him so much. This time, knowing he loved me—it changed everything.

We dusted the sand off the best we could and fixed each other's hair before we headed back to the house. We could see people piling out of the front doors as we approached. We'd made it back just in time.

"You want to go in first so your mom doesn't see us?"

No. I didn't. I wanted to walk in there holding Preston Drake's hand and daring her to say anything about it. Was she really going to tell everyone about his past? Because I wasn't going to leave him, so they'd all know that her daughter was dating a former gigolo. I wasn't so sure my mom was that self-destructive. Her social circle would eat that information up. Also, she'd have to rat the mayor's wife out, and that would cause all kinds of drama.

"I want to walk in there holding your hand. I'm tired of hiding things because I'm scared of my mom's reaction. She is going to be against this, but I don't care. She'll learn to live with it. And once she's around you for any amount of time, she's going to be charmed. You have that way about you. It is impossible for a female to not like you."

Preston pulled me up against his chest and cupped my face in his hands. "I love you. I love you so damn much it consumes me. I don't deserve you, but I'm gonna become the man who does deserve you. I promise you. I'll make you proud of me."

I reached up and ran my thumb over his lips. "I am and will always be proud of you. I want the world to know you're mine."

ABBI GLINES is the author of *The Vincent Boys*, *The Vincent Brothers*, the *New York Times* bestseller *Fallen Too Far*, in addition to several other YA novels. A devoted book lover, Abbi lives with her family in Alabama. She maintains a Twitter addiction at @AbbiGlines and can also be found at AbbiGlines.com.

Want more Abbi Glines?
Then turn the page for a sneak peek at

the vincent boys

the vincent boys ABBI GLINES

from the author of
the vincent brothers

SEVEN YEARS AGO . . .

"You notice anything different about Ash?" my cousin Sawyer asked as he climbed up the tree to sit beside me on our favorite limb overlooking the lake. I shrugged, not sure how to answer his question. Sure, I'd noticed things about Ash lately. Like the way her eyes kind of sparkled when she laughed and how pretty her legs looked in shorts. But there was no way I was confessing those things to Sawyer. He'd tell Ash, and they'd both laugh their butts off.

"No," I replied, not looking at Sawyer for fear he'd be able to tell I was lying.

"I heard Mom talking to Dad the other day, saying how you and me would start noticing Ash differently real soon. She said Ash was turning into a beauty, and things between the three of us would change. I don't want things to change," Sawyer said with a touch of concern in his voice. I couldn't look him at him. Instead I kept my eyes fixed on the lake.

"I wouldn't worry about it. Ash is Ash. Sure, she's always been pretty, I guess, but that's not what's important. She can climb a tree faster than either of us, she baits her own hook, and she can fill up water balloons like a pro. The three of us have been best friends since preschool. That won't change." I chanced a glance at Sawyer. My speech sounded pretty convincing, even to me.

Sawyer smiled and nodded. "You're right. Who cares that she's got hair like some kind of fairy princess? She's Ash. Speaking of water balloons, could you two please stop sneaking out and throwing them at cars right outside my house at night? My parents are gonna catch y'all one of these days, and I won't be able to get y'all outta trouble."

I grinned, thinking about Ash covering her mouth to silence her giggles last night when we'd snuck down there to fill up the balloons. That girl sure loved to break rules—almost as much as I did.

"I heard my name." Ash's voice startled me. "You two better not still be making fun of me about this stupid bra Mama's making me wear. I've had it with the jokes. I'll break both your noses if it doesn't stop." She was standing at the bottom of the tree with a bucket of crickets in one hand and a fishing pole in the other. "Are we gonna fish or had y'all rather just stare down at me like I've grown another head?"

Chapter 1

ASHTON

Why couldn't I have just made it home without seeing them? I wasn't in the mood to play good freaking Samaritan to Beau and his trashy girlfriend. Although he wasn't here, Sawyer would expect me to stop. With a frustrated groan, I slowed down and pulled up beside Beau, who had put some distance between him and his vomiting girlfriend. Apparently, throw up wasn't a mating call for him. "Where's your truck parked, Beau?" I asked in the most annoyed tone I could muster. He flashed me that stupid sexy grin that he knew made every female in town melt at his feet. I'd like to believe I was immune after all these years, but I wasn't. Being immune to the town's bad boy was impossible.

"Don't tell me perfect little Ashton Gray is gonna offer to

help me out," he drawled, leaning down to stare at me through my open window.

"Sawyer's out of town, so the privilege falls to me. He wouldn't let you drive home drunk and neither will I."

He chuckled sending a shiver of pleasure down my spine. God. He even *laughed* sexy.

"Thanks, beautiful, but I can handle this. Once Nic stops puking, I'll throw her in my truck. I can drive the three miles to her house. You run on along now. Don't you have a bible study somewhere you should be at?"

Arguing with him was pointless. He would just start throwing out more snide comments until he had me so mad I couldn't see straight. I pressed the gas and turned into the parking lot. Like I was going to be able to just leave and let him drive home drunk. He could infuriate me with a wink of his eye, and I worked real hard at being nice to everyone. I scanned the parked cars for his old, black Chevy truck. Once I spotted it, I walked over to him and held out my hand.

"Either you can give me the keys to your truck or I can go digging for them. What's it going to be, Beau? You want me searching your pockets?"

A crooked grin touched his face. "As a matter of fact, I think I might just enjoy you digging around in my pockets, Ash. Why don't we go with option number two?"

Heat rose up my neck and left splotches of color on my

cheeks. I didn't need a mirror to know I was blushing like an idiot. Beau never made suggestive comments to me or even flirted with me. I happened to be the only reasonably attractive female at school he completely ignored.

"Don't you dare touch him, you stupid bitch. His keys are in the ignition of his truck." Nicole, Beau's on-again-off-again girlfriend, lifted her head, slinging her dark brown hair back over her shoulder, and snarled at me. Bloodshot blue eyes filled with hate watched me as if daring me to touch what was hers. I didn't respond to her nor did I look back up at Beau. Instead I turned and headed for his truck, reminding myself I was doing this for Sawyer.

"Come on then and get in the truck," I barked at both of them before sliding into the driver's seat. It was really hard not to focus on the fact this was the first time I'd ever been in Beau's truck. After countless nights of lying on my roof with him, talking about the day we'd get our driver's licenses and all the places we would go, I was just now, at seventeen years old, sitting inside his truck. Beau picked Nicole up and dumped her in the back.

"Lie down unless you get sick again. Then make sure you puke over the side," he snapped while opening the driver's side door.

"Hop out, princess. She's about to pass out; she won't care if I'm driving."

I gripped the steering wheel tighter.

"I'm not going to let you drive. You're slurring your words. You don't need to drive."

He opened his mouth to argue then mumbled something that sounded like a curse word before slamming the door and walking around the front of the truck to get in on the passenger's side. He didn't say anything, and I didn't glance over at him. Without Sawyer around, Beau made me nervous.

"I'm tired of arguing with females tonight. That's the only reason I'm letting you drive," he grumbled, without a slur this time. It wasn't surprising that he could control the slurring. The boy had been getting drunk before most the kids our age had tasted their first beer. When a guy had a face like Beau's, older girls took notice. He'd been snagging invites to the field parties way before the rest of us.

I managed a shrug. "You wouldn't have to argue with me if you didn't drink so much."

He let out a hard laugh. "You really are a perfect little preacher's daughter, aren't you, Ash? Once upon a time you were a helluva lot more fun. Before you started sucking face with Sawyer, we use to have some good times together." He was watching me for a reaction. Knowing his eyes were directed at me made it hard to focus on driving. "You were my partner in crime, Ash. Sawyer was the good guy. But the two of us, we were the troublemakers. What happened?"

How do I respond to that? No one knows the girl who used to steal bubble gum from the Quick Stop or abduct the paperboy to tie him up so we could take all his papers and dip them in blue paint before leaving them on the front door steps of houses. No one knew the girl who snuck out of her house at two in the morning to go toilet-paper yards and throw water balloons at cars from behind the bushes. No one would even believe I'd done all those things if I told them. . . . No one but Beau.

"I grew up," I finally replied.

"You completely changed, Ash."

"We were kids, Beau. Yes, you and I got into trouble, and Sawyer got us out of trouble, but we were just kids. I'm different now."

For a moment he didn't respond. He shifted in his seat, and I knew his gaze was no longer focused on me. We'd never had this conversation before. Even if it was uncomfortable, I knew it was way overdue. Sawyer always stood in the way of Beau and me mending our fences, fences that had crumbled, and I never knew why. One day he was Beau, my best friend. The next day he was just my boyfriend's cousin.

"I miss that girl, you know. She was exciting. She knew how to have fun. This perfect little preacher's daughter who took her place sucks."

His words hurt. Maybe because they were coming from him or maybe because I understood what he was saying. It wasn't as if I never thought about that girl. I hated him for making me miss her too. I worked really hard at keeping her locked away. Having someone actually want her to be set loose made it so much harder to keep her under control.

"I'd rather be a preacher's daughter than a drunk whore who vomits all over herself," I snapped before I could stop myself. A low chuckle startled me, and I glanced over as Beau sunk down low enough in his seat so his head rested on the worn leather instead of the hard window behind him.

"I guess you're not completely perfect. Sawyer'd never call someone a name. Does he know you use the word *whore*?"

This time I gripped the steering wheel so tightly my knuckles turned white. He was trying to make me mad and he was doing a fabulous job. I had no response to his question. The truth was, Sawyer would be shocked that I'd called someone a whore. Especially his cousin's girlfriend.

"Loosen up, Ash, it's not like I'm gonna tell on you. I've been keeping your secrets for years. I like knowing my Ash is still there somewhere underneath that perfect facade."

I refused to look at him. This conversation was going somewhere I didn't want it to go.

"No one is perfect. I don't pretend to be," I said, which was a lie and we both knew it. Sawyer was perfect, and I worked hard to be worthy. The whole town knew I fell short of his glowing reputation.

Beau let out a short, hard laugh. "Yes, Ash, you do pretend to be."

I pulled into Nicole's driveway. Beau didn't move.

"She's passed out. You're going to have to help her," I whispered, afraid he'd hear the hurt in my voice.

"You want me to help a vomiting whore?" he asked with an amused tone.

I sighed and finally glanced over at him. He reminded me of a fallen angel as the moonlight casted a glow on his sun-kissed blond hair. His eyelids were heavier than usual, and his thick eyelashes almost concealed the hazel color of his eyes underneath.

"She's your girlfriend. Help her." I managed to sound angry. When I let myself study Beau this closely, it was hard to get disgusted with him. I could still see the little boy I'd once thought hung the moon, staring back at me. Our past would always be there, keeping us from ever really being close again.

"Thanks for reminding me," he said, reaching for the door handle without breaking his eye contact with me. I dropped my gaze to study my hands, which were now folded in my lap. Nicole fumbled around in the back of the truck, causing it to shake gently and reminding us that she was back there. After a few more silent moments, he finally opened the door.

Beau carried Nicole's limp body to the door and knocked. It opened and he walked inside. I wondered who opened the door. Was it Nicole's mom? Did she care her daughter was passed out drunk? Was she letting Beau take her up to her room? Would Beau stay with her? Crawl in bed with her and fall asleep? Beau reappeared in the doorway before my imagination got too carried away.

Once he was back inside the truck, I cranked it up and headed for the trailer park where he lived.

"So tell me, Ash, is your insistence to drive the drunk guy and his whore girlfriend home because you're the perpetual good girl who helps everyone? 'Cause I know you don't like me much, so I'm curious as to why you want to make sure I get home safe."

"Beau, you're my friend. Of course I like you. We've been friends since we were five. Sure we don't hang out anymore or go terrorizing the neighborhood together, but I still care about you."

"Since when?"

"Since when what?"

"Since when do you care about me?"

"That is a stupid question, Beau. You know I've always cared about you," I replied. Even though I knew he wouldn't let such a vague answer fly. The truth was that I never really talked to him much anymore. Nicole was normally wrapped around one of his body parts. And when he spoke to me, it was always to make some wisecrack.

"You hardly acknowledge my existence," he replied.

"That's not true."

He chuckled. "We sat by each other in history all year, and you hardly ever glanced my way. At lunch you never look at me, and I sit at the same table you do. We're at the field parties every weekend, and if you ever turn your superior gaze in my direction, it's normally with a disgusted expression. So I'm a little shocked you still consider me a friend."

The large live oak trees signaled the turn into the trailer park where Beau had lived all is life. The sight of the rich beauty of the southern landscape as you pulled onto the gravel road was deceiving. Once I drove passed the large trees, the scenery drastically changed. Weathered trailers with old cars were up on blocks, and battered toys scattered the yards. More than one window was covered with wood or plastic. I didn't gawk at my surroundings. Even the man sitting on his porch steps with a cigarette hanging out of his mouth and wearing nothing but his underwear didn't surprise me. I knew this trailer park well. It was a part of my childhood. I came to a stop in front of Beau's trailer. It would be easier to believe that this was the alcohol talking, but I knew it wasn't. We hadn't been alone in over four years. Since the moment I became Sawyer's girlfriend, our relationship had changed.

I took a deep breath, then turned to look at Beau. "I never talk in class. Not to anyone but the teacher. You never talk to me at lunch, so I have no reason to look your way. Attracting your attention leads to you making fun of me. And, at the field, I'm not looking at you with disgust. I'm looking at Nicole with disgust. You could really do much better than her." I stopped myself before I said anything stupid.

He tilted his head to the side as if studying me. "You don't like Nicole much, do you? You don't have to worry about her hang-up with Sawyer. He knows what he's got, and he isn't going to mess it up. Nicole can't compete with you."

Nicole had a thing for Sawyer? She was normally mauling Beau. I'd never picked up on her liking Sawyer. I knew they'd been an item in seventh grade for, like, a couple of weeks, but that was junior high school. It didn't really count. Besides, she was with Beau. Why would she be interested in anyone else?

"I didn't know she liked Sawyer," I replied, still not sure I believed him. Sawyer was so not her type.

"You sound surprised," Beau replied.

"Well, I am, actually. I mean, she has you. Why does she want Sawyer?"

A pleased smile touched his lips making his hazel eyes light up. I realized I hadn't exactly meant to say something that he could misconstrue in the way he was obviously doing.

He reached for the door handle before pausing and glancing back at me.

"I didn't know my teasing bothered you, Ash. I'll stop."

That hadn't been what I was expecting him to say. Unable to think of a response, I sat there holding his gaze.

"I'll get your car switched back before your parents see my truck at your house in the morning." He stepped out of the truck, and I watched him walk toward the door of his trailer